Chosen Subject

Iain Welsh-Shaw

ISBNs:
Paperback: 978-1-80227-073-0
eBook: 978-1-80227-074-7

To my sons

Chapter 1

'It's so... ' Jed let his eyes wander round the grey slabs of the gaunt gothic structure in front of him, searching for a word. He liked words. Didn't get much chance to use them, but he liked words.

'Old?'

'Yes, but there's something else. These blocks are just, just... 'grim."

Had he read it, Jed might have likened it to 'Bleak House' and would have been wise to do so. In just an hour, he had been removed from his familiar semi, cheek by jowl with other semis, to a mansion in its own grounds with not another building in sight. The drive was sweeping and covered in small stones. The lawn was close cut and had hoops and wooden balls on it. He pushed the car door closed and waited for Maggie, his aunt, to accompany him. They walked up the short flight of steps carved out of a similar grey stone, past the two pillars, through a door with peeling black paint and finger-smudged glass and onto the dulled mosaics of the vestibule floor. Maggie pulled a metal rod which summoned a distant bell. Footsteps clicked along a passageway on the other side of a closed cream door.

'You must be Jed and Mrs McKay. Do come through. We've been looking forward to your visit.'

The cream door opened into a parquet-floored colonnaded hall with a sweeping staircase leading to a minstrels' gallery. A floor polisher whirred unseen, and an aroma of disinfectant-mixed-with-polish, with an undertone of vomit, suffused the room.

'So, Jed, you're the star of the show today. Let's see what you make of us.'

The Headmaster, for that is whom Jed assumed him to be, swept in front of them. His black gown clipped ledges that had escaped the attentions of a duster, giving flight to tiny particles that reflected in the shafts of light streaming through stained-glass windows that spoke of the mansion's former life.

'Yes, it's certainly seen better days, this place.' The Head had anticipated any observation that either of his visitors might care to make on the faded elegance that surrounded them. 'But that's just the fabric. What's really important is the atmosphere: the camaraderie, the community spirit. And there's plenty of that. Come into the study. I'll be guiding the conversation. Here we are. Take these chairs.'

'The Study' was a sparsely furnished, green-carpeted room with two desks, behind one of which sat an elderly man. He glanced at them briefly and then looked down at the papers covering the green leather that distinguished it from the desk by its side from behind which the Headmaster pulled a chair, lifted his gown and sat.

'I'm Mr Freeman, the Headmaster. This,' he briefly motioned to the man at the other desk, still engrossed in looking at papers, 'is the owner of Finchingham School, Captain Cassell.'

'Captain Cassell,' Jed rolled the alliterative title and surname in his head. He didn't look like the sort who had a first name. He also didn't look like the sort who welcomed the intrusion of strangers into his domain. There was a slight grunt at the mention of his name, which may have been a muffled 'Morning,' but did not invite any response. There was no other recognition of the visitors nor any eye contact. 'Maybe he's shy. Wonder why he's here.'

'As I said, I'll be conducting the interview. Captain Cassell is here to observe. We shall swap notes later.'

Jed expected the older man to have a pen poised, ready to take them, but his hands remained out of sight, his eyes cast down, his face without expression.

'Mr Freeman.' Jed thought about this, too. His mother had told him that you never called yourself 'Mr.' That it was a title other people gave you and not one that you gave yourself. It had a name that he couldn't quite recall, but something to do with honour, and he assumed it was the honourable thing not to call yourself 'mister'. But Mr Freeman did. He wondered why.

'Finchingham School,' Brian Freeman pulled his gown tightly around him and stiffened his back, 'is a small school. Deliberately kept small so we can offer individual attention to our boys and enable them to flourish in a supportive environment.'

Here we go, thought Jed. A school's a school. I have to go to one, so let's just get on with it.

'What we offer is a bracing environment with plenty of sports activities. Education is what's most important in life. That's what Aristotle says. ' He always liked to get that in at some point as it suggested a classical background. This audience was unresponsive.

'And the fees.' Mrs McKay spoke for the first time. 'They are remarkably competitive. My brother-in-law couldn't possibly afford the normal prices on his army salary.'

Jed had always been aware that money was an issue. His father was the breadwinner. His mother looked after him and his older sister, Gill. She was the constant presence in their lives, a woman younger than most of the army wives with an unintended social superiority that could not be concealed. From her RP accent to her stylish clothes and even the way one foot was placed before the other when she walked, there was a poise and confidence that he had not noticed in the other children's mums. He knew that she had been privately educated herself and had read English at university. One day, it would be the 'Ancrene Wisse' - 'This is 'Middle English', Jed, you can see how our language developed'. The next, a George Elliot novel - 'Yes, George Elliot was a woman who had to keep her gender a secret to get taken seriously.'

She had married the love of her life and accepted the comparative penury that resulted. 'Sometimes, living here, I feel like an anchoress without the belief myself, but the last thing I want for you is to become an anchorite. I want you to meet stimulating people. Plato said that teachers were the most important members of society. They educated the upcoming generation. Listen and learn, and you won't go far wrong.'

'Wasn't it Plato?' Jed wanted to correct the man in charge of the interview. 'I thought Aristotle was the one with ideas about the theory of tragedy,' The words remained unspoken. He had his doubts about this confident Headmaster.

With a sister ten years his senior, Jed had been like an only child most of his young life. He researched what the life of an anchorite might be like and saw similarities. His mother did, too, and saw only pitfalls. It was his mother who had inculcated in him a curiosity that belied his years. 'The goodies are good, and the baddies are horribly bad' was her introduction to 'Macbeth.' 'Here's where you see someone who's on top of his game come crashing down to the lowest of depths, and all because of a flaw in his character. That's what Aristotle says. ' From an early age, Jed had known about fatal flaws. He was determined to avoid them.

Now her husband had been posted overseas, and she had joined him; a boarding school was a necessity for their son.

'Yes, we keep in mind the forces bursary and understand that the government is prepared to pay for boarding education for the children of forces personnel. So important that these children have continuity, of course, which is exactly why you chose us, and it's a great choice you have made - or will be, of course,' the Head chuckled, 'when you have made your decision.'

'But what this costs is exactly what the grant is. To the pound. How can you afford to do this?' She blushed at her straightforwardness. 'If I may ask?'

'Well, of course, we value our armed forces. Captain Cassell here was in the army. He fought in the last war. He is prepared to take the financial loss that this represents, and he ensures that the full fees paid by other parents subsidise the fees of forces' boys. It really is a wonderful opportunity, and we are so pleased you found us on the list of recommended schools.'

'I'd imagine that lots of forces' families would send their boys here.'

'They do.' Brian Freeman opened his mouth to continue, but the words came from the man on his left.

'Just a few.'

'Exactly,' Brian Freeman interjected. Jed sensed that the Headmaster was rescuing himself from a near-faux pas and felt his desperation. 'We are a broad church. We have boys from all sorts of families and value the varied contributions that they make. I'm sure you don't want to sit here talking to me. We'll take the tour.' The Head's bottle-bottom glasses magnified the intensity of his stare. The pair rose obediently and followed in the dust-cloud of the swirling gown.

Past rooms, along corridors, down some stairs, up some stairs. All was a blur. Words came to him distantly: 'Fellow-feeling', 'friendship' - all variations on the same theme. Jed waited in vain for any repetition. The patter was well-rehearsed, the delivery emollient. The language came from a thesaurus. The vowels were fruity. Here was a small, proprietorial boarding school. All around were the trappings of a public school. Jed and his aunt were feted, given every attention. Any word they might utter, although they spoke hardly at all, so comprehensive was their guide, was seized on, repeated and elaborated on. This apparently erudite man was devoting an hour of his valuable time to them - a boy and his aunt from a semi-detached house in a market town.

A wooden floor, a tiled floor, wood-panelled walls, tiled walls, painted walls, walls that needed repairs. Dorms with iron bedsteads, rails from which hung jackets, curtainless windows, unshaded lightbulbs. On and on, the tour proceeded. Here was a glimpse of boarding school life. It was bracing indeed, even with the June sun streaming in through the windows.

Freeman and his aunt were deep in a one-sided conversation about values of the 'House' system: 'Of course, you know, it gives the Housemasters the chance to offer the boys even more individual attention, to really get to know them and to develop them,' when Jed, walking some way behind them heard the noise of falling water. A door, painted in the same cream as the door he had come through in the building, was ajar. He gently pushed it with his foot.

'Hello?'

'Oh, hello. I'm sorry. I didn't expect to see anyone,' Jed looked the young man straight in the eye and tried to fix his gaze on his face.

'It's OK. I'm Baxter G.'

'That's a strange name.'

'No, it isn't. Oh. I see. There's a space between 'Baxter' and 'G'. That's so you know I'm not 'Baxter D'. He's my brother.'

'Is that your first name?'

'No. We don't have first names.'

'Oh?'

There was enough of a question mark in Jed's acceptance of the fact that the boys had no first names to warrant an explanation.

'We have them, of course, but we never use them.'

'Oh. I'd better go. I'm on the tour.'

'OK. May see you if you come.'

Jed closed the door that had been ajar. He felt he should. Although Baxter G. had conducted what had clearly been for him a normal conversation with a stranger, Jed felt he should let him get on with what he was doing in private. The water was from a shower. The boy who had faced him throughout their brief encounter was naked under its flow.

'So, no more questions? I hope I've shown you enough to let you see beyond the bricks and mortar and get an insight into the special atmosphere we create. Tailored, as we say in our prospectus, to the individual boy. Lessons given by professional, dedicated teachers. It's all a matter of trust, isn't it?' Freeman paused so that the words following the rhetorical question would have an impact. 'Absolute trust.'

'Oh, yes. Of course.' Maggie hunted for a question, so comprehensive had been their guide. She felt she ought to ask one and wasn't doing her duty by her nephew if she didn't ask something, anything. She knew nothing of boarding schools and had only her own experience of teachers as a yardstick.

'I suppose you teach. I mean, you're a qualified teacher. No, that's not what I mean. Sorry. I mean, do you teach as well as be the Headmaster? Something like Maths, or English?' Maggie felt her voice trail away. The Head had been so articulate, so eloquent, so charming that her question appeared intrusive, rude even.

'No. Sorry. I didn't mean to question you. I just asked out of interest. It's OK. Yes, of course, we'll come. All right, Jed? You like it, don't you? I'm sure the other boys are all very friendly and will help you. You'll meet them when you start in September. And you'll love boarding. I've read all the Enid Blyton stories. It's such a lot of fun. Boarding, I mean. And learning, too, of course. Not just fun. Jed likes to learn. Do you want to test him?'

'No, that's fine. He seems like a great chap. He'll do well. You can be sure I'll keep a special eye on him.'

'Thanks very much for your time.' She felt like adding 'Sir' to the end of her sentence. The man's name momentarily escaped her. 'There isn't a ladies' room, is there?'

'There's a washroom down the tiled corridor,' Jed interjected. 'I saw it.'

'No, no. We have a special loo for visitors. Let me take you. Stay here, Jed.'

In the room Freeman and his aunt had left, the man at the other desk continued to look at papers. After a while, as nothing was happening outside, Jed diverted his gaze from the window to the assorted stationery that was so engaging the attention of the other occupant of the room. From the columns of figures, he sensed that they were bills. He could even read most of them. They were upside down. Jed wondered what he would say if he told him he'd seen they were upside down. How could he read upside-down figures? Small hands grabbed at the papers, made them into a bundle and tapped them on the leather to make the edges meet. Corners and edges met. He tapped again, and the bundle separated, deposited half of itself on the floor. Jed shifted in his chair, unsure if he should break the silence and pick them up, anxious that he might be perceived as being curious to know their contents. At the slight movement, the man coughed nervously, lifted himself from his chair, walked to the strewn papers, knelt and gathered them up. Jed could see that he was old and that his eyes were two dark beads set in a face of grey translucent skin. They moved briefly in his direction, then back to the task in hand.

'You a new boy.' With its absence of intonation, it was neither a question nor a statement. As he was the only other person in the room, Jed felt it must have been directed at him and that there was a need for some response.

'I think I am now, sir.'

The eyes continued to read the reorganised but still upside-down papers. The silence was, by now, oppressive. Jed felt there should be some communication but that it shouldn't come from him. After all, he had uttered the last sentence. It was the man's turn now. Jed felt and then heard his stomach rumble. He had not felt like breakfast that morning, and now his tummy was telling him it was lunchtime. He heard a distant gong, like at the start of some films. He assumed it signified the start of a meal, but felt he could - should, even - break the ice by asking what it was for. But he was a child, and a good child shouldn't speak until spoken to. He waited to be addressed. The silence continued. He was sure Cassell must hear the workings of his digestive system, but it was as if he wasn't there. His stomach rumbled again more loudly. He shifted in his chair and cleared his throat to disguise his inner workings.

For want of anything else to occupy his mind, Jed recalled his aunt's awkwardly-phrased question to the Headmaster. Grown-ups could be so embarrassing, and she brought it on herself. Why did she try to fill the silence by saying the first thing that came into her head? Far easier to be a 12-year-old no one expected anything of. He would just sit there and wait for this old man to say something - or not.

The aunt and the Headmaster returned. Freeman never did answer the question. That he taught Maths was stated in the prospectus, but Mrs McKay's assumption that he was qualified was a false premise. Brian Freeman was not a graduate; he had never attended university. He had been thrilled when he had been offered a Headship as he had never dreamed that this would be possible. Having been in the post for six years, however, he knew why none of the other candidates had wished to be appointed and had already submitted his resignation.

'See you in September, Jed' were his parting words. He knew that he would never set eyes on this family again. And this had made the interview bearable.

The water had turned cold long ago. Grant Baxter towelled himself dry, picked up his sponge bag, hung the towel on a peg and walked up the stone backstairs to the prefects' dorm.

Chapter 2

'Trunks in the cellar when you've unpacked. Sports kit in the changing rooms.' Instructions were barked by various members of staff at parents, boys and the empty air.

Parents busied themselves in car boots; boys tried to keep their distance from them, certain they would do or say something embarrassing and, if they did not, the very presence of a parent was an embarrassment in itself. Clothes were hung on rails, sweets hidden under pillows, loved teddy bears sent back with parents - 'Thought it'd remind you of home' - and, for this brief moment, there was laughter, the bright dresses and perfume of the mothers, and the warmth of familial hugs and kisses.

Jed's parents were miles away in Germany, where his father had been posted some while ago. Their son had spent a few days with his aunt. 'Just to get yourself used to the UK, Jed. You'll be back for the holidays before you know it, and you'll be able to tell us about all the exciting things you've done, subjects you've learned and people you've met.'

His aunt had told them how important they had felt at the interview and how solicitous had been the authorities. 'Such a pity the old Headmaster didn't stay. Such a nice man.'

His aunt had also told them that the owner of the school had been there to meet them, too, but that he was shy. 'A poppet. But so shy. I'm sure he'll be there when we arrive.'

He was. 'Good afternoon.' This was more of a mutter than a greeting. Captain Philip Cassell was mingling with the parents. The small beady eyes darted across the floor. 'Good afternoon.' They remained fixed to the floor. 'Good afternoon.' On he shuffled, with never a glance at his audience.

The new Headmaster was in his element. 'So lovely to meet you. I do look forward to getting to know your family. Such a lovely day to start the new academic year. Oh, Chaplain, a word in your shell-like, if I may.' The bonhomie was lost on Jed. He was fixated by the one discordant note that no one else seemed to have noticed. No one had remarked on. There was the Emperor, and he had no clothes. But no one told him. They all carried on as though it was perfectly normal. Jed could not take his eyes off them.

Cassell was wearing grey and brown check bedroom slippers. They were Marks and Spencer's bedroom slippers made of plush and with a furry lining. They shuffled between the polished leather, the brown suede and the stiletto heels. He felt sorry for them. In their place, at home, they were fine, comfy slippers. But in this place, they were... Again he struggled for the word. In a few years' time, he might have observed that they were jarringly out of context, incongruous even, but right now, they were just out-of-place. The parents seemed not to know who he was. He melted between them. 'Excuse me' alternated with 'Good afternoon.' There was the owner, and there were the owner's slippers. What could he make of that?

'Are you new?' His musings were interrupted by a man's voice. It was a warm voice, deep and with a Scouse twang. The voice belonged to a man with brown hair that touched his collar and a brown beard. At his age, all grown-ups were just grown-ups. They were of an indeterminate age and just old. But he could tell that this one was younger than his parents and more smiley. He nodded assent.

'I'm a new boy, too.' He held out his hand. 'Alan Watson. I teach Music.'

No 'Mr'. Here was someone who knew the rules. Momentarily nonplussed, Jed shook his hand. 'Thank you, sir.'

'We'll have to look out for each other,' Watson laughed.

'Yes, sir.'

'Jed, everyone's going to the parents' meeting they're having in a room across the hall. I don't think I want to get involved with these people, so I'll say goodbye now. Come and give your auntie a farewell kiss.'

Alan Watson slipped away without greeting the aunt as if absorbed into the throng.

Hot with embarrassment, Jed accompanied his aunt out of the front door and hoped that no one had noticed. In the driveway, several boys his age, identically dressed in pale grey tweed jackets, grey shirts, grey trousers, and red ties, were seeing their parents off. Identical that is except for the shoes. They were all booted in smooth black leather.

'I'm sure I read 'brown brogues',' his aunt had said by way of an excuse, 'but never mind, it's just a little thing, and we can get new ones during the holidays.'

By putting first one foot and then the other behind a leg, Jed tried to minimise the impact of the brown brogues, the badge that made him different, odd, an outsider. Everyone would notice. They would rib him. He just wanted to be anonymous. If he said nothing, maybe no one would notice him. Yes, that's what he'd do. He would try to be invisible. Then no one would see his shame.

'Now make sure you behave yourself and do as you're told. Your mum and dad and me, we want to be proud of you. This is a great opportunity. The teachers are really clever, so listen to them and follow their example. Be good. Bye, Jed.'

Jed thought he would be ashamed of his aunt's little car. He imagined the drive would be clogged with Bentleys and Rollses. But no. Small cars that had seen better days were bumper to bumper in front of this stately home that must have seen horse-drawn carriages in its day. He was not sure whether to be relieved or disappointed.

He waved until the dust settled.

'You! Get moving. Gong's gone for tea.' A large man in a black gown was gesticulating at him.

'Sorry, sir. Didn't hear. I was saying...'

'No matter. What's your name?'

'Jed, sir.'

'Not your first name. What's your surname?'

'Massie, sir.'

'Right, Massie. Being late for tea deserves a debit point.'

'But, sir, I was just...'

'Enough excuses. You're responsible for your own timekeeping here. But you're new and can be forgiven for being stupid. Just this once, mind. I won't be so merciful next time.'

'Thank you, sir. I'll try not to be late again.'

'I hope you'll do better than 'try'. You'll need to succeed, young man.'

'Yes, sir.'

Tea in the dining room had finished. A few limp sandwiches were all that remained.

'They started out that way, too, you know. No one seemed to want any. I saved you some cake, though.'

The bearded man who had introduced himself earlier was holding a plate.

'Take it. Tuck in.'

'Thank you, sir, but I think I'll have a lie-down.'

'Bit cream-crackered, are you?'

'Cream-crackered?'

'Tired. It's cockney rhyming slang.'

'But 'tired' doesn't rhyme with 'crackered.''

'I'll tell you later.'

Alan Watson walked off. Jed thought better of refusing the cake and tucked in.

'But 'crackered' and 'tired' don't rhyme. Don't see how he can say they do.' Jed was speaking aloud to himself in an empty dining room. But they must rhyme. A teacher had told him so. It must be true, but he couldn't see it. For the moment, all he knew was that he was wearing the wrong shoes and that he knew no one.

The room smelled of old food, boys and dust. The school's crest hung above the staff table. '*Melius Esse Conamur*'. Jed wondered what it might mean. The picture above it was of a sheaf of corn with an open book covering waves. On the end wall facing him was a huge mirror. A painted growth of decorative ivy crawled across it like some grotesque excrescence. In a room that was essentially stripped of anything that resembled softness, its presence was incongruous. He looked more closely. On one of the leaves was a huge chip out of the glass. A tendril radiating from this followed the crack that emanated from the source. Near the chip was a bowl full of used cutlery. He assumed someone had chucked something in at it and missed. He would discover some decades later that it had been no accident.

'No entry' read the sign that had now appeared at the foot of the massive wooden staircase that swept up to the minstrels' gallery and the rank of dormitory doors - 'Use stone backstairs'. Jed turned away.

'Have to look out for each other, won't we?' The brown-haired teacher was shaking hands with a lost-looking boy whose eyes were red and whose face was streaked with tears.

Chapter 3

'I'm having a good time and learning things, but I miss you very much. The teachers are nice and most of the boys. I have a friend called Richard. He is very homesick all the time, though, and the others ignore him. I really, really need a pair of black shoes. Please, please, will you send me some? I think I'm size 4.'

What else could he write? Jed put another tooth mark on the yellow and black of his Staedtler HB pencil and practised twirling it from finger to finger. He was just managing to retrieve it from his little finger when it dropped onto the desk. Heads shot round. The library that had been heavy with breathing and the scratching of writing implements on Basildon Bond now rang to the shout of the master in charge.

'That was you, Massie. Everyone else can knuckle down to writing their Sunday letter home, but you have to make a noise. Is this really the best you can do to make a mark on the school? Come back here after lunch, and you can write me a letter about what you intend to do to make a success of your time here at Finchingham School. Same goes for anyone else who makes noise. Back to your letter-writing, boys. You have another 15 minutes.'

Maybe, thought Jed, when he got his black shoes, people would start to like him. It wasn't that they were nasty to him, except for Poynton, but no one seemed to have much time for him. They were busy with their football practice or disappeared into the woods or went into town or just couldn't be found.

'Messy Massie', Poynton had called him. 'They're covered in dog pooh,' he had roared outside the classroom. 'That's why they're brown, and they're all rotten. That's why they've got holes in them,' Jed reddened in front of the pointed finger. He felt warmth creep up his back and his stomach tighten. Most of the twenty or so 12-year-olds standing in front of the Nissen hut that housed the room in which they were to learn history laughed along with him; a flat laugh, humourless, but it humoured Poynton. 'Get those smelly shoes away from us.'

A sudden silence descended when the teacher appeared with his key and let them in. Poynton, a clumsy boy with a tendency to fall over his own feet, pushed his way forward to the front, grabbed a chair at the very back, twirled it around on one leg and plonked down heavily, hands in pockets, legs apart with the chair back in front of him, and him slumped forward onto it.

'Never one not to make an entrance, Poynton. Turn the chair around and look interested even if you're not. Any new boys? Ah yes, Massie and Woods. Books for both of you.'

Two books flew in quick succession from an experienced hand and landed on each desk.

'Last term, I told you we would start on the Civil War. Dates, please.' Several hands shot up. 'Redding, let's see what you've come up with.'

'1642 to 1651, sir.'

'Splendid. And the protagonists? Jamieson, you try.'

'Roundheads and Cavaliers, sir.'

Benny Jamieson could always be relied on. He waited for Poynton to show his only skill, his talent for disruption.

'Sir.' Poynton was keen to make a point. His hand was not up. Both remained in his pockets. 'Sir. Are you a Roundhead or a Cavalier? I'm really interested. I'm a Cavalier.' He looked around. 'I think Massie's a Roundhead, though. Aren't you, Massie? We need to know.' He laughed at his joke. The one or two who understood the point he was making tittered. A few of the rest who had no idea tittered, too.

Poynton was the sort of boy you didn't cross. He smelled, Jed observed to himself. He had an incipient moustache and a ripening pustule on his forehead. 'Are you going to take Spot for a walk?' Oh, how Jed wanted to say this.

Poynton thrust his chest forward, enormously pleased at his display of rudeness thinly disguised as wit and even more thinly disguised as a relevant question. It was the kind of jibe one might almost get away with and one that Poynton employed on occasion to show how clever he was. At least it passed the time. He looked around for the approval of his classmates and started to lean back into the chair.

Jed saw it coming. He thought momentarily that if he yelled a warning, he could stop it, but he would not. It was not a step he wished to take. He would luxuriate in letting it happen, see his tormentor get his comeuppance, see how he recovered from it. Too late, Poynton realised that the back was in front of him. The chair shot from under him, and the boy fell backwards with the full force of his ten stone, his splayed legs thrust forward, too late to pull his hands from his pockets to steady himself with his arms, the side seams of both pulled apart. Poynton uttered a word that Jed had rarely heard before. The class shrieked and clapped.

'Well, I guess the answer to your question will have to wait while you go to Matron and get yourself sorted out, Poynton. No hurry. Now would be a good idea, though.'

The class relaxed with Poynton's departure. The basic facts about the protagonists in the Civil War were briefly taught, and homework was set.

'Sir. Can't you get something done about Poynton? He's just spoiling the subject for the rest of us. He couldn't care less about anything historical, and this is a subject I love.' Benny Jamieson had waited until the end to make his polite request.

'I've spoken to Captain Cassell and Mr Brookfield about him, but they put it down to – what did they call it? – 'youthful exuberance' – so I'm afraid the answer is no. Look, I know you want to get into university and read history. You might ask your parents to take this up with the management. Don't tell them I told you.'

Benny was an obedient child and did as he was told. History became a subject he taught himself the following term as he correctly detected that the new teacher brought in quickly as a replacement seemed to have no knowledge of the subject.

'Why did Poynton think I was a Roundhead?' Jed asked Richard Braine as they walked out. 'I think I'd have supported the king. Cromwell's lot were pretty miserable.'

'Dunno,' said Braine.

'I think it can't have been something nice, though. Poynton doesn't think nice thoughts, does he? He seems to have it in for me. Does he like you?'

'Never see him,' Braine replied. 'He just goes off to the woods or disappears. What are Roundheads and Cavaliers anyway? I thought they were cats and dogs.'

'They're Shorthairs and Spaniels,' Jed replied, surprising himself at his quickness of thought. 'These are supporters of the king and parliament. You've got to write about them for homework. 500 words. Weren't you listening?'

'I don't listen,' said Richard and shrugged his thin shoulders. 'That's why I don't get good marks. My parents make me have a tutor every holiday.'

'One of the teachers here?'

'Kempson. He lives in the house and teaches me French, English and piano.'

'You're lucky. Mine couldn't afford anything like that. I bet he costs a lot.'

'Dunno. I s'pose they think it's worth it. My marks are still rubbish, but it gets me out of my parents' way. They don't like me very much. Well, I think my mum does, but she's drunk most of the time. She doesn't notice what's...'

'Enough of this mothers' meeting. Didn't you hear the gong? It's lunchingtons.' As if on cue, Kempson swept past the huts, his wavy hair just touching his shoulders, his gown billowing open to show a dimpled purple tie against a lilac shirt. 'Chop, chop. I'll be on your table, Braine.'

'Doesn't he call you 'Richard' when he's at your home?'

Kempson had stopped and turned around. 'Stop twittering, boys, and hasten to the refectory. Time and tide and all that.'

Was Richard a friend, Jed wondered? This tall thin boy with translucent skin was as close as anyone at his new school had become to fulfilling this role, and maybe he was just quiet by nature. He'd only known him for a few days, and he seemed as lost as he was, even though he had been at school since he was 11 and so had a year's advantage. And he had started telling him about his family. That's something Jed would never have done. 'If you can't say something good about someone, don't say anything at all,' is what his mother had told him from as far back as he could remember, and he had never questioned those words.

'Drunk.' Jed shuddered. He could no more imagine either of his parents or his aunt being in that state than flying in the air. Couldn't see the point. Why did anyone want to make themselves ill? His aunt had told him it was 'the demon drink' that did for her marriage and that his uncle wasn't himself when he was in his cups. For a long while, he had imagined cups of tea and that too many of them went to your head. 'Oh no, love,' his aunt had said, 'It wasn't the tea that got to him. It was the hard stuff.' But how could it be hard when it was liquid?

There were so many things about adult life that he found hard to comprehend. 'Why don't you stay for a cup of tea?' his aunt always said to his parents when they came to collect him. 'Oh no, we couldn't possibly,' was their standard reply, but they always did. Why didn't they just say 'Oh yes, please, let's'? Saying the opposite of what you mean just makes life complicated. Grown-ups were, he decided, unfathomable. In the meantime, he'd see if anyone else was nice, nicer maybe than Richard Braine, who quite probably wasn't his type and whom he didn't really have much to do with outside lessons.

He needed the loo and, assuming there would be a queue for lunch, diverted to the washroom. It was the room where he made the diversion from the Head's tour, a room that wasn't on the itinerary. He could see why. Its white tiles made it appear bright, although the only natural illumination came from a skylight that ran almost the length of the room with handles dropping from a metal frame that surrounded it and which, he assumed, could have been turned to open it. The mechanism was corroded with years of steam from the rank of 12 shower heads above a long tray. There were no curtains, no separate cubicles. These were communal showers. The baths were communal, too. All six of them were in a row with a couple of feet between each. The lavatories at the end of the room were separated by partitioning, and most had doors. The locks had failed years ago, it seemed.

Jed picked his moments to go when he reckoned no one else would be there. What would he do when he needed a bath or a shower, though? He'd have to wear his swimming trunks or have a special pair of underpants for getting wet. He pushed one of the lavatory doors that was ajar and pushed open another and another. He chose one that he thought would clean up with just a flush and reached to grab and pull the dangling chain. It's all so... What word could he use? 'Huggermugger'. He said the word aloud and let it roll round his mouth. He couldn't remember where he had learned it, but it seemed to be right: a sort of close-together-in-a-tight-group sort of word; cheek-by-jowl.

Traces of the previous user remained. He would help whoever had to clean these. He aimed a stream of his wee at a gash of excrement that had escaped the separated jets of the flush and some spots that clung to a rim just above the jets, dislodging a few. Why would people leave it like that for someone else to clean up? What did the cleaner think when she saw this? How did she cope with removing it? It didn't bear thinking about. He flushed again. Nothing. The cistern re-filled slowly.

'Huggermugger'. It had a warm and cosy ring to it. No, this room was cold and harsh. And that boy he'd met on interview day, Baxter G, he hadn't been worried at all. Maybe that was because he was older, but then again, maybe he should have been more worried because he had been older and he wasn't a child. He was a sort of man. Jed hadn't seen anything quite like that. But he hadn't worried. Just carried on talking, so maybe he shouldn't be worried. He'd make a decision about it when he had to. In the meantime, he'd see how long he could go without washing. Would he be able to make it half-term? That was almost two months away. He doubted it. He tried the flush again, although the cistern was still filling up. There was a trickle of water from behind it down the wall, which must be contributing to its slowness.

'What the hell are you doing? Your table prefect told me to find you, and my meal's bloody going cold!'

Jed shot out of his reverie and swung around from the lavatory. Silhouetted in the doorway was a figure that was starting to stride in his direction. A hand swung out and connected with the side of his head, knocking him against the flimsy partition and bringing it down into the next cubicle.

'Now look what you've done, you little shit. Get that board up, wipe that blood off your nose and report to your tutor. And do your zip up, you disgusting little perv.'

Jed had fallen across the remains of the partition, his head against the lavatory bowl of the next cubicle. Momentarily dazed, he saw only a blurred shape in front of him. He shook his head and blinked hard. He looked up into a black jacket with a gilt badge on its lapel. 'Head Boy', he read. 'I was just going to the loo. I'm sorry. I didn't mean to cause trouble, sir,'

Jed pushed himself back into his underpants and pulled his zip closed. He reddened at the knowledge that he had exposed himself to the shape towering over him.

'Don't 'sir' me; I'm not a teacher. You caused trouble for me, and I'll be causing it for you. You make my food cold, and I'll make you cold. Be here at 5 sharp, with a towel. What's your name?'

'Jed, sir. Sorry. Jed. And I'm sorry about the sir, sir. I mean not sir.'

'Don't be funny with me.' The hand lashed out again across his head, cracking it against the lavatory seat, which parted company with the bowl and smacked into the opposite partition. 'I couldn't give a shit what your first name is. Give me your surname.'

'Massie, sir. Sorry. I didn't mean it. It just came out.' Jed put his hands up to his head to guard against the next blow that he sensed would come. He was just bringing his knees up to his chest as an instinctive protection when a foot struck him in the stomach.

'And you just came out - from under a stone. You make me sick.'

The foot, the leg, the body, the whole being that had intruded into his world turned and strode out. A small boy was coming in through the door. 'Out of my way, scum.' The small boy yelled in pain as he was pushed back into a row of coat pegs. 'Stop it, Poynton. That's bullying.'

Poynton? Not the Poynton whose path he'd crossed earlier that day. This was an even bigger version. Maybe a brother. Jed picked himself up and surveyed the wreckage around him.

'What's all this?' A man had appeared at the door. He was not wearing a gown, but he had the voice of authority, clipped, superior and loaded with contempt. The words were spat out of lips that curled in a sneer. 'You're a vandal. That's what you are. This'll be a pretty penny for your parents to shell out. Go to the Head's Study. Now!'

Chapter 4

Pushing his brown brogues under the thinly upholstered bench seat, Jed squeezed himself as far away from the Head Boy, Poynton, as the fixed wooden armrest would allow. Poynton sat upright, staring into the middle distance, his head elevated, chiselled features, ice-blue eyes, smooth skin, a shadow on his upper lip that spoke of a recent encounter with a razor, the slightest hint of nicotine. He was a boy on the brink of man-hood. Out of the corner of his eye, Jed could see no facial resemblance between this Poynton and his other tormentor. Just the absence of any warmth.

'Head's busy. Wait,' were the only words spoken.

Almost immediately, the door opened.

'So nice to have met you, Captain Tonge,' the Head radiated bonhomie. 'And Mrs Tonge and Graham. Now do consider all the factors and weigh them up, so you make the right decision. And remember, the most important aspects of a boarding school are what you don't see, but what you feel. It's a partnership. Captain Cassell and I would love you to join us in a partnership to bring out the very best in young Graham. I'm sure we can all achieve this.'

'Thank you so much, Mr Brookfield. We'll let you know when we've all had the chance to have a chat, but what you've said has been... Has been...' Mrs Tonge's eyes were watering, and her voice wavered. 'Insipid. No. Inspired. No, not that either.'

'Inspirational?' Mr Brookfield suggested. 'I try to help.'

'Yes. That's it. Inspirational. We'll just check that the Forces' Bursary covers all the Fees so we can be sure.'

'It will, Mrs Tonge. You can be sure of that.'

'Brown shoes, Mr Brookfield? While casting around for the right word, Mrs Tonge's eyes had ranged from ceiling to floor and taken in Jed's feet, hidden though he thought they were. 'I thought they had to be black.'

'Indeed, how astute you are to spot this, Mrs Tonge. Naughty little Jake here made a mistake. We'll have to chide him gently, won't we?'

Mrs Tonge giggled and smiled at both boys sitting awkwardly on the straight-backed bench placed just outside the study door. ''Chide'. What a word. Mr Brookfield, you put it all so well.'

'Too kind, Mrs. T. Adieu.'

The Tonge family trouped out of the black front door, and St. John Brookfield turned his attention to the boy and man-boy sitting in front of him. 'Well, you'd better come in, hadn't you? I sense some chiding may be called for. Oh, Boyce, um, Nicholas,' Brookfield picked on the first person he saw passing by. 'Show Captain and Mrs Tonge and Graham to their car.'

It was as Jed had remembered it from the awkward meeting with Cassell and Brookfield's predecessor a few months before. The room was illuminated by dust-flecked shafts of light from huge sash windows, a thick green carpet topped by two basic wooden desks at one of which Captain Cassell sat as if he had not moved since their first encounter. Jed imagined that the papers he was turning over were the same. The only difference was a changed wingman. Brookfield sat on the edge of his desk and motioned with his wrist the other two to stand before him. His black hair was Brylcreemed flat, his pince-nez hung from a cord to his waist and from his waistcoat pocket protruded a gold chain. He crossed his legs and examined his shoes. They were brown brogues.

'I see we have something in common, but I sense it not this you wish to speak to me about Master Poynton.'

'No, sir. This boy is a vandal.'

'Oh, dear. You give Goths and Vandals such a bad name. I had heard as much from Mr Martin. He dropped me a note while I was interviewing. Massie, aren't you? Massie, a new boy who wants to make his mark on the school by smashing it up. Massie, a boy who is here on a grant courtesy of Captain Cassell here, who shows his gratitude by destroying what Captain Cassell has provided him with, and who imagines that Captain Cassell is going to make good what he has violated out of his own pocket. Do I have it in a nutshell, Massie?'

'Yes, sir. I mean no, not really.'

'Well, Massie, here's how I see it. There you were, deliberately late for lunch, in the lavatories, smashing them up, as witnessed by the Head Boy and Mr Martin. Not so much a smoking gun as a leaking lavatory, certainly after you had - how shall I phrase it? - kicked it in.'

Brookfield slid from the desk and sashayed to his chair. He placed both elbows on the barrier of his desk, placed his hands together and rested his chin on them. He paused for dramatic effect.

'Or are the Head Boy and the Captain of our Cadet Force both lying through their teeth?'

'Sir. I didn't mean to.'

'Oh, dear, Massie. How unfortunate. There you were looking at the lavatory cubicle, and it all fell to pieces around you. Sad. And expensive. No, Massie. Captain Cassell here,' Brookfield turned to him and smiled. Cassell remained focussed on his task. 'Captain Cassell here won't be paying. Burden is getting a costing together as we speak, as we speak, boy, which he will present to me within the hour, and which I shall present to your tutor who will, of course, commiserate with your regrettable situation when it all so unfortunately fell down around you, and who will extract that sum from your pocket money and, if a top-up to your funds is required, as I suspect it will be, will assist you to write a letter to request that same top-up of funds from your father in wherever he is, who will, I am sure, be impressed that his son has chosen to waste his money in such a manner.'

There the Head, realising that the sentence he had been carried away with creating was just a tad too long without a breath even though the effect might be diminished thereby, paused momentarily. 'His, I dare say, hard-earned money thrown away by a child who decides on a whim, a mere caprice, to do as he wishes, to etch his pathetic little personality on the fabric of our building, and who, I may well assume, is also responsible for the graffiti we see around us day to day which you will, in addition to whatever punishment Poynton sees fit to mete out to you, remove with a scrubbing brush for the next month until it is all removed.'

Brookfield pulled himself from his desk and stood at full height, hands on the lapels of his light brown jacket. He smiled at Jed. 'I do hope I make myself clear.' He erased the smile and turned to the other boy. 'I assume I can leave the modus operandi to you, Poynton?'

He sensed what 'modus operandi' might mean and nodded his agreement. 'He made my dinner cold, so I'm going to make him cold. He'll be seeing me at 5.'

'No, Poynton. Listen to me. You should always strike while the iron's hot. The boy has done wrong and needs to know this. The time will be now. You may leave.'

Along the corridor, down a flight of steps, past the staff room, onto a tiled section and through the door into the changing room. Poynton pulled at a lever on the wall and turned a dial from red to blue. 'Strip. Get under. Two minutes.'

'But what do I wear and what do I dry myself with?'

'Nothing - to both your stupid questions.'

'I'm keeping my pants on.'

'Who cares? Get under.'

Hot with embarrassment, flushed with rage, Jed removed his clothes, folding them before placing them on the floor. He stood at the side of the torrent. 'Get your head under.'

Jed clutched his hands around himself and let the cascade cover him. On and on it went.

'That's two minutes, Poynton. Let me out.'

The older boy turned his back on him.

'Don't cheek me. That's another two.'

He had not seen his skin blue before. He thought of home, of kindness, of the warmth of the fire in the sitting room there.

The love of his family. Everything that was important to him was away from this place.

'Get out. Get dressed.'

'But I have nothing to dry myself with.'

'Drip dry.'

Jed pulled his clothes on over his wetness. He had not walked in wet clothes before. He made slow progress towards the door.

'Well done, Poynton. He needs discipline.' The Head was there in the doorway.

'Yes, sir,' said Poynton. His back stiffened, and his heels clicked together.

'Get to your tutor's flat, Massie. There's a bill waiting for you.'

Chapter 5

'Enter.' The voice was purposeful. Jed had not yet met his tutor. Maybe he was a kind man. Mr Freeman had told him that a boy's tutor was there to look after him and help him in his journey through the school. He felt he really needed help now.

'Oh, dear. You look sad. Before you start, I have to tell you that the Head has sent me a little billet-doux - that's a note - outlining what has happened. And Mr Burden, he's the clerk of the works here, has also sent me a note with a list of the materials required and what his labour will cost. The Head has told me the full cost is to come out of your pocket money allowance.'

'I didn't do it, sir. It was an accident.'

'Now, Massie... Jed... one thing we have to do as we grow up is admit to our mistakes. The way I see it is that there was no damage when you went in, and there was plenty of damage when you left. That's the way I see it, but I'm a simple sort of a fellow, and I just see things as they are.'

His tutor smiled at him and beckoned him to take a seat. The man had a youngish, full face. Jed thought he looked a bit like drawings of Moonface in 'The Faraway Tree' books he used to have. His room was a little like Moonface's room in the tree, small and softly furnished. The carpet felt thick, and two armchairs were upholstered in a green floral pattern. A small table stood between them on which were placed a wine bottle and an ashtray. Bookshelves lined one wall and three elongated school photographs, one over the other, decorated the wall facing him. A sash window overlooked the front lawn. The room's tranquillity came as a relief and filled Jed with the hope that a little piece of home did, indeed, exist in this harsh building. He started to feel safe.

Conscious of his dampness, Jed said, 'If it all right with you, sir, I'd rather stand.'

'As you wish. Just relax. I'm your tutor. My name is Alex Stanhope. You aren't in any of my classes yet, but you may be in a couple of years. I'm also in charge of the cadets. You may want to join them. We do exciting things like have campfires where we toast marshmallows.'

'No, mister.' He knows the rule.

'Now, I have to show you Mr Burden's bill. Here it is.'

Jed extended a shaky hand and took the small piece of paper, dreading what it might contain. There were lines of scribbled writing with a number at the end of each line. He had never seen a bill before, so he had no idea what it all meant. Mr Stanhope extended a helpful finger. 'This is the business part of the bill. It's the total. As you can see, it's £334,' Stanhope paused to lets its significance take effect. 'Three hundred and thirty-four pounds,' he enunciated slowly. 'That's what you have done will cost to repair.'

'But I don't know what that means.'

'What it means, my boy, is that you will pay the school this amount from your pocket money. What's your weekly allowance?'

'I think it's £5, but I'm not sure. I haven't spent any.'

'Well, let's put your maths to good use, shall we? Five into thirty-three?'

'Six and carry three.'

'Good. Five into thirty-four?'

'Almost seven.'

'Yes. Almost seven. That's the number of weeks it'll take you to pay the bill. Almost 67 weeks. If there are 52 weeks in a year, that's more than a year, but we have to reckon on the holidays.'

'Why do we have to do this?'

'Because,' Stanhope gently explained, 'you only get £5 a week when you're here. In fact, it'll take you two years to repay the bill, and I can assure you that Mr Burden's suppliers of the materials he needs won't wait two years to be paid, nor will Mr Burden wait two years to be paid for his labour. So what should we do?'

'I don't know, sir.'

'Well, Jed, I do. I shall have to write to your dad, tell him what's happened and ask him to send the money.'

'Oh, no! Please, sir, don't. My dad would find it really hard to pay all that, and he'd be so ashamed of me. I've never been in any trouble before. Isn't there a way of not telling him?'

Stanhope reached for a packet of tissues that he kept handy on one of his shelves. 'Dry your eyes. I don't see a way. Oh dear, this all seems to have come as a shock. Let me put my thinking cap on. I tell you what. This is all very unfortunate, being your first offence and all that,' he sighed and rubbed his forehead. 'Look, here's what I'll do for you. You're a nice enough young fellow, and I'm here to help, so... I don't make a habit of this, you know... I'll take it on myself to pay this bill out of my own pocket for now... No, don't interrupt; let me finish. I'll pay it out of my own pocket, and you can pay me back. We can keep your parents out of it. I don't want to wait two years, mind.'

'You're very kind, sir. It's so nice of you, but how can I pay you back?'

'You know, young Massie,' said Alex Stanhope, sliding deeper into his chair and stretching his legs out, visibly relaxing, 'School is a growing-up process. One of the good things about being away from home is that you have to make your own decisions. I had to do this when I was at my public school. One of the teachers was horrible to me, but I knew I had to deal with it myself. I did, and I think it made a man of me. Look at what's happened this way. It may help make a man of you.'

'But I still don't know how I can pay you back.'

'Go away and have a good think about it. Come back in three days and tell me what you've come up with. Off you go. I'll do my best for you.'

'Thank you, sir. I'll have a think and tell you.' But Jed knew that he would not be able to come up with a plan to magic the problem away, however hard he thought about it. And think hard he would. But at least he had an ally. Mr Freeman had been right about his tutor. He was a man Jed could rely on.

Chapter 6

In the days that followed, little else entered his head. He wouldn't buy any sweets. He wouldn't spend any of his money on himself. That would save something. He considered selling his toys, clothes he had grown out of, books he'd read, but had no idea how to do about this and suspected that the amount raised would be tiny. Three hundred and thirty-four pounds. He had no comprehension of such a huge sum.

'Do you agree?'

'Agree with what, sir?'

'With the statement I've just given to you and the class?'

'Sorry, sir. I really didn't hear it.'

'Come off it. You've shown real insight in the last lessons. I thought you were getting to understand why David signed himself off in his prayers with 'I am David'. Please don't prove me wrong.'

The rest of the lesson passed in a blur. Try as he might, Jed could not get out of his head the enormous debt he owed, and that it had become a debt of gratitude made it even worse. 'Never a borrower or a lender be,' his mother had told him, but he had become a borrower. He didn't want to, but he had seen no other way out. The money had been offered. Should he have refused it? That would've been rude. No, he must've done the right thing.

So much damage. He'd done so much damage. He hadn't meant to. Should he tell someone? Maybe his tutor. He might understand. Maybe he would intercede - he thought that was the word - yes, maybe he would agree to interceding with the Headmaster. But that meant telling tales. He shouldn't do that. He shouldn't get someone else into trouble. He would have to make up a reason for what happened. That would mean telling someone something that wasn't true. That would be a bad thing, but he was protecting someone else from getting into trouble, so that would be a good thing. It would be one of those 'white lies' that his mum had talked to him about.

His mum's friend had given them an ornament for looking after their house once. It was an ashtray with 'Duporth Holiday Camp' written on it and a small colour picture of little chalets. 'Oh, how lovely,' his mother had said and had stroked it and looked at it with affection. She adjusted her language to suit her visitor. 'That's a lovely thought. Thank you so much.' His parents didn't smoke.

'You do smoke, don't you?' the friend had asked.

'Well, no, but we really could use one for visitors, so this is just the ticket. Here, we'll give it pride of place on the coffee table in the lounge. You must tell me all about,' his mother picked up the ashtray and read from it with interest ''Duporth Holiday Camp'. We'd love to hear all about it.'

And they did. The stories were long and detailed. They learned all about the competitions, were instructed in the finer points of 'cork 'n ball', discovered what their friend had found on the 'scavenger hunt', heard about the Brown Windsor soup they enjoyed at almost every meal, the dances, the events, until his mum announced in the middle of a sentence, 'My goodness, I almost forgot! Dad's tea. I need to pop to the shop for some ham before it closes. I'd forgotten it's early closing day. I'm so sorry, Beth. Just when it was getting so interesting. Be a good boy and nip and get my purse, Jed. I'll see you out, Beth, my dear. So sorry. Must get my shoes.'

Jed's mum had got to her feet and made for the door. When her friend had disappeared from view, she sank back into the uncut moquette. Jed handed her the purse.

'You don't need this now, do you? he had asked rhetorically. 'Was that a 'white lie?' You said a 'white lie' was told to make someone feel better, but that didn't make her feel better, did it?'

'No, but it's made me feel a whole lot better. Put that thing in a drawer, will you?'

The Duporth Holiday Camp ashtray, in all its awfulness, would never see the light of day again.

Jed smiled at the recollection. His mum's pale grey lie had shown him a way to relate to people that had stood him in good stead so far. 'Such a polite boy,' people had told his mother. 'He always likes to make people feel comfortable,' and this had made life more comfortable for him, too. 'Just think what the other person would think,' his mother had told him, 'and then you can say it.' The friend had left, and the friend would return, 'not too soon,' his mum had added, but the relationship would continue.

Jed observed the way his mum conducted her social relationships safe in the knowledge that whatever she did had been thought-through first. 'You need stability, Jed,' she had said when her husband announced yet another transfer. 'It's not good for you, going from school to school, so what do you say that I take a look at the list of private boarding schools that your dad can get for us? They'll all be recommended as being fine, and I'm sure the experience will be good for you. It'll be strange for us not having you here, but your education is the most important thing we have to think about. Your auntie has told me she'd be happy to have you come over and take you to see whatever we decide on, and you can spend short breaks with her.'

That was how it had all begun. They had gone through the approved list, checked the fees and seen what each of the schools wrote about themselves. It was the 'small school' and 'small classes' that had struck his parents as being special about Finchingham School. The word 'individual' had appeared several times. 'It reads in such a reassuring way,' his parents had said. His aunt had fed them back her impressions about what she had seen. The Fees were far lower than other schools and matched the bursary they were allowed when relocating overseas. All of them had decided that this was the place to go. They were the grown-ups, and the adults in his life had always been right, always steered him in the right direction. They must be right now. What he had seen couldn't be important; it must be what his dad had told him was 'character-forming.' He didn't see it now, but he had to believe that everything he was living through had to lead to some goal at the end and that the goal was 'character formation'. He wasn't sure what it was, but he knew that it was something his parents aspired to for him, and so, as he was a dutiful child, he would give it to them. Yes, everything was 'character building', and it wasn't built yet, so he'd run with it and let it develop him.

His mind made up, Jed closed the door on his inner self and fixed his mind on what was happening around him. The room was empty. The lesson must have ended. His teacher was still in situ at his desk, looking at him.

'I wondered when you'd re-join us. Too late for the lesson, I fear. You may well be a boy with some ability. I don't know. You didn't show much today, but the keenness I saw right at the beginning augured well for the future.' The young teacher looked at him quizzically. 'Now it all seems to have gone out of the window - where your thoughts are right now.'

'Sorry, sir.'

'Well, an apology is something, but it isn't doing you any good, is it? I'm going to put you in detention, partly as a punishment and partly so you can read about what you missed this morning. It's not good for a new pupil to get a detention in his second week, is it? It'll be on your record, and your parents will know. Who's your tutor?'

'Mr Stanhope, sir.'

'OK. Are you able to talk to him about what's wrong? I sense there's something troubling you.'

'He's very kind, sir.'

'He's a resident teacher. I'm only part-time, so he's the one to turn to. OK?'

'Yes, sir.'

'And you're getting on with everyone else?'

'Not sure about Captain Cassell, sir.'

'No? Well, I can't talk about him. He must speak for himself.'

Jed sensed an undertone, a sudden coldness. Maybe he had seen the slippers on the first day. He thought he would go just a little bit further.

'Or Mr Brookfield.'

'Yes. I see.'

There was the same coldness. Stanhope was OK, but not the others. Should he go further? The decision not to was taken from him.

'I have to whizz off now. I hope you get whatever it is sorted out, Jed.'

'Jed'. Hardly anyone used his proper name. It was his. It was special. He loved reading 'I am David' in his English lessons, and he had a feeling for how David kept himself together during his lonely travels across Europe, although he did not feel like communing with God about it. 'I am Jed.' He had only a vague realisation that he was the sum total of the experiences that had given him his moral code and no conception that he would shortly reach a crossroads in his young life. He enjoyed his English lessons and liked his English teacher. He felt ashamed that he had disappointed him.

The fresh-faced teacher who sat in front of him had no idea that this young man would, in thirty-five years' time, articulate to him the entire story from its beginning and transform his life.

Chapter 7

'Cold crud, that's what I got. Waste of my time. Who does he think he is, swanning around? Not a care in the world. Little runt. Dreams his way around the school. I'll give him something to worry about.'

Baxter G. looked up from his essay writing, saw the familiar curling lip on the palely handsome face, knew a rant was starting and looked down again. 'I'm busy, Poynton. Go and tell Stanhope.'

'It's loud enough that gong. Makes the windows rattle if it's beaten properly. Goes off at the same time for every lunch. No excuse for not hearing it. Just…'

What it just was, Baxter G. was not in a mood to discover. 'My dad says I can invite you for half-term if you want.'

'Yeah? Great! Oh. Hang on. I can't. Anyway, my brother won't have anyone to look after him.'

'Isn't that what you've got parents for?'

'They won't be around. They're off somewhere,' Poynton didn't know where they were off to, and Baxter knew he didn't know and knew not to ask.

No one had met Poynton's parents, either separately or together. Unlike the other services families, they were not based

44

abroad. They lived somewhere near the east coast. Neither Baxter nor anyone else in Poynton's circle had been told the name of the town, let alone the address. If conversation ever drifted towards a consideration of parents, neither Poynton acknowledged they had any. Their views were not offered, their opinions, their attitudes, their words were not referred to. Their two sons lived in a world uninhabited by parents. They appeared not to resent them; they just did not feature. The other boys assumed that they provided their two sons with a roof and four walls. In this, they were correct.

Mrs Poynton was not one to waste words. 'I've spent pounds on this bouffant and make-over, just blow a kiss to me. I'm out until after your bedtime. Put the lasagne in the micro at six just for five minutes. Wash up after you and make sure your brother's in bed by nine. You can have another hour and a half, and I expect you to be asleep when I'm home. I'll check, you know.'

His father had fewer words to waste. 'Unsociable hours. That's what they're called,' his father had told him. It was one of their longer conversations.

'What's 'unsociable'?' the older son had asked.

'Look it up, or ask one of those teachers that all my money goes to pay. I'm not a walking dictionary.'

Brett Poynton never did look it up. 'Unsociable hours' were what they were, and were all the hours of every day of every holiday. It was his normality. There were no arguments. His father was out with his work, and his mother was just out. They passed in a corridor from time to time, but did not greet each other or exchange a word because there was nothing to say. There was also nothing to do. At least, there was nothing to do at home. This was an irrelevance. 'Are you here for the holidays or away?' his mother would ask casually. Generally, the answer was 'away'. His social circle from school gave him an entrée into a lifestyle that his mother would have envied had she asked about it. The problem was his brother.

'Look,' Brett told his brother, 'you're 13. You don't need me hanging around babysitting you, do you? Well, I'm telling you that you don't. 'Bout time you grew up anyway. No need for the parents to know anything. Just make yourself scarce, and I'll make it worth your while. This school trip you're going on for a couple of weeks...'

'I'm not going on any trip. No one's told me about it. Where's it to?'

'It's to wherever you want it to be. Go and stay with a friend. Go and make a friend. I'll give you some money, and you can just go somewhere for a couple of weeks.'

'Where are you going?'

'Out and about. You wouldn't like it. It's too grown-up for you. You'd be bored. You know what you're like.' The boy smiled at the thought of the freedom ahead of him.

Jerome Poynton rarely saw his brother smile. 'Can't I come with you?'

'No. You aren't invited.'

Baxter G. paused for an answer to his question. 'Isn't it?'

'Isn't what?'

'Isn't looking after your brother what parents do?'

'No, Baxter, he'll be OK. It's just that I'll be away most of the time. I think we're going to London. Alex has been talking about taking us to the Liberal Club. We have to get DJs. No, not disk jockeys, you spas. Dinner jackets. They're being hired for us. And he's told me to learn some quotes so I can sound clever when I talk to important people. 'Think not for whom the bell tolls. It tolls for thee."

'What does it mean?'

'That we're all going to die, or something.'

'Sounds stupid to me.'

'Well, it would. You aren't one of us and, unless you buck your ideas up, you won't ever be. You're too bourgeois.' Poynton strutted to a mirror and ran his finger over his upper lip. 'Now that I have to shave at least once a week, I may well grow a moustache. Alex says it would suit me.'

'It's such a bore shaving, sir,' he had told his tutor.

'Shows you're a big boy. Ask your folks for one of those little Philishave things for Christmas.'

'They don't know that I have to use a razor. They don't know that I'm growing up. Anyway, I don't want to ask them for anything, and I don't think they'll want to buy it for me.'

'You need parents, Brett. Don't be hard on them. If you have a problem, they're the first people you should go to. They're the ones who understand you, who love you. Parents are the sort of people who will do anything for you. As I know mine would have done for me.'

The catch in the man's voice was lost on the boy.

'They're not the sort of people I can turn to. Don't need to anyway. I'm OK as I am.'

Alex Stanhope felt the tense he had used would have given the boy enough of a clue about his own status as an orphan. Maybe it had been too subtle. Poynton was not noted for his sensitivity. He would try again in a voice more tinged with regret.

'Well, I'm sure mine would have been.'

'They have their own lives, and that's OK by me. We get on fine. They don't bother me, and I don't bother them. There's food in the micro and a roof over my head. I do very well, sir.'

'You'll know how much you love them when they're gone, Brett. That's what I realised.'

'They're only 39, sir. I don't think they'll be going anywhere soon. Well, not to heaven anyway.'

'It was a canal.'

'Yes, sir.'

'A canal. In Amsterdam.'

Brett Poynton looked puzzled. 'I've never been to Amsterdam, sir'.

'My parents. It was a canal in the centre of Amsterdam that their car went into.'

'That was a bit silly.'

'They were there for the weekend. They must've rented a car and slid on the cobbles or something, and they never came home.'

'I did that once. When my dad was posted somewhere, the place was full of cobbles, and I came off my bike. Did my knee in. Was off footy for a month.'

'My parents were killed in Amsterdam when I was quite young. I was brought up by relatives. I missed them every day. Still do.'

'I don't know if I'd miss mine. Don't really know them.'

'My only point, Brett, is that you have to have someone to talk to. Someone with whom you can be completely frank. Growing up isn't easy. You have to make choices and be guided by what you believe in. This is what parents do for their kids, and this is what I, as an ersatz parent, in my '*loco parentis*' role, am expected to do for you. Your parents would expect no less.'

'But it's still a bore, shaving'.

'Well, grow a moustache. It'd suit you.'

Baxter G. accepted that his invitation had been declined.

'Funny thing is,' Poynton turned away from the mirror. 'I'm sure he told me his parents were killed in a shootout in Beirut.'

Chapter 8

'Stanhope's expecting you. Something about wanting an answer to your predicament.'

A Land Rover had scrunched the gravel on the drive, enveloping him in a cloud of its dust. The driver's window slid open, and Jerome Poynton's head emerged from it. 'Give me a hand with my stuff, will you?' In the back were trays of Coke and boxes of crisps.

Had he not been so preoccupied with his dilemma, Jed would have noticed that his erstwhile tormentor had been absent from his life for a while. Classes were quieter, and the joint Heads were untroubled by his frequent visits to be disciplined. Jed might also have wondered what a 13-year-old boy was doing driving a car. In fact, Jerome Poynton's status had changed from schoolboy to entrepreneur, starting with half-dozen packs of Coke from the shop in the town, which he sold individually at twice the price to the boys from a counter in the cellar. Such was the demand that, within a week, he had added a range of crisps and sweets bought in bulk from the cash-and-carry warehouse with the school's trade card.

So busy with buying and selling was he that he absented himself from all lessons.

'Is Jerome Poynton still a boy at the school?' had been asked at one of the staff meetings.

'Yes. He's now under Captain Cassell's guidance.'

Jed had expected boarding school to be different and accepted unquestioningly what he found around him. That a boy had vanished from his classes was a fact in the same way that the same boy had been a constant disruption was something to adjust to. He just got on with lessons. Or he would have done had the question of how to raise a large sum of money not blotted out every other thought. More than three days, now two weeks had passed since his meeting with his tutor. He knew he would have to climb those stairs, knock on the door and say something, but whatever the thing was that he was going to say had still not formulated itself. His brain churned with the issue night and day. What could he do?

'Another detention, Massie.' His history teacher assumed an expression of resignation. 'Although it really doesn't seem to work.'

'He says he wants you to see him this evening after prep,' Jerome Poynton pressed a coin into his hand. 'Thanks for the help.'

'You're actually being nice,' Jed said to the boy's back. He was stacking a shelf with all kinds of delights.

'Don't push it. Just go and see Stanhope. He told me to tell you, and I said I would. Here, you can have these mints. They don't sell as well as the sweet things.'

'OK, I'll go, but I don't know what to say to him.'

'You'll find some way.'

Jed walked up the stone stairs and out of the cellar. Just attend prep, and then he'd have to say something. He still had no suggestions to make. 'You'll find some way.' The words unsettled him, and he wondered why. 'Some way.' That was it. Some path forward, some road to take. That's what he needed, and the other boy in some way knew it.

'This door.' The master on duty stood in his way, his left arm extended to the open door of the dining room in which prep had already started.

Two hours later, Jed knocked tentatively at the cream door that led off the minstrel's gallery behind which he knew his tutor would be waiting.

'Come.'

Jed obeyed. His eyes were cast down, and he saw only a pair of shoes, brown shoes slightly muddied. In a flash, it came to him.

'I can clean, sir. I can clean your flat and polish your shoes. I can do this, sir, and I can keep on doing it all the time I'm here.'

His tutor beckoned him to sit and moved the winged chair slightly towards him.

'Jed, Jed, Jed,' he sighed. 'Yes, we'll give that a try, but things aren't going well for you, are they? I've had reports about inattention in class, work of poor quality, preps done late or not done. Shall I continue? Your mind hasn't been on your work, has it?'

'No, sir. I'm sorry. I just keep thinking.'

'I've promised the other teachers that I'll come up with a solution. Yes? With me so far? Good. The thing is, you aren't getting on with your prep in the dining room, so I think we'll put a desk up here on the minstrel's gallery specially for you, and I'll pop out from time to time to see how you're getting on. If you have any questions about your work, you can knock on my door and, if I can't help you, I'll send someone to ask a teacher who can. Does this seem like a fair arrangement to you?'

'Yes, sir. Thank you, sir.'

'And after your prep, you can come in and do some of the cleaning you suggested. I'll keep a tally of the hours, we'll work out an hourly rate, and we'll deduct it from the money you owe. If we say a pound an hour, that would seem to be reasonable for a boy your age, wouldn't it? In fact, you can start with these shoes. Just let me get another pair.'

Alex Stanhope disappeared into the bedroom part of his lodgings, reappearing with the encrusted brown shoes in his hand and shiny black shoes on his feet.

'Someone's at the door. You'll find a knife for the mud, a tin of polish and dusters under the sink over there.'

The visitor was the larger Poynton accompanied by another large boy whom Jed did not recognise.

'Ah, good,' Stanhope rubbed his hands with mock glee, 'you've come for your fittings. Here they are.'

With his back to the proceedings, Jed could only guess what was happening. The two boys scooped up what sounded like tissue paper and disappeared past him into the bedroom area to emerge a few minutes later with a 'Da-raaa!'

'Now you look absolutely the part: both of you young gents. Perfect fits. Now for the final touch, the bow tie. Some people would go for a clip-on, but not us. We'll do it the proper way. The way I'm used to, and nothing less would be expected for your first visit to the Liberal Club. Watch and learn. Stand by me, and we'll go through the ups and overs in the mirror. Here and through here and here and pull, *et voila!*'

Jed turned to see two boys in black suits with bow ties, the penguin effect spoiled only by their regulation grey shirts.

'I think Massie here will be the one to shine your shoes. I'll teach him the military way with a warm spoon and polish. You'll be able to see your faces in them. Now you look the part; you'll have to sound it as well. Let's practise. Someone extends his hand and says, 'How do you do?' What do you do and say?'

The unknown large boy grasped Stanhope's offered hand with 'Very well, thank you.' Stanhope became quite exercised about this, his voice rising an octave.

'Wrong! Let Brett try. Here you are, Brett, take my hand. 'How do you do?''

Brett Poynton bowed slightly, leaving Stanhope with a hand extended. 'I'm fine, and you?'

'Wrong again!' Was there a little jump, or did Jed imagine it? He was trying to appear not to be taking notice and kept his eyes fixed on the caked mud crumbling into the sink.

'Here I am like a prat with my hand out and nothing in it. You must take the extended appendage' - here, the last syllable was drawn out to rhyme with 'large' - 'and simply repeat what's been said. 'How do you do?' elicits the standard response, 'How do you do?' Only the very ignorant would actually answer the question.'

Stanhope's small audience was transfixed. They were learning from a master.

'Now, let's say you need a wee. How do you find out where to go?'

'Where's the toilet?' suggested one.

'Never a 'toilet,'' said Stanhope, positively beaming. He was really enjoying this. 'It's a 'lavatory'. Only the really vulgar say 'toilet'. A 'toilet' is where one did one's 'toilette' in the past. That's to say one's make-up, and that doesn't really apply to you, does it? You could try this one; 'You couldn't possibly tell me where the lavatory is, could you? That's the proper way to do it. As you know,' Stanhope chuckled knowingly, 'saying the negative is a way of stating the positive.'

An extension phone rang. 'Yes. This is Mr Stanhope. Who is this? Yes, the suits are perfect. Send me the bill, please. Thanks. Goodbye.'

So he doesn't know the rule, Jed realised. He did with me when we met, but he's forgotten it now. The word suddenly came to him.

'Honorific prefix. It's a title other people give you, but not one you give to yourself. That's what my mum said.'

He looked up from his scraping to see heads swung towards him and eyes meeting his. He knew he had given voice to his thought, and he averted his glance in shame. It was a monumental gaffe that he knew discomfited everyone in the room. He could not unsay it, so he grasped for other words - another idea that might supersede the original expression and get them to concentrate on that.

'I mean people with honours, titled people, they just call themselves by their last name. 'Cardigan'. He met my sister where she works,' The eyes remained fixed on him. 'It's a gallery near the Liberal Club. He came up to my sister and said 'Cardigan'. She turned to my mum and me and said, 'This is Lord Cardigan.' But he just said 'Cardigan.' I mean, how do you know that he's not 'Mr Cardigan?' I just...'

'Enough, Massie. You're talking nonsense. But tell me more about your sister. Older, I assume?'

'Yes, sir, she's 22 and lives in London. She's got a job there.'

'Well, gentlemen, maybe we should arrange to meet her while we're in town. A bit old for you, but maybe there's a chance for me. A pound for her name and address, Massie. How does that sound to you? Write it on this.' The master handed him a pad from beside his telephone.

'You're a cad, sir.'

'Am I now?'

'Yes, sir.' Jed thought he would try something he had read in the paper his mother had delivered. 'There's a difference between a cad and a bounder, sir. Did you know? I read it. In the paper. Once.'

All eyes were on him. He wondered what the effect would be of being a little clever, risqué even. It would at least help to pass the time.

'A bounder is the sort of officer who would sleep with a brother officer's wife but might then go out and win a VC, whereas a cad would sleep with the lady while his brother officer was out winning the VC.'

Jed heard the blood in his head pound through the blanket of silence that fell on that small room.

'That's what I read.'

'What's a 'VC?'' asked Poynton directing his question at Stanhope rather than Jed.

'Very Clever,' Stanhope replied. 'Just get on with it, Massie. Leave the banter to me.'

'Sorry, sir. My mother said that 'banter' was essentially unkind and that a witty exchange was more 'badinage.' Like a tennis match. One clever remark batted away with another.'

Jed had noticed this in himself. When he could say something he thought was clever, he could not let go. He simply wanted to develop the theme. He remembered the conversations he had with his mother of an evening. They just went on from one topic to another. The words and ideas flowed.

'Ow!' Jed blinked away a flurry of particles. Stanhope had blown into the sink, sending flying the smaller particles of mud there.

'Just do what you're here for.'

He had gone too far. Jed knew this and knew also that he had wanted to test the boundaries of this self-important man.

His mother had admonished him for this tendency. 'OK, so you find out how far you can go and that they're maybe not as clever as you are. So what? No one wants to be shown up by a child. Oh yes, before you say it, that wasn't your intention, but that's the effect. Remember - 'so wise so young, they say, do ne'er live long."

Was that 'Macbeth'? No, 'Richard III.' He couldn't think which, and while he was thinking, Stanhope pressed the bristles of the shoe brush onto his hand.

'Do it now and get out.'

Chapter 9

'He was the perfect gentleman.' Gill's voice sounded excited. Jed had chosen to call her rather than his mother for his one permitted phone call that Sunday. 'I'd forgotten they existed.'

'What does a 'perfect gentleman' do, then?'

'It's more a case of what he didn't do. He wasn't pushy. He didn't make a pass. Even when Poynton wasn't there, he didn't. I asked him about himself and eventually, managed to get him to tell me about his Russian heritage. You never told me this, Jed.'

'Well, I didn't because I didn't know it. He doesn't seem to like talking to me. I have the feeling he finds me - what can I say? - sort of intimidating.'

'Can't imagine why. Anyway, his great-grandparents were Russian and were displaced after 1917. They lost all their fortune and escaped to England. It was because of his connections that they approached him.'

Gill paused on the assumption that her brother would be so intrigued that he would beg her to carry on. He didn't.

'To be a spy.'

The silence at the other end of the line needed to be broken.

'Well, he refused. Said he couldn't betray his country.'

'Which one?'

'I don't know. His, I suppose. Russia. Or maybe England. That's not important. What is, is that he was asked. And declined - because of his...'

'Integrity?'

'Yes. He is a man of honour.'

'Alex Stanhope. A man of honour?'

'Exactly.'

'If you say so.'

'Jed, you're honoured, really privileged, to have such a man as your tutor or whatever it's called. You can learn from him. And I rather think he likes you.'

'He hides it well.'

'That's his professionalism. He told me he found you charming. He can't let on that he likes someone he teaches. He has to appear impartial.'

'He certainly does that.'

'Such a man of honour. And so admired. I could see that Poynton looked up to him.'

'So Poynton was there?'

'Yes, he took him on an educational visit. All at his own expense. So generous. And he bought us a wonderful dinner. But it gets better.'

'Can it?'

'Oh yes. When I told him that our mother was into Anglo-Saxon texts, his eyes just lit up. 'That's my passion', he said. 'My passion.''

'Passion,' Jed repeated.

'He had to wipe his eyes. His hankie had 'A.S.' on it, but that's not what I wanted to say. He was so overcome. He said,

'I couldn't. No. I shouldn't be saying this.' I said to him to go on. And he said, 'I couldn't possibly meet her, could I?' And he paused after 'possibly' and 'meet' came out so sheepishly that I almost shed a tear. He's so...'

'Unassuming?'

'Exactly. It was as if there could be no greater thrill for him than meeting mother. More so than any of the famous people he's met. He wouldn't name names, of course, but he's met some real celebrities.'

'And he wants to spend time with Mum?'

'Yes. Talking about learned texts. Next weekend.'

'What?'

'Yes, dad's still in Germany, she's back to see to the house, and I was going up to keep her company, so I've invited Alex to come, too.'

'That's nice.'

'Say it as if you mean it. Jed. It'll be fun.'

'That's nice.'

He's a strange one, thought Jed after he had replaced the receiver and walked into the open air. He just seems to like to lord it in front of the sixth-formers. Must have got him all wrong. There I was thinking there was less to him than meets the eye, and he has this secret passion. It all seems a bit... He knew there was a word for it. A single word that captured the idea he had about Stanhope's passion for Anglo-Saxon texts.

'May I ask you a question, sir?' Jed asked his English teacher.

'Fire away.'

'I think there's a single word for. It's when someone is interested in something that hardly anyone else is interested in. Well, only people who are really sophisticated. Something that's quite complicated and sort of 'deep', but the funny thing is that they're not really interested.'

'So it's a word describing the subject you're after? The 'not being really interested' is another word entirely and has something to do with 'deception' perhaps. But something that's obscure, esoteric and a bit over the top is, well...' The young man looked in the sky for inspiration. '*Recherché*'. That's the word I'd use, but that's a bit recherché, too. And a touch pompous. It's one of those words that the French do rather well; that we don't have quite the '*mot juste*' for. That means the 'exact phrase', like '*sympatique*'. That means that you feel for someone. Our 'sympathetic' isn't the same. That's when you feel sorry for someone - which is quite different, of course.'

Jed let the words roll round in his head. Pompous, yes. He knew he would have to find a situation to use them in.

'Did you do Anglo-Saxon at school, sir?'

'No, Jed, everything was in modern English. I'm not that old. But seriously, I did it at uni. Othere, Wulfstan, Beowulf, Gawain - the lot. You can borrow one of my old books if you like.'

Chapter 10

'Shit!' Poynton the larger had just spluttered his red wine over himself and another boy sitting opposite him. 'You tell me the punch line just when I've got a mouthful.'

'Then just sip it, Poynton. Let it roll around your mouth. Don't fill your gob'.

'Gob' wasn't a word Jed associated with Alex Stanhope. Maybe that's why he used it: for dramatic effect. Whatever the reason, Poynton and the other boy were vainly using spit and their fingers to get the pink stains out of the white shirts they had acquired for their London visit.

'Get them off,' Stanhope muttered from the depths of his winged chair. 'Massie will spot wash them for you.'

Jed removed the wellington boots from the basin and rinsed out the muddy water. White fabric slapped him round the ear. 'Yeah!' said Poynton's side-kick. 'Right round the ear'. Poynton's shirt landed on the floor.

Poynton rubbed his chest. 'Got hair coming there,' he said. 'How 'bout you, Benson?' He looked critically at the other boy and answered his own question. 'Nah, you're not a man.'

'It's called the 17-year-old human body.' Stanhope affected a sigh, 'And whether it's covered or not is all the same to me. Those trousers are stained, too. My dressing gown's in the wardrobe. Stick that on. Massie, wash the whites separately. That'll reduce your fine a bit. You should be grateful. Brett, give Massie your socks, so he'll have the full Monty.'

Brett Poynton pulled off his socks, strolled to Jed at the basin and flicked one at each ear before dropping the two blue socks in with the shirts. 'Get a move on, Dame Washalot.' Poynton raised an arm to flick the already reddened ear.

'You stink, Poynton.'

Jed knew that he would pay for those words.

'For once, Massie's right. Just walk straight on and go into my bathroom. There's a towel on the stool.'

The water in the small basin was turning blue. Jed took out the socks, let the water drain and refilled the basin. Poynton and his smell disappeared into the bathroom.

'You're a bit whiffy, too, Mark,' Stanhope motioned his hand towards the study door. The other youth took the hint.

'Met your sister, Massie.'

There was a pause, so Jed assumed he should respond in some way. With his arms in soap suds up to the elbows, all he could think of was, 'Yes, sir.'

'She's nice.'

'Yes, sir.'

'I'll be meeting her again.'

'Yes, sir.'

'Well, I expect you can come up with something more interesting than 'Yes, sir', can't you?'

'Yes, sir. I mean, yes, I understand.'

'What's she interested in?'

Jed's mind raced. It was like 'Mastermind' on TV. What was Gill's specialist subject? He would have to think of something exotic. Yes. He knew what he was doing. 'The Voyages of Ohthere and Wulfstan,' he paused, 'Sir.'

'Who the hell are they?'

'And 'Beowulf',' he paused again, 'Sir.'

'What are you talking about?'

'Your passion, sir'.

'Talk sense, boy. What's this rubbish? I just wanted to know what she's interested in so I can have some good conversations with her if I see her again.'

''If' sir?'

'Yes. I may, and I'd like to have some topics of conversation, so who are these people?'

'They're travellers, sir. They go on journeys, long journeys, into Russia and places. I think they're Scandinavian. That's Otter. Stan Woolfe and his sister, Bea. Or maybe she's Spanish. In which case, I guess her brother is, too. I thought you'd've heard of them. They're her passion.'

'What's all this about 'passion', Massie?'

'I just thought you might have one, sir. A passion, I mean.'

'Get on with earning the money you owe me. And you, Poynton, get yourself decent.'

Poynton had emerged from the bathroom, drying his hair with a white towel. He draped it around his waist and tucked it in.

'Stink, do I? Long cold shower at eight tomorrow. You can drip dry. You drip.'

A young man of few words, Jed thought. Mostly crude, short and stupid. It was almost worth it. And Stanhope didn't have a clue about his passion. He had given him the three best-known characters from Anglo-Saxon literature, and he hadn't a clue. His mention of Russia had gone unnoticed. If there were a passion, that was likely directed at his sister. Yet that didn't sit right either.

A fist smacked into the side of his head. 'Get those blue socks away from the whites. You'll ruin them, you moron. If you have, you can buy us each a new white shirt. You have! They've turned blue. Idiot. Sir, tell him to pay for new shirts.'

Shaken by the abrupt end to his reverie, Jed looked at the blue laundry. Poynton snatched both shirts and slapped them across his face. 'Ruined!' he yelled. 'Ruined!'

He grabbed both points of Jed's shirt collar and pulled upwards and out. Eight buttons popped out of their buttonholes and shot across the room. Stanhope ducked instinctively. The raging hands pulled downwards and the placket shredded from the body of the shirt; the yoke split from the back. Jed screamed in pain as the cuffs were tugged from his wrists, and the fabric bit into his armpits. The fingers scrabbled for more fabric and, failing this, found skin. Jed was on the floor, hands covering his head, his back exposed to the clawing nails.

'Enough, Brett,' Stanhope yelled. 'He won't be doing that again.'

'You bet he won't'. Poynton crouched over Jed, now prone, on his back. The face above him red and glistening; a drool of snot hanging from the nose; the teeth bared; the eyes fixed and bulging. The towel was on the carpet. Poynton was a naked wild animal. His belly was heaving.

'Ever!' Poynton spat from curled lips.

'Enough. Out.'

Poynton threw the towel over a shoulder, grabbed his dripping laundry and left without a backwards glance.

'Up. Show me.'

Two vivid striations ran the length of Jed's spine. Stanhope took cotton wool balls from his bathroom cabinet, dampened them and touched the wounds. Jed winced slightly.

'They'll heal. No need to trouble Matron. If he touches you, tell me. I'll speak to him and make sure he keeps his distance. Consider the 8 a.m. appointment cancelled. Let me have those rags. You won't be wearing that one again.'

The fibres of his pullover against his skin were a strange sensation. Jed hoped the others would not notice the absence of a shirt. He kept his head down and headed straight for his dorm, burrowing down in the familiar sheets and pulling on his pyjamas under their cover. On emerging, he saw specks of red sullying them. How was he going to explain that? Yes, a spot that he had picked. That would have to do. Another white lie. He was getting better at this.

'Massie,' A voice at the head of his bed sang out in a whining tone. 'I...'

The lost-looking boy with the red eyes he remembered from his first day and whom he had not seen since had clearly prepared something that had disappeared between his arrival and the emergence of Jed's head from the sheets. 'I...'

Jed sensed the boy's embarrassment and sought to fill the silence.

'Haven't seen you since the first day. You were going off with someone, as I recall. A member of staff wasn't it? Yes, he had a chat with me. It's coming back to me. He was new. He told me he was new, too. I mean, he was new, and he saw that I was new, and then he said something I haven't heard a grown-up say before. He said: 'We'll have to look out for each other, won't we? And then things happened to me, and somehow it all went out of my head.'

The red eyes were bulging now with an intensity that told Jed that he had said something significant. Whether this was a good thing or not, the boy's expression gave no indication of. The lost look had changed imperceptibly to one of something else. Jed couldn't put his finger on it. Hunted. That was it. The boy was pressed against the wall, backed into it. Trapped, yet held there by his own volition.

'I...'

'What? Jed saw at once that, no matter how gently he enunciated the word to be as unthreatening as he could manage to be, it was too blunt, too brief. That the boy had something to say was evident. It was how to get him to relax enough to say it that was the challenge. Maybe something tactile. The boy flinched from Jed's extended arm.

'I saw you.'

'OK?'

'I knew what he said to you.'

'Yes. He said the same to you.'

'And he did.'

'Did what?'

'Look out for me.'

'Well, that's a good thing, isn't it? You were new. He was new. So he gave you a helping hand.'

'Yes.'

Whatever more there was, was not going to come out immediately, so Jed took the initiative.

'I think I want to sleep now.'

'OK.'

'But come and chat to me when you want.'

'Yes, but you're with Mr Stanhope a lot, aren't you?'

'He's employing me to do jobs for him. He's my tutor, you know.'

'I know.'

'Well, you can see me when I'm not there.'

'He's helping you, isn't he?'

'Well, yes, sort of.'

'Then I know.'

The boy kept his mouth open. Whatever it was he wanted to say remained trapped in his head. He looked at the floor and slid along the wall to the door, eyes fixed on his shoes.

It wasn't so much that the boy 'knew'. It was the 'then' that struck Jed as the significant word in their brief exchange. As though the boy's knowing hinged on the helping that Jed had just agreed was happening. 'Because he knows my tutor is helping me, he also knows something else,' Jed let his imagination roam. What could it be that the boy knew because he knew Jed was being helped? That there was something to know made Jed think even harder.

'He's using me to get to my sister.'

Chapter 11

'What can I say, Jed? Gill and I have had the most delightful weekend with Alex. He is such an easy guest. And I had no idea, really no idea that he and I shared so many interests. I thought I was unusual in my tastes, but there they are, reflected in a man young enough to be my son. I've put him onto Sir Gawain. He's the one who chopped the Green Knight's head off, you know. It's all about alliteration- 'all grey grew the grass that was green before' – morality and nobility. But this man has it all. In spades. Such a courteous gentleman. Gill and I so enjoyed his company. And he tells us he'd love to come again. Can't imagine why. Maybe he has a soft spot for Gill. He was so attentive.'

'Lucky you.'

'No, Jed, that's ungenerous. He's not only charming but selfless, too, having to look after those boys. They certainly aren't his type, but he felt he had to do his duty.'

'What do you mean 'those boys?''

'The brothers. What were they called? Pontoon? No, that's a card game.'

'Poynton? Not the Poyntons, surely?'

'Brent and Jeremy, I think they were called. Very quiet. No conversation. Apparently, Alex is guardian to them, and the younger one can't be left on his own, some underdevelopment or something, so they came, too. Quite out of their depth, I'm afraid, although Alex, Gill and I tried really hard to engage them in our conversation. They just didn't seem to know very much.'

'Anything?'

'Jed, that's unworthy of you. No, they weren't - how shall I put it? Curious? Inquiring? - Well, just not interested.'

'So you had three visitors to accommodate. Where did you put them?'

'Well, there's the guest room and your bedroom.'

'There's just one double bed in the guest room and a single in mine.'

'Well, yes. They didn't want to put me to any trouble, so I had two in the double and the younger brother in the single. I thought when Gill brought her first young man home, I might be having to tell them they couldn't share, but Alex made it all so easy for me.'

'Gill's young man?'

'Well, I'm jumping the gun, but he is certainly attentive. Can't do enough for her. But, look, Jed, there is something else I need to talk to you about. I had a long chat with Alex about you. About your well-being. He tells me you're tending to be picked on and that you've got yourself into a little bit of trouble already. Is that so?'

'Some, but not my fault. I...'

'Look, Jed, I know it's hard with your parents at a distance and just your sister and aunt in the country. Well, I think - especially after a conversation I had with Alex - that you need a male role model closer to you geographically. I asked Alex if he could think of someone, and he said he would be willing to take on the responsibility.'

'No, mum, I don't need anyone. Not him. Not anyone. I'm fine as I am.'

'This is such an opportunity for you, Jed, and a weight off my mind.'

'But you didn't have a weight on your mind before. It wasn't an issue.'

'Talking to Alex was so helpful. He knows so much about young people. I had no idea how difficult it is to be at boarding school alone. I thought you could manage, but that was just wishful thinking. I can see how that poor Ponton boy has suffered.'

'But that's with Stanhope. Stanhope's his guardian, and look where it's got him.'

'He used to be far worse, Alex told me. It was all in confidence, though. I can't be talking to you about another pupil. Alex told me everything he said was in confidence. He's right. He's so professional.'

'Is he now?'

'OK, Jed, I'm sure his relationship with Gill has something to do with it, but be that as it may, it's such a relief to talk things through with him. Like having another member of the family. Consider it done. I've talked it through with dad, and he thinks it's a great idea. He's sending a signed letter to Captain Cassell to tell him that Alex can take decisions for him regarding your welfare. I've already given Alex a cheque for your pocket money for safe-keeping. Look, Gill's right by me. She'll have a word with you.'

'Jed? Yes, OK, I know: you don't need a guardian; you can manage on your own perfectly well; you already have a dad, and you don't need another one. Blah, blah. Well, this is a golden opportunity for you to have someone really academic close to you. There he was with mum talking about passion and with passion. Yes. He was on and on about these texts and Norsemen and Arthurian legends, and what a backstory. That awful day in Beirut. Both his parents killed, caught in the crossfire.'

'No, they weren't. They died in a canal In Amsterdam. Someone heard it from Baxter G, who heard it from Poynton.'

'Yes, I know. Alex was telling us, and Poynton said just that. 'Sorry, sir,' - isn't it sweet when they call him 'sir' - 'But you told me they were in a car that crashed into a canal.'

'Ah, Brett,' he said, 'but that's the story the security forces told me to tell. No one is supposed to know that my father was really undercover in Beirut. There are no records. Expunged. Redacted.' That's so weird. Everything about him is so mysterious.'

''Nothing is but what is not.''

'OK. Don't show your 'Macbeth' off to me.'

'No record of anything?'

'Look, he's got a brilliant First from Cambridge and a deep knowledge of early English texts. He's a cut above your ordinary secondary schoolteacher. Anyway, he's 'in *loco parentis*'. Just like a member of the family. And who knows?'

'Who knows what?'

'Just 'who knows?''

''Who knows? Who knows if he's really going to be a member of the family? Is that what you're saying?'

'Not yet. But I like him. Jed, I really do. I've seen him with young people, how kind he is, how he listens to them. Can't do enough for them. And offering to take you under his wing. That was so kind. Mum didn't know what to say.'

''No,' would've done for a start.'

'Jed, it was a brilliant suggestion. Mum just couldn't say no. You'll get to like him. You'll see. Anyway, 'what's done is done...''

''And cannot be undone,' Yes, I know how it goes.'

'The letter's written, the agreement's signed. You're Alex's ward now.'

'Alex's ward,' It didn't sit right with Jed. 'Stanhope's ward?' He tried this with as little success. He didn't see Stanhope as Alex. Hadn't imagined he had a first name apart from 'Mr'. 'Mr Stanhope's ward?' Yes, he could imagine that written on an official document. Why would his parents think he needed a guardian? He wondered about 'ward'. 'To ward off evil spirits? He asked his English teacher.

'Ward?' The young man rolled the word in his head. 'I think it's Old English 'weard'. I'll check, but I'm pretty sure it's right. A 'weard' is a 'protector'.'

'Well, I'm one now.'

'That's a surprise. What do you need to be protected from? I thought you had parents for that sort of thing.'

'It's Stanhope.'

The English teacher coughed gently.

'Sorry, sir. Mr Stanhope. He offered, and my parents accepted. They're out of the country a lot, and they thought it would be a good idea.'

'Maybe. Where did the idea come from?'

'Mr Stanhope, sir. He suggested it to my parents. Apparently, he's guardian to the Poyntons.'

The silence that followed told Jed everything. He knew that his English teacher could say nothing. His English teacher knew that he knew that.

'I don't want it, sir.'

'Well, you're not exactly in a position to say no.'

'I think he wants to be part of our family. He seems to be getting on well with my sister.'

Jed could sense surprise fleeting across the young man's face.

'Mr Stanhope is very involved with people, Jed. He, how shall I put it? - 'engages'. On a personal level, I mean. I told you before; I don't. Partly because I'm not resident, and partly because I keep a distance. I'm sure it's different for a resident master. And he's also your tutor, so he sees you on a different level. A more personal level.'

'But I find it easier to talk to you, sir. Let's put it this way: I've never actually had a conversation with Mr Stanhope. I'm often in his flat, but we don't talk.'

'So, why are you there?'

Why do I think the arrangement with Stanhope is a secret? Jed thought. I feel that it is. I know it is. But why is it? Why do I feel I have to keep a secret that Stanhope has created?

Jed felt a tear trickle down his cheek. He wanted to say. Oh, how he wanted to say, 'I'm paying off a debt for something that wasn't my fault by doing chores and being bullied by prefects and a teacher,' but the words wouldn't come. It wasn't loyalty to Stanhope or because he didn't trust the man standing in front of him. He knew that if he could tell someone, it would be him. For reasons that defied the logic that had guided Jed through the almost thirteen years of his life, he had to keep the secret.

'He helps me with work, sir.'

'I know that your tutor is there if you have a problem, but you can talk to any of the teachers if you want. And to your parents.'

'Yes, sir. Thank you. I ...'

'Look, Jed. Let me be straight with you. You know I know. I know that you know I know. We're knowledgeable people. The thing is, I just know it's something, and I don't know precisely what. If you want to talk about it, it has to come from you. I can't put words into your mouth. I'm offering, for goodness sake.' Paul Mason paused significantly. 'Up to you. If you want a chat, you know where I am.'

Stupid, stupid! How could I let myself down like that? How is it that I don't know why I feel like this? Guilty. But I'm not guilty. So why couldn't I tell him why I'm up there? I know it's all part of Stanhope's plan to get together with Gill. But she's not his type, so why is he bothering? I should have said something to him.

'Massie.' It was the lost-looking boy. 'You've been blubbing.'

'Something in my eye.'

'I do that quite a bit. I know I should be grateful, but sometimes I just want to cry. That's weak, isn't it?'

'Probably, but I think everyone does it sometimes. The thing is, you can't let anyone see you, can you? Anything that's weak here is wrong. But there are other wrong things. Things that feel wrong. I don't know why. They just feel wrong.'

'Anyway, Mr Watson is taking me to the Dutch Masters' exhibition at the National. I showed him my drawings, and he told me I really had a flair for art. He's got books and books of paintings. He gets me to do drawings.'

'What do you draw?'

'He calls them 'life drawings'. You know, real people.'

'You mean he gets you to draw people? People here?'

'Oh, no. Not yet. I'm still practising.'

'So who do you draw?'

'Him.'

'Oh.'

'He's very patient. Sits for ages without moving.'

'You must show me.'

'Oh, no. Can't do that.'

'Why ever not?'

'Alan says they're not quite good enough yet. That I need to practise more.'

'You call him 'Alan?''

'That's his name. I call him 'Mr Watson' in public, but he wants me to call him 'Alan' in his free time.'

'What does he call you?'

'Bunny.'

'But you're Michael O'Hare, aren't you? Is that what they call you at home? Your parents?'

'Oh no. No one's ever called me that. But I like it. It's a cuddly name. Don't tell anyone. They'll use it against me and make it horrible. It's something special that Alan and I have got.'

'It's a secret? Yes?'

'Yes, let it be our secret, too.'

Jed couldn't call Michael O'Hare the lost-looking boy any longer. He wasn't lost. He had a spring in his step. And a new name. A name that he had to keep a secret. Another boy with a secret. But a secret he had told him. Should he tell Michael his secret? Maybe he would. Later. Much later.

Chapter 12

'I felt like a celebrity. It was the most wonderful surprise ever. He told me to put my glad rags on and to meet him outside Harrods. 'What's it going to be?' I asked him all along Brompton Road. I was a girl again. 'Do tell me. Come on, tell me. Is it Harvey Nics?' I said. We walked past that. I was a little bit sorry. I'd've loved to have gone in, but no, we came to Piccadilly and then. Oh, go on, Jed, guess. You must have an idea by now. OK. Well, I'll tell you. We had tea at The Ritz! Yes, cucumber sandwiches, scones with jam and cream, little cakes. The lot. And then... You won't believe it. He took a little box out of his pocket and...'

'Oh, for God's sake, you're not going to tell me...'

'It was a brooch - a silver brooch with green stones. 'To go with your eyes,' he said. But not just any old brooch. It was his great-great-aunt's. 'Been in the family for generations,' he said. 'Sitting in a jewellery box. About time it went out and about.'

'Which great-great-aunt was this? The one from Moscow or Beirut? Or maybe the one from Canvey Island who won it at a side-show at the fair. Come off it, Gill. He's not going to give someone he hardly knows a jewel of great prize, is he?'

'We didn't speak about its value. It's vulgar to talk about money. And, anyway, he's simply the most spontaneous person I've ever met. He told me he'd suddenly decided to drop those brothers off and steal a few minutes for himself and for me.'

'Drop them off to shoplift in Harrods? They'd've jumped at the chance.'

'Stop being cynical. He had to take them to London for some reason or other and just took a little time off.'

'Yes, I thought it was peaceful here.'

'Look, you could at least make an effort not to be sarcastic about him all the time. He's your guardian. He'll look after your welfare. He often mentions you.'

'He doesn't like me.'

'Come off it. The older Poynton tells me you're always in his room of an evening, hanging about. Why do you spend so much time with him if you don't like each other? I know. It's for protection. Alex told me how the other boys get at you. Bully you even. Someone pulled at your clothes. He stopped them. Jed, he's a good man. And I like him. That's an end to it.'

After his weekly phone call, Jed made his way to Stanhope's flat to do his chores. He decided to ask the man how much he still owed. He paused outside the door and poised himself before knocking.

'Just begging for it,' Standish was saying.

'Yeah, go for it,' came the guffaw of the older Poynton.

'Good on yer, sir.' That was Baxter G.

'Come!' bellowed Stanhope.

A fourth boy Jed recognised as the one whose hairless chest Poynton disapproved of was making up and down movements with his fist above his groin.

Four pairs of eyes followed him in the room. 'Go, Massie. Massie, Massie, Massie', chanted Poynton. Baxter G. sniggered.

'Right, Massie. There's some grubby things for you to clean. Then you can dust the bookshelves. Look lively!'

'You know what grubby is, sir, don't you?'

'Enough, Grant, get back to your 'Beano'. You can use Desperate Dan as a role model.'

So Baxter G. did have a first name, after all. Jed opened his mouth. Should he? Why not?

It's 'The Dandy,' Jed paused just for long enough, 'sir'. He let another second pass.

'What?' Stanhope retorted.

'He's in 'The Dandy' not 'Beano'. Desperate Dan. Baxter can use Dennis the Menace as his role model. And Beryl the Peril. They're both in the 'Beano."

With unaccustomed alacrity, Alex Stanhope rose from his winged armchair and put his face up to Jed's. There were flecks of spittle around his curled lips. Jed blinked as a slight shower went into his eyes. The man's face, generally red, was puce now. At zero distance, Jed took in the open pores on the nose, a sprinkling of blackheads and some whiskers missed by the razor that morning. The breath was rancid. Teeth stained. Red veins stood out in the no-colour eyes.

Stanhope pulled Jed towards him by the knot in his tie.

'If I say it, it's true. Whatever I say is true, whether it is or not. I'm the teacher; you're the pupil. I'm the man; you're the boy. You do as you're told. Whatever you're told. And you can shove 'The Dandy' where the sun doesn't shine, lad.' Stanhope gave the knot a twist and pulled him closer. 'Get it?' Stanhope's other hand slid down into Jed's trousers. Jed gasped and then yelled in agony as the grip tightened into a fist. Stanhope removed his hand and pushed him backwards into one of the hardbacked dining chairs. He pulled off his shoes and flung them at the prone boy. 'Polish these. Then clean the flat.'

My guardian, thought Jed. The man who's there to protect me. This jumped-up would-be tyrant. I know there's less to you than everyone thinks. Sooner or later, everyone will see you for who you are.

Chapter 13

Jed had never considered doing anything underhand. Straightforwardness was prized in his family. Maybe not so much prized as assumed. One did as one was told. Everything he had been told to do was sensible, so it had never occurred to him to operate outside its parameters. What was sensible, indeed, what was right at Finchingham School, was stood on its head. He was used to seeing adults operating in the best interests of the child, him. Here and now, it was the adults' self-indulgence that was paramount.

It was another thirty-five years before he could put this into these precise words. Until that point, it was just a feeling, but one strong enough for him to know that he had to grow up quickly, keep his misgivings to himself and cover himself with a hard shell. Always, he had seen his parents as his protectors. Now they had become part of the problem. Not through any fault of their own, but they had been traduced by something powerful, seductive, and, he knew, wrong.

He tended to think things through in words, but his thoughts were too complex for his current vocabulary. It was so much harder to think through feelings: words concretised thoughts. Like David in his book, he would have to be guided by what he knew was right. When he came up against something - and someone - not right, he would think it through and act against it. As most of what was around him fell into the category of not right, that would be a challenge. The alternative was to accept what was all around him. So what was screaming to be challenged? He would start with his guardian.

Stanhope was a fraud. There were plenty of clues to take this viewpoint. Logically, if he exposed him, his parents would see his unsuitability for guardianship. His sister would realise that his intentions were not good for her. Where to begin? Let's challenge the assumptions. The first one to look at must be his qualification. Gill had mentioned Cambridge and a First. There must be proof somewhere, a sort of certificate. Yes, he would write to the University and ask for it. No one would look twice at a handwritten letter written by a not-quite-thirteen-year-old, so it would have to be typed. He decided to embark on his new mission of being not-quite-straightforward.

'Miss.' With no idea of her name, he was at a loss how to address the grey-haired lady in the office. Perhaps she would fall for what was utterly genuine about him - his naiveté. 'I don't know what to call you.' How would she respond? Would she simply tell him or brush him away? All could be lost at this stage. The response was midway between his hope and expectation.

'Well let's start with Mrs van Hofstadter, shall we?'

How he would have loved to do his spiel on honorific prefixes. Now was not the occasion. Anyway, its use told him she was married.

'Please, Mrs van Hofstadter, may I ask a favour?'

'You can try.'

Was that a faint smile starting to crack the makeup around the mouth? He had her attention now. The trick was to keep it. This was not going to be a white lie. It would be the first time he had ever attempted an out-and-out untruth. He smiled.

'I would really like to impress my parents with something. Something that I have thought up all by myself. That would make them see that I was really taking the opportunity of being away from home to try new things.'

It was too long. He was losing her.

'Come along then. What is it? I've got the minutes of the staff meeting to get out by lunchtime.'

'Well, I was wondering if I could type my next letter home. Only a short one. Just to surprise them.'

'Look, I'm far too busy to wait around while you clack away. Sorry, but no.'

Jed thought quickly. 'You mentioned lunchtime. Might I have a few minutes at your typewriter while you have lunch? I would be so, so grateful.'

He felt the charm oozing out of him and hoped he hadn't gone too far. He looked her in the eye for a clue as to any reciprocity.

'I know they would love it.'

The pause was just long enough to know that there would be no outright refusal. There would be conditions. He knew they were coming.

'Well, you certainly know how to express yourself politely, which is more than I can say for most people here - and not just boys.'

Now that was an unexpected chink in the armour.

'So, tell you what. Come here at 12.59, and I'll let you have the key. After lunch, I'll be in the Staff Common Room until 13.45, so knock on the door and ask for me.'

'Oh yes, of course. I'll be here on the dot.'

There was something else. She was wavering.

'Don't look at anything else. The files are in a locked cabinet, but there may be pieces of paper not yet filed hanging around. They are not for your eyes. OK?'

'Yes, of course. It hadn't occurred to me.' That was true. But now that she mentioned it...

'And something else.'

Oh, dear. What next?

Mrs van Hofstadter smiled. 'Type slowly and don't jam my keys.'

'I promise I'll be ever so careful. Thank you very much.'

Jed sat through the morning's lessons with growing excitement. It was naughty, duplicitous and fundamentally wrong. For the first time in his life, he had manipulated someone. He saw how easy it was. Was it because he had seen almost everyone around him doing the same? Was it the first step to being as corrupt as they were? He needed to justify it in his own head, convince himself that he was still the decent person he needed to feel himself to be. He was trying to right a wrong. To show that someone was not who he pretended to be. To reveal corruption. He struggled with the concept of ends justifying means and knew that such abstractions would have to wait until he had the maturity and vocabulary to deal with them. Until that point, he would be guided, like David, by his inner voice. Yes, David would show him the way, without the

God-thing, though. He couldn't see the point of that. It was a comfort to David to confide in someone, though. Who could he confide in?

'Well, Massie, answer the question!' The music teacher's voice was raised an octave. 'Or I'll keep you in at lunchtime.'

'Well, some would agree, and some would disagree, and many would have no views either way, but it's really a matter of personal taste.' It was something and nothing. It just came out. Instinctively. At least it covered up his unawareness of what had been asked. It was also another lie. Well, almost. It was going to become second nature.

'Absolutely. At last, a reasonable answer and, Jed Massie, as I firmly suspect that you were miles away in a brown study, a clever one that I personally agree with. For your information, it was about the similarity between Pachelbel's 'Canon in D' and Kylie Minogue's 'I should be so lucky.''

'I know, sir. Johann Pachelbel would be thrilled to know that his work has inspired a pop song. Imitation is, after all, the sincerest form of flattery.'

Alan Watson stroked his beard. 'Indeed, he just might.' He paused, still stroking, and fixed him in the eye. 'A clever boy, aren't you? 'So wise so young do never live long.' They say.'

'Thank you, sir,' Jed couldn't resist. Actually, it's 'So wise so young, they say, do never live long.' Or so they say. It preserves the scansion.'

'Or, as I would say, don't push it. Mate.'

Had he not had the conversation with Michael-cum-Bunny a few days ago, he might have quite liked Alan Watson. Now he simply saw him as a danger. Maybe he should look into him after Alex Stanhope. Same age as Stanhope, mid-twenties. Just a little more subtle. In the event, Alan Watson would die by his own hand thirty-three years later.

'12.59, Mrs van Hofstadter'. Jed was punctual to the second. 'I was afraid I might be late - or early.'

Mrs van Hofstadter smiled. She knew the quote. Jed could tell she was warming to him.

'Here you are.'

'Thanks.'

'What's your name?'

'Jed. Jed Massie'.

'Well, Jed, let's let this be our little secret, shall we? Wouldn't want everyone asking for typing practice, would we?'

'You can count on me, Mrs van Hofstadter.'

'Yes. I rather think I can.'

And Jed rather thought he liked this lady with the foreign-sounding name and had the feeling that she might actually approve of what he was about to do.

Chapter 14

It was all his own work. It had taken the best part of half an hour. He had tried to get into the head of the adult writer and adopt the sort of casual but firm tone that an employer might take. Without the benefit of an address, he hoped the Post Office would know where it was to go. He would ensure that it was graced with a first-class stamp, so they knew it meant business.

Jed read through it again.

The Person in charge of Qualifications
The University of Cambridge
Cambridge

Dear Sir.

We are considering employing as a teacher a certain Mr Alexander Stanhope. He tells us he has a First Class degree from your university but cannot find the certificate.

Please can you confirm that Mr Alexander Stanhope has the degree that he tells us he has.

Yours faithfully.

J. Massie

He knew it was 'faithfully' with Dear Sir' and 'sincerely' with 'Dear Mr/Mrs' and that the 'f' would not be capitalised. It should be to the point but polite. The more he looked, the more he liked it. And it was on official school letterhead. He had found a few sheets on Mrs van Hofstadter's desk and took one. Well, maybe another couple. They might come in handy, he thought.

He was just about to leave when there was a double knock on the door. An adult voice said, 'Maartje, are you there?'

Jed froze. He hadn't thought to lock the door. His mind raced to grab something he might say if the teacher outside decided to open the door anyway. He wanted to shout 'No' as an answer. He held his breath. The handle turned slightly. Then it stopped. Whoever was there thought better of entering an empty office and walked off. Jed waited until the footsteps were no more, opened the door a crack and slipped out, clutching a single sheet of paper folded into thirds to fit a DL envelope. The spare sheets were flat inside his pullover. He knocked on the Staff Common Room door.

'May I speak to Mrs van Hofstadter, please?'

She appeared with a mug of tea in her hand.

'I wonder if I might trouble you for an envelope, please,' said Jed. 'And might I buy a first-class stamp from you? Perhaps it could come out of my pocket money account.'

They walked together to her office.

'Mission accomplished?'

'Yes. Thanks. It was quite an experience.'

'I can't debit your pocket money, I'm afraid. Your tutor has given instructions that, as your official guardian, he will assume control over your spending, so you'll have to get the money from him, but here's an envelope for you.'

Jed looked crestfallen. His plan was about to be wrecked. Stanhope would want to know why he was writing a letter that wasn't the permitted weekly letter that went with all the other letters to the study to be given second-class stamps and put in the box that the post van collected each evening.

'Oh, I can't do that. I mean, I don't want to, rather I can't ask him. I don't want to ask him for anything.'

The smile disappeared from the woman's face. She could hear the fear in the boy's voice, see it in his eyes.

'I understand. I'll get you a stamp. I'm sure the Head wouldn't mind.'

'Oh, thank you so much.'

'I trust your parents will be impressed.'

'What?'

'With the letter to them you've typed.'

'Oh yes. I'm sure they will. It could make quite a difference.'

Jed hoped he hadn't given anything away. He hurriedly folded the letter and put it in the envelope, making sure the address could be read through the little window, straightened the stamp, secured an exeat from the master on duty and walked briskly to the post box down the hill. The envelope pitter-pattered down the cylinder of the box. He knew that he had crossed the line. No turning back.

As he walked back, he felt the papers in his pullover crinkle and knew they would spoil if he left them there. He gently eased them out. Three sheets. He separated them and saw that there was a fourth - a different, thinner paper that was not letterhead.

There was faint printing on it, which is presumably why it had been discarded. It can't have gone through the Roneo properly. His immediate reaction was not to look. 'Eavesdroppers never hear any good of themselves,' he had been taught, and this was tantamount to listening at a door and equally irresistible. In for a penny, he thought.

Jed looked around to make sure no one was looking, left the main track and wandered into the undergrowth. If he held the paper in the light, he could just make out the printing. 'Minutes of Staff Meeting' was the title. Within a few minutes, his body was trembling. What he held in his hand was a time-bomb. He realised its import, but it was of the adult world: a world he knew little of. He was still at the stage at which things were done for him, and if he forgot any of the few things he did for himself, someone would rescue him. These were mundane things like remembering when it was a mealtime, bedtime, time to put his washing in the laundry basket. If he were unsure, he would ask, and the answer would be given.

Never had he felt so alone. Here was information that he didn't want, hadn't asked for and didn't know what to do with. All he had to do was throw the paper into a bush, and the problem would disappear. Except that it wouldn't. He had seen it, and he could not unsee it. He knew it and could not unknow it. The day before his thirteenth birthday, he had become part of the adult world. It was complicated and drew on skills he had not yet practised, and there was no one to guide him.

He sat down, overwhelmed with the importance of it all. The landscape around him was spinning; there was noise in his head; his breathing was rapid. He pinched his hand. Right, I'm going to be like David. If I haven't anyone to talk to, I'll talk to myself. I know I can rely on myself not to do anything stupid. They tell me I've done stupid things, and I started to believe them, but I didn't. I didn't do anything they said I'd done, so why did I believe them? Yes. It was because they were grown-ups, and they had power. That's what it's all about. Why didn't I think of that? They had power, power over me. But there again, all adults have power, and they don't all make me feel bad like these adults. Why don't they do this? What makes them different?

Ideas were racing through Jed's mind, still unformed and without all the vocabulary to comprehend the difference between the exercise of power for someone else's good and using that power for one's own good. He was getting it but was still a blur. Maybe if he just put it in terms of right and wrong. Right was a thing that was good for people, and wrong was the opposite. He had to do the right thing when all around him were wrong things done for reasons he could not understand. This is what growing up was about. This is the difference between twelve and thirteen. Now I'll be thirteen.

Yes, he would read the information in his hand and then decide which was the best way forward. David would tell God. He would tell his inner self.

Jed read the faint print. There was his English teacher's name and afterwards what he had said: 'said that Richard Braine had come to see him in some distress saying that he did not want Mr Kempson to tutor him or come to his house in the holidays and that he sensed the boy was afraid.'

He read on: 'Mr Stanhope said that the boy was lazy and just wanted to do nothing in the holidays.'

The next line had his English teacher's response: 'I made this point to Richard. He burst into tears and said that

Mr Kempson made him do things he didn't want to do. This is the point at which we need, at least, to involve Richard's parents. These are serious allegations.'

The next line was an invitation to Mr Kempson to respond. 'Mr Kempson replied that it was stuff and nonsense.'

'Mr Stanhope made the point that several boys found it funny to make allegations against members of staff and that this needed to be stamped out firmly.'

'The Headmaster agreed and said that the very future of the school would be thrown into doubt if these rumours persisted. Staff were instructed to bring any child making allegations straight to Captain Cassell, that staff were to take no action themselves and that, if they did not comply, they would be asked to resign.'

Back to his English teacher. The minutes quoted his exact words: 'So I am not to take what Richard told me seriously? I am to refer this to Captain Cassell? What action, may I ask Mr Cassell, will he take?'

The minutes went on: 'Captain Cassell declined to answer the question. He said that there was a drop in pupil numbers and that he would have to consider reducing staff numbers. He further said that any adverse publicity would jeopardise the school's existence.'

His English teacher: 'Captain Cassell's reaction makes it clear that the information this child has provided will not be acted on. It is not the first time that I have drawn his attention and the Headmaster's to staff favouring certain children to the detriment of their personal happiness. I am unable to continue my employment under these circumstances.'

The Headmaster: 'We regret, but accept this resignation. The post will not be advertised. Now we must move to other matters. We need to decide to whom to award the sports prizes.'

Jed read on. No more mention of allegations. It was as if nothing had been said.

What should he do? Something? Nothing?

Chapter 15

'Richard! Couldn't find you. What in heaven's name are you doing here?' Having hunted over the school, Jed had eventually tracked him down to the games changing room, where the boy was sitting on one of the benches, head in hands.

'Nothing much to do,' he said. 'I'm leaving.'

'Are you really?'

'Well, I've asked my parents if I can leave, but they keep saying no. I've said they can send me to any school but this one. I'm not learning anything. I don't have any friends. I just don't want to be here.'

'Maybe if you told them that a particular person was making life difficult for you, they might reconsider.'

'Tried that. They just think I'm lazy and tell me they'll employ the tutor for every holiday, even half-term. Every holiday. I see him every day. And my parents aren't there. Those are the worst times. I just want to be on my own. I want to be free to do what I want.'

'Is he the problem? Your tutor?'

'I'm not talking about it. I can't talk about it. You don't know anything about it.'

'Try me.'

'No. I tried once, but it didn't work, and it just got the other person into trouble. No one will believe me.'

'But someone did.'

'Yes, but there's no point in talking about if at the end nothing happens that makes things better.'

'Maybe it's worth trying again.'

'Look, if the person I spoke to can't change things, you have no chance. You're a child. People like you and me have no power to change things.'

'What if I told you I knew who you spoke to?'

'He told me he wouldn't tell any of the kids. There you are, I can't even trust him.'

'No. That's not what I meant. I found out by accident. He didn't speak to me. He wouldn't.'

'I can't tell you. I couldn't tell him. Not the whole thing anyway. Please don't push me. It only makes me feel worse. I'll just have to get used to it.'

'Is it Kempson?'

'I'm not telling. Just leave me alone, please.'

'OK. Sorry. You know you can talk to me whenever you want, don't you? I know what some of the people here are like. I've had a taste of how nasty they can be.'

The boy looked up. ''I doubt it. Frankly, you'd be better off not knowing.'

The boy started weeping quietly. Jed saw that his clumsy efforts at helping had been an abject failure and that he had just made things worse.

'I'm sorry, Richard.' He started walking back to his dorm.

'He's making me be like him.'

Jed turned. 'What was that?'

It was decades before he was to find out.

'Jed. May I have a word?'

Mrs van Hofstadter was beckoning him from her open doorway.

'Close the door, please.' She indicated a seat in front of her desk. 'I've just had a phone call. It was from the University of Cambridge. They seem to think you're me but called 'J. Massie'.

Jed's stomach hit his feet. He imagined they'd write to him, not phone the number on the school letterhead. Every piece of his plan unravelled in that single instant.

'It wasn't a letter typed to impress your parents, was it? You lied to me. You wrote a letter asking about Mr Stanhope's qualification.'

'Yes. You're right. I don't know what to say. I lied to you. It was wrong, and I'm ashamed.' Jed hung his head and waited for the justified outburst about how untrustworthy he was. Whatever was coming, he deserved no less.

'Well, he hasn't got one.'

'Hasn't got what?'

'A qualification. Not from Cambridge, at least.'

Jed looked at the grey-haired woman, now white-faced and, yes, he could see it - fearful.

'I won't expose you. I don't know what to do with this information, or what the repercussions on me may be, but the University was clear. They have never had anyone of that name as a student in any subject. They are writing to 'J. Massie' to confirm this.'

'Thank you, Mrs van Hofstadter. Thank you very much. I think I need some moments to take this all in.'

'Well, I think I do, too. If the man's a fraud, Jed, you did the right thing. More than I would have done at your age, or, come to think of it, at mine. As you'll be getting written proof, there's no need to involve me or say how you came to type the letter. I would appreciate it. I'd certainly lose my job if the Head or Cassell found out. They expect loyalty above everything.'

'No. I'll say nothing. I won't get you into trouble.'

'And for what it's worth, let me say well done. The man's a pompous boor. I assume you plan for him to get his comeuppance. Good luck to you.'

'Thank you. Thank you. You don't know how much this means to me.'

Mrs van Hofstadter opened the door. She pressed his hand as he left. 'I think I may do, Jed'.

There was a spring in Jed's step as he left the secretary's office. Someone had praised him for his actions. Although he could never acknowledge the praise, it had happened, and her appreciation and support made him feel that he was no longer alone. He just had to wait for the letter and work off his stupid fine in Stanhope's flat for a few days until the man was exposed as a fraud.

'Come.' Stanhope did not look up from his newspaper. 'I'm going to tell you to make a start on the dishes in the kitchen.'

'Yes, sir.'

'Then, when you've done that, you're going to vacuum the carpet.'

'Yes, sir.'

'Come here first.'

Chapter 16

Jed woke to a different world the following morning. Always he had been able to rely on talking to himself, to know that he could have a sensible conversation with himself and work out a good way forward. Now he knew there was a part of himself that was blanked off, that he dared not enter because to go there would be too painful. Others will see it. He would see it in their eyes and know that they knew. They'll point the finger and make everything so much worse. As if it could be worse. He knew what the worst was. It was screaming inside him so loudly that he couldn't imagine anyone not hearing it.

He decided he would keep out of their way. Yes, to stick to the shadows will be the safest way from here on in. Above everything, he didn't want to be noticed. What should he do with the feelings he had never had before? How could he deal with emotions that he could not put into words because they had never entered his young life? He hardly knew what they were. Inside him was a maelstrom of pent-up anxieties that he needed to pin down, to give words to; otherwise, his head would explode. That's what he'd do. He'd identify them and sort them out one by one.

What was the first? What was the biggest threat to his being? There were two that loomed large. One was shame. Yes, he had touched on that when he hadn't told anyone about the chores he was doing. Even more when he kept the secret that Stanhope had grabbed his genitals. And shame had a close ally. So close that he could not separate them. Guilt. He could hardly separate the two. Guilt and shame. They couldn't be let out, or they would wreck him. They had to be kept inside, chained down. They were horrid feelings that would upset everybody. But there was another one, almost overriding the other two. He had to identify it to deal with it. He bit his lip, hoping the pain would concentrate his mind. It was coming to him. It was huge and black and swamping his very self. Yes, he had it. He knew what it was, and it was so big that he knew it could overwhelm him.

Hate. Jed now knew hate. He felt it become absorbed into the essence of who he was. And he knew without a shadow of a doubt that now it was part of him. It was integral and would have to be lived with; an unwelcome guest. Yesterday he thought he had become part of the adult world. Today he knew how cold it could be.

'Happy birthday, Jed!'

He forced a smile to Mrs van Hofstadter.

'It's arrived. I thought I'd hand it to you myself.'

Just as well she did as it had 'University of Cambridge' on the envelope and was addressed to 'Mrs J. Massie, Principal.'

He went straight to his dorm, peeled it open and looked at it. As expected, it read: 'Further to your recent enquiry, we can confirm that this university has not taught or awarded a qualification to a Mr Alexander Stanhope.' He should feel satisfied at what his tenacity had achieved, but it just ratcheted up his hatred another notch. The man had entered his dreams. He wanted him out of the school, out of his head and out of his life. Now he had to think how best to achieve this.

'False face must hide what the false heart doth know' were words he knew only from a play. In his life, he had been expected to be truthful, and it had never occurred to him to be anything else, but dishonesty appeared to be the way of the world here, and, he felt, the only way to achieve his ends. He thought through as many of the possible scenarios as he could, but there was bound to be a surprise. He had to safeguard his information. Yes, that was the first thing to do. Everything was on a single piece of paper. Were that to be lost, all would be lost.

He went back to Mrs van Hofstadter. 'Excuse me, but might I ask you to make a photocopy of something for me, please?'

'I'm so sorry, Jed, but I've been waiting for the engineer to repair it for some days.'

His mind raced.

'You don't happen to know who's in charge of the Photography Club, do you?'

'I'll look it up. It's somewhere in the records. Yes. Here we are. It's run by one of the prefects, Mark Boyce.'

'I don't know him. You haven't got a list of the members, have you?'

'Yes, I should have as there's a small termly charge I have to add to the bill. There are quite a few on the list.'

'May I look?'

Mrs van Hofstadter passed a sheet of paper to him, and he skimmed down the page.

''Richard Braine'. Great. That's what I need. Thanks.'

'Whatever you're doing, please be careful. Nothing here is quite what it seems to be, you know?'

'Yes. I'm starting to realise this.'

Jed waited until the long break to catch Richard on his own.

'Look, I need a big favour, and I don't know who to ask. I have a letter I need copied, but the only way to copy it is to take a photo of it. Could you do this for me?'

'Not sure how many exposures I have left on my film. Let me look after lunch. There should be quite a few. I'll come and find you.'

Jed wanted to deliver the *coup de grace* as soon as possible. One thing he was sure of was that he would never go into that man's flat ever again. Now it was one hurdle after another.

There was someone else he could talk to who would understand. He ran to the English Room. It was empty apart from a cleaner.

'Do you know where Mr Mason is?'

'I am afraid he's gone, young man.'

'Oh, he's finished for the day. OK. I'll see him another time.'

'I'm afraid you won't. He's left. Them two in the office said he should go sooner rather than later. They gave him five minutes to take his things. I was in here working. He was very upset. I'll miss him. Such a kind man.'

Jed felt sick. At the back of his mind, he knew that Paul Mason would give support and not judge him harshly. He sensed he could tell him everything. Now he couldn't.

'Jed, can I speak to you?' Benny Jamieson was interrupting his chain of thought.

'Now's not the time.'

'I think it is, Jed.'

'Well, later. Tomorrow, maybe. I just can't stop at the moment.'

'Find me.' Benny paused. 'Please.'

Jed's head spun. Whatever Benny Jamieson wanted to say remained unspoken.

Richard Braine was true to his word. After lunch, he found Jed. 'Yes, I only have two exposures left. Sorry. I thought I had more.'

'OK. Let's go outside as far away as possible and take a shot.'

They ran to far the side of the field behind the cricket pavilion. Jed held up the sheet. 'Can you focus, so you get the print clearly?'

'Just doing this and keeping my hand really steady.'

There was a click. Richard wound the film on.

'Do you want another? Just in case. There's one left.'

'We'll have to take a chance. There's something else I want you to snap, please.'

Jed turned away from Richard, pulled off his pullover, undid his tie, unbuttoned his shirt and slipped it off.

'Christ. How did you get these?'

'I haven't seen them, but I can imagine there are two long red marks on my back. Can you photograph my back, please? I'll turn my head, so anyone looking at the photo will know that it's me.'

'But the marks don't stop there, They...'

'Yes. Right. Here goes.'

Jed found it so easy to do what he never could have contemplated just a few months before.

'My God, that's awful. I don't know what to say. They must hurt like hell. And there's blood down your legs. Give me a moment. My hand's shaking.'

'Calm down, Richard. You see why we need to take a picture. Deep breaths. Just focus.'

The shutter clicked again.

'How do you get your films developed?'

'Nick Boyce does them for us in the darkroom.'

'Too risky. He's bound to read the letter and anyway you know we can't let anyone else see the other photo. We'll have to think of something. We need a chemist shop. I think there's a Boots in town.'

'We can go there on an exeat at the weekend.'

'No, I need these done now. If Boots shuts at five and lessons end at four, we've just got enough time to run there and be back for dinner. I can go my own, but if you're up for it, it would be good to go together.'

'How are we going to pay?'

Neither boy had any money. They would have to go to Stanhope and Kempson to ask for some, and they wouldn't be given any until Saturday.

'I've got an idea. Leave it to me, Richard. I'll see you at the back door straight after lessons. Don't get kept behind.'

Jed composed the words in his head. He was taking a big chance, but of all the adults in the school, he knew there were two he could trust. Of these, one might be too committed to the ideal of professionalism to bend the rules, even in a good cause, and he had been kicked out anyway, but the other had already given him enough encouragement to suspect that adherence to the rules might be, shall we say, flexible. He had five minutes before the start of afternoon lessons.

He knocked. What if she were out? He crossed his fingers. The door opened. 'Jed?'

'May I come in, please?'

She beckoned him in. The room was empty.

'Look, I need to copy the letter. Just in case, you know. Without a copier, the only way to do this is to take a photo. That's been done, but I need to get the film developed now. Boots shuts at five. I can just get there and back after lessons, but I have no pocket money. I'd have to ask Stanhope, sorry, Mr Stanhope for it and he won't let me have any until the weekend. Could I possibly borrow £2? It's a cheek to ask, I've never done this before, but I just have to make sure no one takes this proof away.'

It was all too much. Jed's body shuddered with sobs. Everything came rushing into him at once. A concatenation of emotions. Maartje van Hofstadter opened her arms and clutched him to her. 'There, there. I won't let them... I mean, I can't imagine what you're going through, but I have the most awful idea.' She stroked his back. The sobs subsided. 'This is no way to spend your birthday.'

'Is this what growing up is?'

'No, no, my dear. It isn't. It can't be.'

'You know, don't you?'

'Do what you must. Just be very careful. Please.' She slipped a five-pound note into his hand.

'Good luck.' She hugged him. It was the only kind touch he had felt in weeks. It meant more to him than anyone could ever imagine.

Chapter 17

'No. He's a minor, and I have full responsibility. You may not speak to my ward without my being present.'

Stanhope was at his most authoritative, hands on hips, barking at the young police constable.

'Please bring him in, sir. We will speak to him in your presence.'

Rumours had been rife all that morning. One of the prefects out on an early morning run had seen Cassell being taken away in a police car.

'Someone blew the whistle on him. Found some photos. Brookfield's in a right state. Says the school may have to close.'

This was not the impression the Head was giving. After breakfast, he summoned all the boys to the Hall.

'There have been rumours. Rumours. Pernicious rumours that events have happened that jeopardise the future of Finchingham School. Our school, indeed, our home. Rumours can give a false story legs. These rumours are false. F-A-L-S-E. False.' He paused to let the message sink in. 'I will give you the facts. They are not as interesting as the rumours, but they are the truth. T-R-U-T-H. Truth. Someone has made a false allegation to the police about events that have simply not happened. As the owner of the school, Captain Cassell has been asked by the police to refute these stories, and this is precisely what he is doing as we speak. As he is a guest of the local police, they offered to send a car for him. This is what they have done. So, boys, he was not 'bundled into a police car' as someone has informed someone else, starting the rumour. He was ushered in. Normally they would send a car with a chauffeur, but on this occasion, it was not available, so a car with police markings was sent. That is all there is to it.'

Michael O'Hare raised a hand. Heads swung round.

'Yes, boy?'

'But there are some police in the school. I've seen them.' The boy's voice quavered.

'Yes. There are. They will be speaking to individuals to try to get to the bottom of how these foul rumours started. Whoever has been telling lies will be punished. The police and I will make sure of this. Normal lessons will continue, and the school will be back to as was very quickly. Staff have been instructed not to talk about this and to punish anyone who tries to continue the unpleasantness that some lying individual has started.'

St. John Brookfield swept his gown round him and gathered it up prior to his departure from the stage.

'You are dismissed. Leave immediately.'

'Stand not upon the order of your going, but go at once,' thought Jed. As he recalled decades later, the air was, indeed, thick with the sound of chickens coming home to roost.

The Head stopped in his tracks. 'All except Massie. For some reason, they want to interview you. Mr Stanhope, will you kindly come to my study?'

Jed shrank into himself as Stanhope approached him against the tide of boys leaving the room. He pulled him by the shoulder. 'Come with me.'

The boy pulled away.

'Get off me. I'll follow.'

The study door shut behind Stanhope and all Jed heard were muffled voices, Brookfield's emollient; Stanhope's emphatic. Jed sat on the thinly upholstered bench outside the door and looked at the incongruously springlike floral print fabric covering it, worn and stained with many behinds it had accommodated. I bet it could tell some stories, Jed thought.

'What's your name, young man? Jed looked up. A young policeman was pulling a notebook from his pocket.

'Massie, sir.'

'That's OK, no need to 'sir' me. I can't call you 'Massie', though. I assume that with an 'ey', isn't it? And you must have a first name.'

'Yes, sir. I mean, yes, I have one. It's Jed. And it's 'ie'. Massie, I mean'.

'Good.' The policeman smiled. 'Well, Jed Massie, you must be wondering what I'm doing here.'

'Well, Mr Brookfield has told us that Captain Cassell is stopping some rumours.'

The policeman's smile contracted slightly. 'Well, let's say he's helping us. Helping us with our enquiries. Now, my name is Stephen Hope. P.C. Stephen Hope. How do you feel about helping us with our enquiries?'

'Oh yes, please. I'd like that very much. I...'

'Hang on a moment. I just need to get an adult's permission to speak to you. This is the way we have to do things with a child. How old are you?'

'I was 13 yesterday.'

'So whatever you want to say will have to wait. Is that OK?'

'Well, no, not really. I need to talk to someone. There's so much I want to...'

Stanhope opened the study door quickly and was nonplussed by a uniformed police officer taking to Jed.

'We would like to interview this young man here, sir.'

The master gathered his thoughts quickly.

'No. He's a minor, and I have full responsibility. You may not speak to my ward without my being present.'

'That's fine, sir.'

'Anyway, you're wasting your time with him. He has nothing to say that will be of any help to you.'

'Well, sir, please let us decide that.'

'All I'm saying, officer, is that... How shall I put it? The truth and Jed Massie are miles apart. He's a disturbed child. So much so that his parents decided he should be sent away to school and that he should have a guardian to keep a close eye on him in case he got into more trouble. That guardian is me. If you need proof, I have a signed document.'

'Thank you, sir. I'll take the boy to classroom five, which I am told is empty and can be used as an interview room. If you could get the document, that will allow you to be the responsible adult present.'

'With respect, sir. That will leave you alone with the boy, and who knows what he might say.'

'With equal respect, sir, I can assure you that the interview will not commence without your being there.'

'Well, we're stuck, aren't we? I have no intention of leaving you alone with the boy.'

'Then I'll accompany you, and we'll leave Jed to wait here.'

In the silence the followed their departure, Jed caught the sound of a raised voice from the study. It was Brookfield.

'Just go. It'll blow over, and then we'll take stock. Let's put it this way. You're mentioned in dispatches. The silly woman circulated the minutes verbatim without reference to me. I've given instructions for them all to be returned, and I've counted them, but they will have been read. Yes, of course, I've destroyed them. Yes, the original stencil, too. Physically it's as though it never happened. The worst that can happen is that someone will remember something. There's no proof. No. None whatsoever. Don't start this again. We can all play at that game, but you're the one potentially in the firing line, so a sick relative, preferably a long way away, overseas even, would be a good idea at this stage, don't you think? Yes. Now. They're here and talking to people. No, don't get a taxi. Pack a bag and start walking. The sooner you're off the premises, the better.'

Jed had the sense of a receiver being slammed down. The door flew open.

'Oh. You're here. Why?'

'I'm waiting for P.C. Hope to return with Mr Stanhope.' The two 'Hopes' seemed an unfortunate configuration. 'Mr Stanhope wouldn't leave me with P.C. Hope'. Should he push it? 'He was afraid I might say something.'

'And what might you have to say that could possibly be of interest to anyone, Massie? From what I hear, you've been trouble right from the start. Smashing up the lavatories; cheeking prefects - shall I go on?'

'Well, sir, let me put it this way. When I arrived, I was a shy little boy who thought schools existed to help their pupils grow up, who accepted everything that was thrown at him and who wouldn't say boo to a goose. Your school has certainly helped me grow up. It has made me realise that it's full of people whose only power is over people weaker than they are; people whose interests are only in how they can make themselves big by making other people feel small. When I started here, I would never have dared even to think of something like this, let alone say it. I didn't know it existed, but now this is all I can think of. This is my growing up, and I hope my parents will take me as far away from this place as they can.'

'How dare you!'

'There you are. I have dared.'

He saw the Hopes approaching down the corridor. He felt strangely surreal after his outburst. It had been a long time coming.

'Right. I have the necessary document, so we'll go to Classroom 5.'

Stanhope was at his most self-righteous.

'I have taken this boy under my wing against my own better judgement because of my friendship with his family. He's a bad egg. His parents know it, so they asked me to help. He has destroyed school property quite deliberately on his first day. He has told a prefect that he stank...'

'Sir... Mr Stanhope, let me stop you there, please. I just want to ask Jed here some questions. May I start?'

Stanhope motioned P.C. Hope to proceed.

'Now, Jed. How would you say your time at the school has been?'

'A kind of hell.'

'Can you explain why you say this?'

Stanhope interjected. 'It's a waste of time talking to this boy. He's lazy. A kind of hell for him is getting up in the morning.'

'Sir, I must caution you not to interrupt. The boy has a right to answer my questions.'

'I've been falsely accused of things I didn't do. I've been forced to do cleaning. I've been hit - and worse.'

'Right, so let's go through these allegations one by one. The false accusation?'

'I was knocked about in the lavatory by a bigger boy. He threw me against the partition. It broke, and when he hit me again, the lavatory seat broke. One of the masters saw it, but I was fined anyway, and Mr Stanhope told me...'

'I simply will not have an interview conducted in this way. The boy is clearly out to cause trouble and to waste your time and mine. If you won't stop, I shall report you to your superior.'

'Sir, I will continue. Now. Jed, what did Mr Stanhope tell you?'

'Out.' Stanhope pulled Jed from his chair. 'Get out. This line of questioning is utterly improper, and I refuse to allow my ward to be subjected to it. I shall telephone the police station immediately and report you.'

'Sir. You are not letting me do my job. Kindly do not manhandle the boy in this way, or I shall be obliged to report you.'

Jed feared what would happen if Stanhope prevailed over the policeman. He ran into the main building. Mrs van Hofstadter's door was open, and there were raised voices inside her room.

'No, Mr Brookfield. That was not my doing. Please do not make these allegations. You have always asked me to send out the minutes straight after the meetings, and these were a true record of what was said. I have never been unprofessional in my life.'

'You overstepped the mark, Mrs van Hofstadter. You knew how incendiary the minutes were, yet you were happy to let them fly to the four winds regardless of the consequences. That was unprofessional and disloyal.'

'Mr Brookfield, as we seem to be in the mood for truth-telling, I should say that your first loyalty is to the children and their parents. A point was raised, in good faith, I believe, about the appropriateness of the behaviour of a named member of staff towards a child. No action has been taken about these allegations. The parents have not been told. The master has not been questioned. Your only concern is that this information is now known to others apart from you.'

'How dare you question my judgement!'

'I wondered when I would dare. Now I do, Mr Brookfield. I dare because I am right to question it. I dare because, unlike you, it seems, I have the interests of the children at heart. And don't believe for one moment that people who know right from wrong will stand idly by and watch you let sadistic teachers wreck their lives, because they will not. They know how to expose people like you and your kind.'

'Get out. Talk to no one. Your salary will be paid in full until the end of the term, which is more than generous. Tell anyone these lies, and I shall tell Captain Cassell to sue. You know he can. I shall make sure, personally sure, he does.'

Mrs van Hofstadter put a few personal items from her desk into her bag. She took her jacket from the hook and walked past Brookfield without a glance. Jed knew where she was going and took a circuitous route to get there. She was just reversing her car when Jed tapped on her window.

'You were magnificent,' he said through the glass. She rolled the window down.

'I knew it was going to happen one day. There is so much that's wrong with this place. I just couldn't be part of the lies any longer.'

'Look. I have to get away, too. Can I get in?'

She reached behind and opened the rear door.

'Crouch down so no one will see you.'

The tyres crunched on the gravel then, to Jed's relief, the smooth tarmac. He was out.

Chapter 18

'Alex has already phoned me. You've had some kind of melt-down. It was all getting too much for you, being in trouble all the time and getting criticised for it. He's happy to have you back. I'll come and take you there. Just tell me where you are.'

'Gill, don't believe anything this man tells you. Cassell's been arrested. The place is falling apart. I have evidence about what's going on.'

'Yes, yes, I know all about this. It's a huge mistake. Captain Cassell is back. The police have apologised, and everything's back to normal. It seems a woman caused all this by making wholly unfounded allegations without a shred of evidence. An unsavoury character, if you ask me. The school's well rid of her. That teacher you liked, Paul Mason, he's been sacked and replaced within a day or two by a Mr Warburton who's much more experienced, they say. No professional would take up a new position in a place that's falling apart, as you put it. It's changing. Change is sometimes hard to accept.'

'Well, I'm sitting in the unsavoury woman's house at the moment, using her phone to speak to you, drinking a cup of tea she made for me and stroking her cat. As you're talking about unsavoury characters, I think you'll find them elsewhere. Oh, Mr Mason resigned. He wasn't sacked. He took a stand about what was happening to one of the boys.'

'Be that as it may, Jed, you are a child. You're Alex's ward. He's there to protect you, and he's willing to take you back. Just accept that you've been wrong, make your apologies and go back. He'll sort things out.'

'No, Gill. You're my sister, and you have to take over now and, please, do as I ask. Contact mum and tell her you're collecting me from the school, that the place is full of crooks and that her son, your brother, is a victim of some pretty awful crimes. There's more, but I can't do this over the phone. When I know which train you're getting, I'll meet you at the station. I'll phone you in ten minutes. Please do as I ask. I haven't had a meltdown. I know exactly what I'm doing and what I'll do after this. Just believe me. That's all I ask. Ten minutes, Gill.'

He clicked the receiver back.

'Thank you so much. I'm sorry he fired you. I'm afraid it's all because of me.'

'Maybe not. The Head called me to come in because of the arrest and then laid into me for circulating the minutes of the last staff meeting. I don't see the connection.'

'Brookfield lets it all happen; Cassell pays for it; Kempson gets protected by Brookfield, and Stanhope thinks he runs the place. Whatever it is, they're all into it. My sister has been swept off her feet by Stanhope, who can do no wrong in her eyes, so she offers me up to him like some sort of prize, which he takes, but he loathes me. That doesn't make sense. There's something I'm missing. He makes a fuss of my sister, but he doesn't get to know her. He wants everyone to know that he's interested, but I don't think he is. I thought I was starting to understand grown-ups, but they're too complicated for me.'

'For me, too, Jed, and I'm one of them.'

'And Poynton and Baxter G. are always there in his room. He makes a fuss of them while my sister makes a fuss of him.'

'And Kempson makes a fuss of Braine.'

'And Watson makes a fuss of O'Hare.'

Mrs van Hofstadter made another cup of tea. Jed mused some more.

'It's all a lot of fuss for no reason, except there must be a reason. And Cassell says the school has no money, but he carries on paying for it. It doesn't make sense.'

'How did you know that?'

'What?'

'That the school has no money.'

'Oh, I read it.'

'Read it? Where?'

'Oh yes, I forgot to mention it. I took two or three sheets of school letterhead, just in case, you know. I thought they might come in handy. What I didn't realise until I separated the sheets was that another sheet had stuck to them. It was a faint copy of the minutes. One that you must have rejected.'

'So there is a copy still extant?'

'Yes, it's under my pullover at the moment along with the letter about Stanhope.'

'You're a resourceful young man.'

'Thank you. I thought all this was bad for me, and one thing really has been, and I've cried a lot, but it's changed me. I don't know if you've read 'I am David'? We did it in English with Mr Mason. It's about a boy who makes his way across

Europe after the war to find his home. He's completely alone, but he makes it by working things out and talking to God. I just work things out. I don't have God to talk to because I'm an atheist, so I talk to my inner self instead. We try to do the right thing. In a way, this isn't difficult because almost everyone else is doing wrong things, selfish things, horrible things, so I know that if I do the opposite, I'm pretty sure to be right. It's not what I thought school would be, but I've learned things, mostly about me. I am Jed. That's what I keep in my head. I'm a decent bloke.'

'And very different from most of the rest. Don't you think you should call your sister?'

'Oh yes.' Jed dialled the number. 'OK. I'll meet you there then.'

'No, Jed,' Gill said when they met at the station. 'I don't want to hear whatever it is you have against Alex. He's a good man. I've told you how he values the relationship you have with him. I fully expect him to propose at any moment, and I shall certainly accept him. So you'll have a guardian who is also your brother-in-law. Jed, I love this man. He's kind and gentle with me.'

'Does he touch you?'

'What sort of a question is that?'

'If he loves you, he'll touch you. He'll hug you, want to be close to you. That's what I'm asking. Does he touch you?'

'He's too much of a gentleman to do that sort of thing at this stage in our relationship.'

''This stage'? Gill, listen to yourself. You love him enough to want to marry him, but he hasn't touched you, and you think it's too soon. He's not interested.'

'You are so wrong. I wish all men were like Alex.'

'You mean you wish they were all liars?'

'What are you saying? Alex doesn't lie.'

'Well, let's put it this way, I'm not sure if he knows what's true from what's a lie. You know his First from Cambridge? Well, that's a lie.'

'Of course it isn't. He told us. It's easy to check.'

'Yes, it is, but no one does. That's how he gets away with it. Have a few posh expressions and a cut-glass accent, and you can get away with most things. He chose to get away with saying he had a Cambridge degree. He doesn't have one. Look here.'

Jed pulled out the letter from inside his pullover.

'Must be a mistake.'

'And that's it? The University says he hasn't got a degree, and you just don't believe them? So they say he hasn't, and he has. No, Gill, see sense. Oh my God, he's here. You told him. God, you don't stop. I never, never want to speak to that man. That letter is one thing, but there's far more. He's beaten me.'

'Alex, thanks for coming. I'm so sorry about this. You were right. Jed has lost his mind. He's making up all sorts of stupid stories about you. He's got this forged letter from Cambridge saying they've never heard of you.'

Jed could see the man blanch. His sister saw and heard only what she wanted. Often when someone is caught out in a lie, their eyes move rapidly. Stanhope's eyes were all over the place.

Now, thought Jed, how's he going to get out of this one? Stanhope beamed and waved his arms expansively. In years to come, he recollected a little jump for joy or was that to heighten the ridiculousness of the performance?

'Of course they say that. MI5 gave me a new identity some years ago. The whole family changed its name and left behind its past life. The name before the secret service changed our lives is there in the vaults. My new identity is unknown to them. It's all so simple.'

There they were in the soft drizzle outside the local station, his sister seeing as if through new eyes the posturing figure in front of her in all its fabricated pomposity. He hadn't listened to her saying it was a forged letter. He knew it was true, so he lied his way out. Realisation hit her like a physical blow. A sudden coldness came over her. Before she had seen him as through a glass, darkly. Now, she saw him face to face.

'Liar!' She surprised herself with her vehemence. She felt only bitterness and betrayal. It was all so clear now. How could she have been so blind? 'You dare to come into our lives, turn them upside down and give me this drivel? Either I'm a fool, or you are, and, as I have never seen things so clearly before, the fool is the one I'm looking at. 'New identity?' Sure. You can be whoever you like and then change again. But you will always be you - a con man, a cheat, a liar. Oh yes, you took us in. We fell for it, all of it, but it's in pieces now, and it takes a 13-year-old boy to do it. He was never taken in, always saw you for what you were. We believed you because we wanted to believe that we were important, special enough to deserve your attention, and you massaged our egos. Now we shall get you out of our lives. You've hurt me and hurt my brother. You've made idiots out of my parents. They trusted you. Really trusted you, and it'll break their hearts when they know. You are disgusting and dangerous. Children shouldn't be exposed to you.'

The two of them turned their backs on him and entered the first car in the taxi rank. They drove off without a backward glance. Jed didn't see Stanhope again.

But he never left him.

Chapter 19

'I don't know if you remember me, but I was a pupil of yours at Finchingham School decades ago. My name is Jed Massie. I've tracked you down via Facebook in the hope that I might speak to you about something that I can't get out of my head.'

It was so easy to click 'send', but it had taken what felt like a lifetime to summon up the courage to do it. How would his old English teacher react? Ever since the school closed down just after he left, he had regretted not speaking to him. Mrs van Hofstadter had been kind enough, but she had been supportive rather than proactive. He sensed that the actions of his English teacher had, if not caused, maybe accelerated the dénouement. Of all the adults in his life, he felt that Paul Mason, a man he had not spoken to since he was 13, was the only person he could talk to. There weren't that many people in his life.

Jed had followed a typical path from sixth-form college to university with a creditable two-one and now worked for himself as an IT consultant. Outwardly successful and now approaching 50, he led a life of almost total isolation. No one came close. Those who may have wanted to were politely but firmly rebuffed. He was charming, convivial, even sociable, but intensely private.

'Sure. Good to hear from you after all this time. Yes, of course, I remember you. You were interested, eloquent and engaging. By all means, let's meet up. I am pretty sure I know what it's about…'

They agreed to meet for lunch at a country house hotel. Jed waited in the car park. He had arrived early, just to be sure. 'It's a black I-Pace,' he had been told. Mr Mason always had swish cars. 'Mine's a silver Polestar,' Jed had told him. At exactly 13.00, a black I-Pace pulled up next to his Polestar. He would have recognised him anywhere. Time had been kind.

'Mr Mason!' Jed offered his hand.

'Paul, please. We're both grown-ups. You look good, Jed. I see we've both gone electric. Whoa. Hang on there…'

Jed looked into his erstwhile teacher's face, and every part of his having been 13 rushed back to him. His eyes flooded with tears. Paul held him steady and sat him in the passenger seat of his car, scrabbling in the glove compartment for the tissues that he knew were there.

'I'm so, so sorry. I had no idea this would happen. I feel utterly stupid and back to being a child again.'

'If it's what I think it is, it's really not surprising. I assume it's that ghastly man, Stanhope. He had some sort of Svengali effect on people. Can we cut straight to the chase? Did he do something to you?'

'Yes. He entered me with the handle of a hairbrush.'

There it was. He had put into words what he had never said to a living soul, not even to himself. It took a couple of seconds, and he had been waiting most of his life to say it.

'Then he touched me. There. You know. And when I reacted, he said, 'You'll never forget that your first time was with me,' and he was right. I have never forgotten it. Nor his voice. It's always there, so smug, so sickeningly self-righteous, that voice softly saying those words into my head.' The tears came again.

Paul held Jed's trembling body. 'You're safe here. Just let it out. It's been a long time coming.'

'Sorry, I...' Jed pulled the door open, a hand over his mouth. He vomited onto the gravel.

'I can't let it go. Can't let him go. God knows I want to. I loathe the man to the depths of my being. I'm intelligent, capable of connected thought, I can articulate ideas, I can function as an adult, but I can never get that moment out of my head. I keep thinking my head will explode. That's why I wrote to you. 'You'll never forget that your first time was with me.' How true. So much so that it was also the last time. OK, I've said it. I'm trusting you, as I have never trusted anyone else in my life. What do I do? I need this to end.'

The autumn sunshine shone through the glass roof of the car. The lawns were manicured. The leaves just turning to orange, and here was Jed sitting next to him, in extremis and terribly wounded.

Paul Mason thought about all the implications. 'There's no making the event unhappen. I can't tell you that it's one of those things one has to get over because it clearly isn't. All that can happen now is that you can get justice, and he can get punished. After all, 'Revenge is a kind of wild justice.''

'Yes, I know the quote. Yes, it's true. I want revenge. I want him to pay for what he's done to me. First of all, he had his hands down my trousers and squeezed my balls 'til I thought they would burst. Then a few weeks later he entered me with a hairbrush and then…' Jed knew that the concatenation of all the horrors that he had kept inside since he was a child were flooding out with tears and sobs and snot onto this man who held him gently in his arms, and who suddenly he knew he had to give it all to. 'And then…' He buried his head in Paul's chest. 'I just want to stop thinking about it. I wish I could forget it.'

'And, may I suggest, you might want him stopped?' Paul Mason was coolly matter-of-fact, in professional mode. 'He did it to you. He may well have done it or even be doing it now to others. For one who has not been a victim of this, I have to say the depth of the damage done is hard to comprehend. Talking to you now and being with you, I know that this has touched the depths of your being. You've been violated. These people don't stop.'

'What should I do now?'

'Well, Jed, you've been the victim of a crime. Yes, it happened thirty-five years ago, but the law is that if you have not previously felt able to reveal the crime because of the nature of the crime, there are no time limitations on when you can make the complaint. So your next step is to make a complaint to the police. Their next step is likely to be to arrest Stanhope.'

'That means talking about it all over again.'

'Of course, but it's never gone away, has it? It's always there. You go over it and over it. And you feel shame and guilt. That's what the abuser has done to you.'

'Yes. Way back when he made me do chores to pay off the debt he told me I had, I knew what he was doing was wrong. I hadn't done the damage I was accused of having done, and he had no right to enslave me. Yet, I couldn't tell anyone what was happening. It was like a secret between the two of us. I was keeping his secret. It was a strange feeling. You know that I so wanted to tell you. I nearly did.'

'That's what these people rely on. The shame and the guilt keep you silent; keep the abuser's secret.'

'But there was something else. Even now, Paul, even though I've told you, it's so difficult for me to talk about the other thing. Oh, Paul, I'm crying again now. God, this is awful. I'm just dumping stuff on you.'

'Go ahead. I know what's coming next. I have to tell you that you aren't the first one who has come to me from that place. Telling me, or anyone really does help some of the shame and guilt go away.'

'OK. Here goes.' Jed swallowed hard. 'When he touched me – I mean, touched me there – my body responded. I was hating every moment of what was happening, but my body seemed to be enjoying it. I was erect, and I ejaculated for the first time. Then he made me touch him, and I was so hard it hurt, and I ejaculated some more. I just hated myself for what I was doing and swore that I would never go through this again. Never. Never. And no one has touched me since. No one. I've never been naked with anyone. Ever. That's not right, is it?'

'No, Jed. You have to trust someone to be naked with them. The problem with boys and men who are abused is that it's a purely physical reaction. In normal circumstances, the body is getting ready for a pleasurable experience. Kind of a reflex. It doesn't distinguish between experiences; it just reacts. There really is nothing to be ashamed of. It's easy to say, and I know men generally don't talk about this, but you have to believe it. This is yet another aspect of abuse that abusers capitalise on. The victim thinks he may have enjoyed it and feels even more guilt and shame. These are yet more reasons why people, especially boys, don't tell.'

'I can look back and think, what if I'd told someone about the debt and the chores at the time?'

'The trouble with that, Jed, is who would you have told? The people running the place were as corrupt as Stanhope. If you'd told me, I'd have referred it upwards, and nothing would've been done. I would then have raised it publicly, as I did with Richard, and you know what happened then. No. People like Stanhope - and Cassell and Brookfield and the rest - need to be kept away from kids.'

'And if I'd told you then what I've just told you now, thirty-five years too late?'

'Gosh. What would I have done? It's as if we're in a different mindset now. Back then, no one thought such things happened. Well, we didn't think they didn't happen; they weren't thought about at all. It was an easy time for abusers. No one imagined they existed, and probably, if they did, people would just tell them to stop and assume they would do that – just stop. Now we know they can't and won't. All the more reason people like Stanhope need to be put away. But if you had come to me then and told me what he'd done to you, I'd have been in shock. I'd have taken you to the police, and I have the dreadful feeling that they'd have taken you back to Cassell and Brookfield and let them deal with it. Really, no one had any idea of how extensive this crime is and how much pain it causes.'

He passed Jed another tissue.

'The thing is, Jed, that you'll have to talk about it. You can't be shy. You mustn't be embarrassed. I know what it took for you to tell me. You'll just have to believe, really know, that you are a victim and Stanhope is a criminal. He was then, and he is now. The man you were in thrall to is a common criminal. The man who enters your head like an uninvited guest is a man who will be a prisoner. The only satisfaction you'll have is that you will be free while he has had his liberty taken away.'

'I don't feel free, though, that's the thing. This guilt just hangs around me.'

'Now that you've let the genie out of the bottle, it should get easier.'

'Do you remember the E.E. Cummings you did with us?'

'"How Town"?'

Jed nodded.

'Since it happened, I've remembered the lines 'children are apt to forget to remember with up so floating many bells down.' I can't forget to remember though, no matter how many bells float up and down.'

'"Only the snow can begin to explain". After this, let some more bells float and, with time and events, your metaphorical footprints in the snow will show you moving farther and farther away from that place. 'And down they forgot as up they grew.' It will happen. I'm sure.'

'I'll try to grow up, then.'

'You will.'

'What's he likely to get, do you think?'

'This is where it's a bit disappointing. The tariff of sentences is the tariff that applied at the time of the crime. When did it happen? 1986 or 1987, wasn't it? So, a length of sentence would have been given then for this sort of crime, but as people didn't know much about it or have any idea how serious a crime it is,

I'm afraid the sentence will be shorter than it would be for a crime committed today. I suppose the logic is that a criminal can look at the menu of time to be served before he decides to go ahead and commit the crime with the off-chance that he might be caught. It makes sense but doesn't help you. You'll go through the whole court ordeal, and all he'll get is a derisory sentence.'

'At least he'll be off the streets, and he'll be on the list, so he won't be able to be with children.'

'Not here anyway, but these people tend to go overseas afterwards. You can only do what you can. There will also be those who won't believe you. No one saw anything. It'll be your word against Stanhope's.'

'Correct, but I'll be telling the truth, and he'll be lying through his teeth.'

'I think his entire life is a lie. All this stuff about his parents and MI5 and so on. Beggars belief. He wasn't my cup of tea then. I just thought he was a latter-day Walter Mitty who wanted my job. Harmless enough. Was I wrong! I think I'll do some checking up on him.'

Jed put his hand on Paul's arm. 'Paul. You know I can't tell you how much this means to me.'

'I know. Don't get me wrong. I feel for you. I really do, but this whole thing is likely to end up in court, and I don't want the defence to accuse you of having me put words into your mouth. I'll be your friend and supporter, but at a distance for the time being. OK?' Jed nodded his understanding. 'Look, I have this lunch reservation. Don't let's let Stanhope spoil this for us. I want to know all about the last thirty-five years. We have a fair bit of catching up to do. Go to the loo and wash your face. I hope they've kept the table.'

Chapter 20

The judge was clear in his appraisal for the jury: 'This is a question of one man's word against another, and it is up to you to decide which one to believe. In a situation where, because of the nature of the offence, there are no witnesses, you have to look at the situation surrounding the events, the testimony of witnesses there at the time, and come to your balanced conclusion.'

Even though thirty-five years separated the accused from his accuser, Jed had accepted the offer of a screen between them. He became 13 going on 48. The first words he heard from Stanhope in all those years suddenly hit him. 'Not guilty.' That voice. It was the same. He might as well have been saying 'your first time.' 'Get out of my life.' screamed his inner voice, so loud that he imagined the entire courtroom would have to be evacuated. And that 'not guilty.' It was so authoritative. Everyone would believe it. There wouldn't be a trial at all. He was surprised when the judge, in a voice that was measured and quiet, invited counsel to proceed. He was relieved to hear any voice but that one. This voice was calm, mollifying, reasoned. It set out the course of the events in factual terms, tracing with precision how the accused had, from the very beginning, set out to put Jed in a situation from which escape would be near-impossible. It was a simple strategy which, right from its inception, was built on lies.

Jed was able to see, in the straightforward, stark even, terms used by his counsel, how a young boy who saw the adults around him in the same way he had grown up seeing all adults – people who knew best – had been duped. As a child, he had no reason to distil what 'best' was, but he could confront this now. 'Best' was what was 'good for you.' 'Best' kept you safe and healthy; happy rather than sad; accepting reality; showing how good judgement should be exercised. The adults in the new world he had entered at the age of 12 were people who knew what was best for them and how they could control events to this end.

Why did these adults act so differently from the adults he had known? What was in their heads? Jed was only too aware of the results of their actions, but he could not understand the motivation. He could have had the same friendly relationship with Stanhope that the man had with his favourites. What was there about him that made him so different from them that the man should want to treat him with contempt, whereas they were pandered to; their every wish granted? Their lives were made comfortable. His life was made a misery.

It was not just Stanhope. Many of the others acted the same. Brookfield loved to make him feel small. He fell over himself to give the prefects what they wanted. Cassell couldn't care less about most of those in his charge, but allowed the younger Poynton to run a business, drive his car, not go to lessons. What was it that drove these people? And they were certainly driven with a passion that seemed to eclipse reason – or at least reason as he, a middle-aged man, perceived it.

Those people were selfish. That was clear. He had been used. He could see that. He had been used and discarded when his usefulness was over. It was the nature of this usefulness that intrigued him. Why was he discarded while the others were retained? Hearing the events that had been of such import that they shaped his life related to the jury in simple factual terms distanced him from them. Is that really me he's talking about? The emotion that was so much part of it was removed and what was left was a clinical dissection.

It was banal. So obvious that he was amazed he had fallen for it. How could anyone not see through it?

'It simply did not happen.'

Defence counsel's authoritative tones rang out. Instantly Jed was back to being a boy. Now he said so, of course it hadn't happened. What was in his head to be making such allegations? He had clearly misinterpreted everything that happened. How misguided of him. Or worse. How cruel and ungrateful of him to even think that those invitations to Mr Stanhope's flat were anything other than giving him a home from home? And the guardianship. A selfless action to help a young man get a good start in his school life. What was the man thinking of to invent stories about what didn't happen thirty-five years ago? What were his evil intentions? And were there other people who had put him up to it?

What was his relationship with Paul Mason, a man with a record of trying to destroy the institution that gave him employment? Here were at least two people with a grudge against the defendant: two unmarried men in their middle years. Say no more. These must be grounds for at least the gravest of doubts. Defence counsel had given the judge the opportunity to dismiss the case at this point as there was no evidence whatsoever. Again, now it was put this way, Jed imagined the judge would seize the opportunity. He was surprised when he declined the chance.

He was sure that, in the face of the arguments presented by prosecuting counsel, the jury would be convinced that Stanhope was quite right. What a vindictive child Jed had been, and as an adult, all he could do was blame this innocent man for all that had gone wrong in his life.

None of it had happened.

Except that it had.

People from his past re-emerged. Some were instantly recognisable. Time had been unkind to others. Brett Poynton was invited to take centre stage. How he had loved to show his superiority as a prefect. He had been the pin-up boy, the sports jock, the swimming star happier in speedos than in uniform. He smelt a bit and did not have a heart of gold; his popularity was probably earned by fear rather than respect; he was the biggest of fishes in that tiny pond. Here he was to strut his hour.

What had Stanhope been like to him when he was growing up?

'He was like a father to me. Like the father I never had. My dad couldn't have cared less. Alex cared for me and my brother. He never asked for anything in return. He took us places, even introduced us to his girlfriend, Gillian. Never said we were getting in the way, even when we stayed with her and her family. Never said he wanted to be alone with her even when she was his fiancée. I've never known anyone as kind as Alex. He did everything for me.'

'Did he ever do anything - how shall I put it? – inappropriate?'

'Course not. Never laid a finger on me. I'd've flattened anyone who tried that on with me.'

Poynton expanded his chest, and Jed could see that his fists were clenched in anticipation of anyone trying it on. What had been an object of desire was now a balding, barrel-chested, tattooed man discomfited by his ill-fitting suit, strangled by his tight collar and tie, proudly showing his loyalty.

Was this a convincing performance, Jed wondered? He didn't come across as authoritative, just blinkered, or was that because he knew how it really had been? He looked forward to the cross-examination.

"Like a father.' How did Mr Stanhope show how paternal he was?'

'How what?'

'His fatherliness. How did he show it to you?'

'He bought things for us.'

'And?'

'He took us places. I told you he took us to his fiancée's house. We met her mum. She liked him. Made him guardian.'

'When you visited, you said that Mr Stanhope never wanted to be alone with her when you were there. Is this correct?'

'Yes. He only thought of us.'

'What were the sleeping arrangements at the Massies' house?'

'What's that got to do with anything?'

'Please just answer my question, Mr Poynton.'

'He didn't sleep with her, if that's what you're getting at.'

'I'm not 'getting at' anything. Mr Poynton. I'm just asking you. As you say you know with whom he didn't sleep, can you tell me where he did sleep?'

At last, Poynton could see where this was going. He coloured and ran his finger around his collar.

'With me.'

'With you, Mr Poynton.'

'He didn't want to. Said I smelt.'

There was the faintest titter of amusement that ran round the court.

'Did you?'

'Did I what?'

'Smell.'

'No. He bought me deodorant.'

'How many beds were in the room he shared with you?'

There was a double.'

'Just the one double?'

'Yes. It wasn't big enough for two doubles.'

'You said that your brother, Jerome, I assume, accompanied you on these visits. Where did he sleep?'

'In the spare room, of course.'

'Was there any discussion about his moving into the double with you, his brother?'

'No.'

'Why not?'

'Why?'

'Well, you were 17 at the time. Your brother was 13, I believe. Mr Stanhope was a grown man of 25. It might be thought that it would be more appropriate for two boys who are brothers to share, rather than a boy and his teacher.'

The word 'objection' rang out. Counsel turned it into a question.

'What did you wear in bed?'

'I didn't.'

'Didn't what?'

'I didn't wear anything in bed. Never have done. Alex agrees with me. He says there's nothing wrong with the human body.'

'I see. And Mr Stanhope?'

'What about him?'

'What did he wear?'

'Told you.'

'No, Mr Poynton, you did not. You told me that Mr Stanhope said there was nothing wrong with the human body. So I repeat my question to you. What did Mr Stanhope wear in the double bed in the Massies' house, which he shared with you when you were naked?'

'Didn't look.'

'Did you see?'

'Maybe.'

'Mr Poynton, let me ask you directly, was Mr Stanhope naked when he was in bed with you?'

'Probably. Yes.'

'Did he touch you at all?'

'Just like a father would. I told you he was more of a father to me than my dad was. If I was unhappy, he'd hold me.'

'Did he kiss you goodnight, for example?'

'That's what a dad does, isn't it?'

Brett Poynton had been a star. Jed was beginning to see where he fitted into this picture of domestic bliss.

Chapter 21

'It's building up a body of evidence that the jury can use to determine whether you or Stanhope are lying. As his honour said, they can only believe one of you. One of you is telling the truth, and one of you is lying. It's that simple. It's working out which one that's the issue.'

The prosecuting counsel was young and keen. Jed was glad he had him. He had been despondent, but he could see a glimmer of light.

'Stanhope fancied Poynton. How does that help me, Hugh?'

'It introduces the idea of his not being entirely straightforward. Poynton wasn't told about Stanhope's feelings. He kept them close. I think there's more to this. I'll be calling his brother, but I have the feeling that's going to introduce a sideshow. It won't harm your case, but there will be more dramatis personae, I think.'

'I'd really like to talk to Paul. Can I?'

'Absolutely not.'

'OK.'

'Look. Defence may call him and aim at proving collusion. As long as there's no contact, they'll find it harder to do this.

Yes, you spoke to him at the beginning, and he put it into your head to go to the police, but that was a perfectly reasonable suggestion. From that point, you acted on your own. If they can suggest that he put any words into your mouth or ideas into your head, that'll cast doubt on every answer you give. If you are asked, and you can give the answer that there has been no contact since your visit to the police, that will remove doubt from the jury's mind. I know Paul has kept his distance. He told me that all his human instincts are to support you throughout, but he knew that the defence would love to cast doubt on your relationship and your ability to think for yourself.'

Time had been kinder to Jerome Poynton. He was slim and looked as if he had street wisdom. Jed was correct in his assumption that several of the years since they last saw each other had been spent in prison. He was just as clumsy as he remembered him and took some time to get his feet into the witness box.

'Mr Poynton. What was your relationship with Mr Stanhope?'

'Never had one.'

'Did he give you any special attention at school?'

'No.'

'Was he like every other teacher?'

'Yeah.'

'Did you like him?'

'No. I don't think he liked me. He kept wanting me to come to his lessons.'

'So he was just like any other teacher?'

'Yeah.'

Defence counsel was quick to consign Jerome Poynton to prosecuting counsel. Nothing to see here. Or was there?

'Mr Poynton.'

Jerome Poynton was unused to having his honorific prefix used. 'Yeah?'

'What sort of relationship did you have with Mr Stanhope?'

'I didn't have one. Don't think he liked me. Said I smelled worse than my brother.'

'Did he buy you deodorant?'

'No way.'

'Let me take you back to something you've just said. You told the court: 'He kept wanting me to come to his lessons.' Was that an unreasonable request? Weren't you at school to go to lessons, Mr Stanhope's included?'

'None of the other teachers cared.'

'So, Mr Stanhope was a caring teacher?'

'No, he just said I should.'

'So why did you not go to lessons?'

'Had permission.'

'Who gave you permission not to go to lessons?'

'Captain Cassell.'

'What reason did he give you for allowing this?'

'Said I was more useful doing other things.'

'"Other things.' What other things did you do?'

'Ran the tuck shop.'

'So you ran a business at Finchingham School?'

'Yeah, and I kept him posted what was going on.'

'So you made money from your business running the tuck shop and being an informant. What information did you provide?'

'He just wanted to know who was with who.'

'"Who was with whom." Counsel repeated his words, but could not resist the correction. It was lost on Jerome Poynton. 'By that, are you saying who was friendly with whom?'

'Yeah. Well, more like who was together with who. Like, well, together. You know.'

'I'm not entirely sure I do know, Mr Poynton. Can you explain what 'together' means in this sense?'

'Look. Cassell paid me a monkey a week to tell him who was having it off with who. OK?'

'A 'monkey?''

'Yeah, five hundred quid.' Jerome Poynton was clearly proud of his business acumen.

'So you told him about the boys?'

'He wasn't into that. He wanted to know about staff. Yeah, like Brookfield and Baxter G, Kempson and Braine, Watson and O'Hare. That lot.'

'Did 'that lot' include your brother and Mr Stanhope?'

'Yeah.'

'Jed Massie and Mr Stanhope?'

'Nah. They weren't together.'

Jerome Poynton had no idea that he had dropped a bombshell in the courtroom. For him, it was all matter-of-fact. There were no moral judgements to be made. It had been purely business.

Chapter 22

'Quite a piece of work, that Jerome Poynton.' Jed had his now customary cup of coffee with prosecuting counsel.

'Amorality on legs. Surprisingly honest, too. Expected us to admire his ability to make money. Clearly, there are more men like you with memories they would prefer not to have. I wonder how many will want to confront them. It's not easy. The court system will put them through the wringer. I'm afraid you can't expect an easy ride.'

'I think some of them may have been in touch with Paul. He knew why some of them wouldn't dare say anything. He knew all about how people like Stanhope transfer the guilt and shame away from them and onto the victim. That's what happened with me, and he managed to make it OK to talk about it.'

'He did a good job. I know you like him, and you have shared with him something incredibly intimate, but leave him right out of this. You were the one to come to the police; you made statements; you were open and honest. That's all that's important. What may or may not have given you the confidence to do this is neither here nor there, so far as the court is concerned. The decision to take this forward was yours alone. If the defence can put into the jury's mind that you wouldn't have done so without the help from Paul Mason, that will damage our case. Save your thanks to him for after the trial. I rather think there'll be more trials to come, too. I hope he's tough enough.'

'Oh yes. He is. The only people with principles there were Paul and the school secretary.'

'What became of her?'

'I think it was all too much for her. She was a sweet woman, and the knowledge that this had been going on around her, and, more than this, that she had been instrumental in saying nice things about the place to parents and encouraging them to send their children into this dangerous hell-hole sent her into a depression. She kept in touch for a while. All she could say in her letters basically was 'sorry''. She said it in different ways, and I told her that she had been really helpful to me, but she just felt really bad. I just wanted to convince her that it was her courage in doing the right thing that helped close the place down. She went back to the Netherlands with her husband. That was in her last letter to me. I think she thought of this as a closing of the chapter. I haven't heard from her for years. She may no longer be alive.'

'I think she isn't. We tried to contact her without success. Towards the end, I'm pretty sure she had a good idea what was going on, and you were just the icing, as it were, on what she knew was an enormous cake.'

'Without her, I don't think the photos would have been printed.'

'The photos? What photos?'

'Richard, Richard Braine that is, and I took a roll of film to Boots to have developed and printed. We didn't have pocket money and knew Stanhope and Kempson wouldn't hand any over until the weekend. She gave us a fiver. We ran down to Boots, handed the roll in and paid for it. With everything that went on after this, we never got to collect them. Wonder where they are.'

'How do the photos on that roll relate to you?'

'Richard had two exposures left. He used one of them taking a photo of the letter that said Stanhope was a fraud. And the other, well, I got him to take one of me, and the marks left by the beating Brett gave me and the caning I got from Stanhope just after 'it' happened.'

Hugh Kennedy pulled his mobile phone from his pocket. His fingers stabbed quickly at the screen. He spoke to whoever had been in its memory. 'You know those photos? Yes, those ones. We wondered about them. They are relevant. Yes, please.'

He turned to Jed. 'We know what happened to the photos. They were what got Cassell arrested. One of the staff at Boots was so shocked that she contacted the police.'

'Yes, I can imagine. I got Richard to photograph me from the back without any clothes on. I was so angry and in pain that I didn't bother about him seeing me like that. Must've been a shock for the chemist, though.'

'What shocked the girl were the other photos on the roll. Your friend may have given his camera to someone else. The photos were of a boy called Nick Boyce and Cassell. The police assumed Boyce was a child. In fact, he had celebrated his 18th the week before, so, although there was an element of duty of care and privileged relationship, they ended up not taking it any further, but the parents and the papers got involved, and the rest, as you know is history.'

'Yes, it took a few months, but the place folded. My parents didn't want to let me follow the news. I thought it was because of that photo.'

'Oh no. We didn't know who it was. Now that we do, we'll take a look at the negative and see what we can do with the clarity.'

'Richard told me his hand was shaking.'

'I can imagine.'

'I told you I stripped completely. That must have thrown him.'

'I doubt it, Jed. There was so much red that we thought it must be fake. You had real wounds on you. That's what must have thrown him. There may be scars to this day.'

Jed felt the tears start. 'There may be. I don't know.' He sighed. 'You may as well know. I've never let anyone look.'

Chapter 23

Richard Braine had to be assisted to the witness stand. He had an oxygen mask to help his breathing.

'Would you like a chair, Mr Braine?'

'Yes, please, your honour.'

When he was suitably ensconced, Hugh Kennedy commenced. 'Mr Braine. Were you acquainted with Jed Massie?'

'Yes, sir. Apart from my partner, I would say he was my only friend. Then and since.'

'Have you met subsequently?'

'No.'

'Were you a member of a photographic club at Finchingham School?'

'Yes, sir.'

'Do you recall taking any photographs at the request of Jed Massie?'

'Yes, sir. I took them the year before the school closed down. I had two exposures left on my camera.'

'Can you describe these photographs?'

'Yes, sir. One was a letter. The other was of Jed. He wanted a shot of him from the back. Naked.'

143

There was a collective intake of breath among the onlookers.

'Can you tell the court, please, Mr Braine, why you photographed Jed Massie in this way?'

'He asked me to. He wanted there to be a record of his injuries.'

'Did he tell you how he came by these injuries?'

'No, sir, but he told me he was afraid Mr Stanhope wouldn't give him pocket money to get the film developed.'

'So how did you get the money to pay for the developing and printing?'

'Jed told me he got it from the school secretary. I forget her name.'

'Is there any chance someone else may have taken photographs with your camera?'

'I think someone must have. I thought I had a full roll of film inside it. I know that Nick, Nick Boyce, had the same type of camera as me, so I thought it must have been him.'

Defence counsel was not so circumlocutory.

'Mr Braine, were you accustomed to taking pictures of people without clothes on?'

'No, sir. The photo of Jed is the only one I have taken – ever.'

'And the other photos on the roll of film, that formed the subject of a police enquiry, were not taken by you, but, you tell the court, by someone else, clandestinely, of the late Captain Cassell and a Nick Boyce. Do you know who this photographer might be?'

'No, sir. As I didn't take those photos, someone else must have.'

'You assume this, Mr Braine?'

'That is the only explanation I can think of.'

'There are other explanations, Mr Braine, as I am sure you know. Is it possible to find out from Mr Boyce who it was who took those photos?'

'No, sir. He's dead. Nick Boyce stood in front of a train. That's what brought the school down.'

'No further questions.'

Jed was next.

'Jed, can we get the question of Mr Braine's photograph out of the way first. May we have it on the screen, please?'

'Is this you?'

'The negative was aged, and there was an element of shake in the way the photograph was taken. We have enhanced it as far as we can. As you can see, the body is taken from the back, but the head is tilted slightly to the right. There is a mole on the nape of the neck in this photograph. Jed, will you show the jury the nape of your neck?'

He lowered his collar fractionally and turned his back to the jury.

'The Court will note the mole on the nape of Jed Massie's neck in the same place as the mole in the photograph. I maintain, therefore, that the court can assume that this photograph is that of Jed Massie taken on 3 July 1987 from the records of Boots the Chemist. Do you concur?'

'Yes. I remember it being taken.'

'Why did you ask for this photograph to be taken?'

'There were two photographs taken. One was of a letter from the University of Cambridge saying that Mr Stanhope did not have a degree from there as he claimed. The other was of injuries he had given me the previous evening and that Brett Poynton had given me some days earlier.'

'How did Mr Poynton give you injuries?'

'He clawed my back with his fingernails. Mr Stanhope was there when it happened. It was in his flat. He didn't stop it.'

'Those are the two striations we see?'

'Yes. The ones on my backside are where Mr Stanhope caned me.'

'And the blood lower down in the photo?'

The answer came out as a matter-of-fact and was not the horror he imagined. 'Mr Stanhope entered me with the handle of a hairbrush.'

'Did he perform any other acts on you?'

Jed heard his voice tremble. Now everyone would know. 'He fondled me, and when it happened, he said, 'you'll never forget that your first time was with me.' Then I grabbed my clothes and ran away.'

He knew he would be interrogated, doubted, questioned, made to relive the horrid moments. He tried to convince himself that defence counsel was only doing his job, quite possibly thought that Stanhope was guilty as sin and was just putting on a show. But there was the defence counsel in his robes and wig, and there he was, a 13-year-old boy in front of a figure of authority for the first time in thirty-five years.

'Mr Massie.' Was that a note of exasperation in the voice? 'You really had it in for Mr Stanhope, didn't you?'

'Yes, sir. He was horrible to me. He made me do chores to pay off a debt that was nothing to do with me. It was a trumped-up situation so that he could have power over me.'

'So, you told him this, of course.'

'No, sir. He was the teacher. I was the child. I believed him.'

'You believed him because it was true.'

'No, sir. I believed him because he told me so.'

'So, armed with your conviction that Mr Stanhope was lying through his teeth, you did chores for him without demur? That was good of you.'

'I had no choice, sir.'

'Mr Stanhope led you in handcuffs to his flat? Chained you to his sink?'

'Objection'.

'Let me rephrase. You willingly went to Mr Stanhope's flat?'

'Yes, sir.'

'And willingly cleaned it and did the dishes?'

'If you say so, sir.'

'Don't take learned Counsel's word for it, Mr Massie. This is your opportunity to respond,' the judge interjected.

This was not a 48-year-old man responding to questions. This was a 13-year-old boy.

'It wasn't that I went willingly, sir. I had no choice. He told me he would tell my parents the bad things I was supposed to have done if I didn't work for him.'

'You accepted his guardianship?'

'My parents did, sir.'

'Sounds like you willingly accepted his hospitality and protection?'

Jed snapped, 'Were you there?'

Oh, God, he thought. What have I done?

'Sorry, sir. I shouldn't've said that. That was wrong. I take it back. I mean, there was no hospitality. He used me like a servant. There was no protection. He created his guardian position that so he could stop me talking to the police. I see it now. I was a child then. I just had to go along with everything.'

'To coin a phrase, Mr Massie, 'recollections may vary', so may that not be the case here?'

'I remember exactly what happened.'

'You seem like a man with spirit, Mr Massie. Are you asking the court to believe that your little outburst just then is not one you would have used had you been treated as shabbily as you maintain?'

'I was a child, sir. I was in awe of authority.'

'Well, that seems to have changed, Mr Massie, doesn't it?'

'What was done to me changed me.'

It was like a tennis match of the mind. The questions and the answers were batted to and fro. On and on. The truth was screaming to be heard, and there was learned counsel trying to make everything the opposite of what it had been.

Eventually, it was over. He was drained. He just wanted to have a conversation with Paul. To get his assurance that he hadn't ruined everything with his unguarded comment. He was getting to know Hugh Kennedy, and he was also, he was finding, someone he could confide in.

'I'm sorry.'

'Don't be. You did fine.'

'I lost my temper.'

'Momentarily. Shows you're human. Put it behind you.'

'Poor Richard.'

'Very sad. What's the back story?'

'Kempson.'

'Aha.'

He could explain Richard Braine's fifty years of history in one word. How sad was that?

Chapter 24

'Sugar, Mr Brookfield?'

'Oh, yes, please. Just the one. Thank you.'

Jed's mum used the sugar tongs she saved for special occasions.

'It's so lovely to have you both together in our home, isn't it, Jed?' She looked from one to the other. 'Mr Brookfield and Captain Cassell. Your names go together like Crosse and Blackwell.'

'St. John and Philip, please, Mrs Massie.'

'Now boys, I have some special treats for you. Jed, dear, please will you give a fairy cake each to Brett and Jeremy? A cucumber sandwich to Richard. A piece of gala pie to Michael. A meringue to Nicholas. A custard tart to Grant. Some Battenberg to Alan and, of course, a packet of crisps to Mr Kempson.'

'Oh, it's Keith, please, Mrs Massie.'

'And, Gillian, don't forget Alex. Some panama violets for him. Daddy, will you be mother? I love saying that.'

Jed's dad poured the tea. Out came Alex's little finger as he held the bone china cup with the filigree gold design.

'Oh, Alex, isn't that a tad outré? Anyway, it's so lovely to have you all here together. I just wish this moment could last forever. Everyone together and happy.' Mrs Massie was at her most beatific. But you, Philip, and you, Sinjun, and you, Keith, and you, Alan, have all been a little naughty, haven't you? It could all have been so nice, but you've smashed up people's lives, and you, Alex, have done your level best to smash up our family. Now how are we going to deal with you?'

Something was coming. A huge machine bearing down on the sitting room. A train?

'It must be a fire engine. There's a bell,' said Jed. 'I need to stop it. Stop, bell.'

Jed rolled over and felt for his phone. He pushed at its side. 'Siri, delete all alarms.'

'Are you sure you want to delete all your alarms?'

'Yes.'

Where had he been? They had all been there. Where? The memory that he had woken with had been pellucid in its clarity. Now it was changing shape, clouding over. All he was left with was an impression of how things might have been. The evanescence was almost complete. Now he saw where he was. A hotel room in Reading. His suitcase on a stand. His suit for the morning ready on a hanger. An hour before the court started. I think I need to be sick. He retched unproductively into the basin. Why do people do these things? They're all so unnecessary. If happiness is the point of life, why do people work so hard to make others unhappy? This probably doesn't make them happy, and they end up being unhappy, too. It's all so counter-productive. It's just as easy to say a kind word as it is to make a cruel remark. Am I being naïve? It all seems so simple.

Jed stepped into the shower and caught sight of himself in the full-length mirrors that were the full-length sliding doors of the wardrobe. Should I look and see if they're still there? The last few days had pushed to the front all those memories that he had suppressed so long. Actions and inactions that had become second nature were being revisited and analysed. It's a crime scene. He gasped internally. That's what it is. His back is the scene of the crime. He imagined SOCO poring over it and shuddered. Just behind him, it had all happened, was happening now. He should look.

He turned his head. It was the first time he had consciously looked at his back since he could remember. He analysed what had become a part of his persona, tried to deconstruct what he had set up as a fortress around himself since childhood. He knew he might be and assumed, maybe childishly, that he would be scarred for life and that seeing what had been done to his skin would be like the mark of Cain that he dared not reveal to anyone. Instinctively, he had never been other than fully-clothed in public. He saw his body as an advertisement of what had been done to him. Part of the ghastliness was that he feared he might have brought it on himself, even have taken a perverse pleasure in it. It had been safer never to let anyone get close to him, close enough to see his body. They might guess what had happened. What had he been doing?

He had wrapped himself in a protective armour. Life was easier that way. There were people he liked, but none too much. No one was able to get to the real him. Not that he had much idea who he really was. He did his work: loved it. Had his clients: liked talking to them. Enjoyed creating a lovely home for himself. Took care to make sure he was well-groomed, trim and smartly-dressed. The image he presented to the world had become what was really him.

Navel-gazing was not for him. No need anyway.

His vision was just on the point of needing the help of glasses or contacts. He had an appointment booked for the following week. His back was slightly out-of-focus. No matter. It was always hidden, even from him.

He clicked the Braun shaver on and ran it over the light stubble. He brushed his teeth until the toothbrush told him his two minutes were up. He sprayed Hugo Boss under each arm. He slipped on the T-shirt he had worn under his shirt every day since the incident. An extra layer of protection. Then the rest of his clothes and a tonal tie with a dimple below the knot. His late father had told him the dimple separated the men who knew how it should be from the boys who didn't have a clue.

He stared in the mirror. People had complimented him on his appearance – the depth of blue in his eyes, the colour of his strawberry-blond hair, the smoothness of his complexion, his bone structure. 'Such a handsome man,' he had overheard a client say. All he wanted was not be conspicuous. He would maintain his sartorial standards so far as his outward appearance was concerned and preserve his own personal integrity, but he avoided anything that made him stand out or appear overtly approachable.

It was to be Stanhope's turn on the stand. He would hear that voice. He retched again. No matter how he presented himself, how pure his own thoughts, everything was sullied with that creature inside him.

'Join me for breakfast.' Hugh Kennedy had noticed him walk by and stood up from his chair.

'Happy to join you, but I couldn't eat anything. My stomach's been churning all morning.'

'Soon be over, and then it'll be in the lap of the jury. It's all a matter of whom they believe: you, or the gross, smug Stanhope. No, I should correct myself. Not so fat now. I see a change from the mug shot in the papers to what I see in the dock. Nothing like contemplating a longish stretch inside to take away one's appetite. He's almost trim now.'

'Still smug, though, I think.'

'Yes, and that's good for us. No one likes to see self-satisfaction writ large, and it doesn't come writ much bigger than in Stanhope.'

'And dare I ask how I have come across?'

'Self-effacing. Sorry, that was a bit direct. I mean, you must know yourself. You are incredibly good-looking and incredibly shy. It's an odd combination. It's the rape, isn't it?'

The word hit him like a physical blow that left him reeling. Jed had never thought of it in connection with himself. No one had used it in relation to what had happened to him. This was something new.

'I wasn't raped.'

'Oh, yes, Jed. You were.'

'But he…'

'Used a hairbrush, I know. Same thing. Whatever it was with, you were penetrated. That's rape.'

'OK.' There was a question in the inflection. This needed to be digested. 'Look, I've come to see myself as a victim: a victim of child abuse. Now you tell me I have to see myself as a rape victim. That makes Stanhope a rapist.'

'Yes, that's just what he is. What he did to you is as bad as it gets. Rapists get into people's souls. The horror of it eats them up from the inside. You have to make sure this doesn't happen to you. You must, absolutely must, see yourself as the victim of a criminal act perpetrated on you, a totally innocent person, by a rapist thug. That's all he is. He speaks perfect RP and knows long words, but he's still a thug.'

'I hate him, Hugh.'

'You should.' Hugh Kennedy looked quizzically at him. 'But don't hate yourself. You're a good man.'

Chapter 25

'It simply did not happen,' Not 'didn't'. It was an emphatic 'did not' with the emphasis on the second word. 'None of it.'

Alex Stanhope was just revving up for the performance of his lifetime. That's what his life had been - all an act. Born the son of a postmaster and a cleaner, he had attended a series of local state schools. Unsuccessful at the 11+, he had proceeded to a comprehensive school and finished his education in a polytechnic. All of this was quite wrong. His parents' appeal against the 11+ result should have been allowed and would have if his parents had listened to him and made their case more cogently. The improvements he had offered to the argument had fallen on deaf ears. Had they not insisted that he made a contribution to the family income with part-time employment, he would have gained better CSE and 'A' level; grades and the dreaming spires would have been his for the taking. Given these misfortunes, he considered it appropriate to be creative and re-work what society had given him. On the basis that 'it isn't what you say, it's the way you say it', he worked on cultivating an accent that was upper class, but with a touch of estuary, so that a listener with an ear for these nuances would assume that he was trying to throw off a privileged background with a few dropped terminal consonants.

The more he did it, the easier it became: fake voice, fake past, fake documents. If you had enough vocal credibility, no one doubted; no one checked. The jury looked like the punters who had rolled up to get a cheap private education. He'd take his chance.

Yes, Massie had been a troubled child. He had been sympathetic. Spent time with him. Made his flat a home from home, and, yes, he'd suggested a few jobs around the place. Good preparation for adult life. He had to do them himself, and, yes, it made a man of him. And, goodness me, didn't the boy need a father figure. Absentee parents and a sister who couldn't cope. Recipe for disaster. And what does he get for his trouble? Unfounded allegations. Deeply saddening. Can't imagine why. Clearly, there were mental health issues. Stanhope had come full circle. All totally plausible. Job done. Jury satisfied. He could see it on their faces. Wished he could see Massie's face. Likely to be in tears by now.

'Well, Mr Stanhope. You make it sound as if you have had a really raw deal. You take this child in, and, in spite of all you have done for him, he ends up trying to ruin your life.'

Alex Stanhope pulled at the lapels of his blue suit and moved his shoulders with just the hint of a swagger.

'Is that a question?'

'It contains an invitation for you to respond.'

'Hmmm,' Stanhope looked as if he were considering whether to respond or not. 'The problem you have, Mr Kennedy, is…' Quite what problem prosecuting counsel had, the court was not to find out.

'Mr Stanhope, I would suggest that you are really not helping yourself by talking to learned counsel in this way.'

'I apologise, your honour.'

Hugh Kennedy continued to pick apart painstakingly the details of the original 'crime', the teacher's threat and the boy's subservience. He separated the details of the sleeping arrangements at the Massies' home from the apparent generosity shown by the teacher to his pupils, and what was left was a sordid pile of manipulation.

'Jed, the jury won't like a witness who is so full of himself. The justice system is a great leveller. After our closing addressees, the jury will retire and, in a nutshell, assess the believability of the two of you. This has to be beyond reasonable doubt. While they may not like Stanhope, they have to ask themselves if it is at all possible that you're making it all up.'

The trial came to a conclusion shortly after this with the two closing arguments.

Hugh Kennedy rose: 'Ladies and gentlemen. Jed Massie had every reason to have it in for Alex Stanhope. He belittled him. He was instrumental in trumping up an allegation against him that he had committed an act of vandalism on school property. He presented him with a fake bill. He falsely told him he would have to pay it off by working. He treated him badly while he could see that other boys were being treated well. And why were they? Mr Stanhope was interested in Brett Poynton. At that time, he was a handsome young man. They shared a bed. Alex Stanhope was attracted, but he did nothing. He was young then, just 25. It is likely he had no experience of how to deal with a situation like this. So how did he deal with it? He looked but dared not touch. Had he done so, he might have ruined everything. Brett Poynton might well reject him altogether. So, what did he do? He cultivated Jed Massie. Not because he liked him. He didn't. Jed Massie, even at his tender age, could see through Alex Stanhope's lies as Brett Poynton could not. Still can't. If Jed Massie were knocked about a bit, so what? No parents on the spot, and, yes, of course, as his guardian, he could make sure that no one listened to him anyway. Jed Massie was punished for not being Brett Poynton.

'You have seen for yourselves how Jed Massie was at the age of 13. That's who he was on the stand just a few days ago when he agreed with learned counsel rather than speak up for himself. Here was a figure in wig and gown; a figure of authority, who, he assumed, had the right to speak for him.

'Now you might think if you were Jed Massie - how could you get Alex Stanhope into as much trouble as possible? An assault would certainly be a way. But a hairbrush? Surely a more straightforward description of a rape would be more plausible. But, no, Jed Massie's assertion has not wavered. No. A hairbrush he often saw on Alex Stanhope's nightstand? No. A hairbrush he had never noticed before. This was a hairbrush he has not described in precise detail as might be expected had he made it up.'

The rest of his peroration and that of defence counsel became a blur in his head. He had done his best, and CPS had done their best for him. Now he just had to wait.

'Paul! Thank you so, so much for coming.' Jed embraced his former teacher.

'Would have missed it for anything. I've been in every day. Strict instructions from the CPS not to have any contact with you. Do you want me to tell you how I think you came across? Mind you; I am prejudiced,'

'Go on.'

'Brilliantly. You let me remember how you were. It was really strange to see you revert to childhood under cross-examination, for instance. I can't imagine how tough everything was for you then, and to rake over it all again now must bring it all back.'

'Not really. It didn't all come back to me. It never went away. My family knew it. You know what happened to them? My mum blamed herself for letting me go there, for not being around, for believing Stanhope, for not listening to me – not that I told her anything – for being too caught up with her own interests and, at the root of it all, for not being a mum. She went to pieces inside. When it all came out in the press, she started losing her reason, you know, forgetting things, letting herself go in her personal habits. My dad couldn't cope. Neither could I. She was put in a hospital for her protection, and she's still there. She doesn't know who she is, let alone who I am. It's so strange. She talks in alliteration like some long medieval poem – 'all grey grows the grass that was green before.' Yes, an extemporisation of 'Sir Gawain', except that she wants him to chop her head off. She wants to die. That's the thrust – and the specialists say this will go on until she does die. That may be what finished my dad off. He couldn't cope with visiting her and couldn't cope with the guilt of not wanting to. He came down with something during the pandemic and gave up trying.'

'And Gillian? That was your sister's name, I think.'

'Yes, alas, poor Gillian. She knew that Stanhope had just used her as a cover. I think it was his jumping for joy when he saw the letter from Cambridge that made her see sense.

She was angry with him, angry with herself and became an angry person. One thing he did do was put her off men. She rebounded quickly enough, though, and became close to an American girl here on holiday with her parents. She was quite a bit younger than her. She thought she was young enough not to have picked up the habit of lying. Anyway, she got in quickly to stop her inventing anything. She took the parents up on their invitation to visit and, you know, one thing led to another, and she's a housewife in Van Nuys in California. Her wife is well-trained and doesn't dare step out of line.'

'Well, Jed, that's the past thirty-five years in a nutshell for your family. Look, I'll be called when there's a verdict. I expect you'll stay in your hotel until then. Hugh told me which one. We'll meet up then. OK?'

Chapter 26

'But what happens if they can't agree? Does the whole thing have to start again?'

'Let's cross that bridge if and when we come to it, Jed. The judge has said he'll accept a majority verdict. So even if there are two who take an opposite view, there will still be a verdict.'

"Recollections may vary'. How dare he say that? I can't get rid of my 'recollections'. Just wish I could.'

He and Hugh Kennedy had decamped to the Carluccio's next to the courthouse. It was all wonderfully normal. People sitting, chatting. The whoosh of espresso machines, waiters bustling, customers chatting. For all the world, they looked like two businessmen taking a break from the office.

'The only trouble with coming here, Jed, is that it's too damn close to the court. Don't turn your head, but just to the right of us, Stanhope and his barrister have sat down. We can leave immediately or stay and carry on our conversation. It's your call.'

Jed froze. He was incapable of thought, let alone speech. Out of the corner of his eye he noticed a blue suit, and knew that it was filled by the thing that he most feared and loathed in his life. He looked away. The blue suit was one thing. What it contained was another. He would not set eyes on the person. To get up would attract attention. He retreated into himself. An idea came to him. He would busy himself with such a normal occupation that no one would notice. He pulled out his iPhone and made eye contact with Hugh, nodding to his phone. Hugh pulled his phone out of his pocket.

'*Can they see us?*' Jed texted.

He could see Hugh's fingers stabbing at the keys. '*I think not. There's a plant in the way, and Stanhope is facing away from us.*'

'*Do you mind if we keep our heads down and text until they go?*'

'*That may be some time.*'

'*I know, but I feel that my legs won't work if I try to stand.*'

'*OK. We'll give it a go. What do you want to text about?*'

'*All I can think about now is what this man has done to me. How can I get him out of my head?*'

'*By seeing him as a liar; someone who is only a proper adult in front of children; a man whom the world will despise when his conviction hits the media. He is a man who did things to you when you were a child, but you will see the law do things to him now that you're a man.*'

'*And what if the jury thinks otherwise?*'

'*Have confidence. You've given it your best shot. I have, too. I think what's happening is that one of the jurors has problems with the one-man's-word-against-another-scenario and is looking for a piece of factual evidence rather than using his ability to analyse character.*'

'*But what about the photo of me with all those marks?*'

'Not easy to rely on that one. Poynton did the marks on your back. As to the marks of the cane on your backside, my immediate thought was that Stanhope acted illegally in using the cane on you in 1987 as its use was made illegal in 1986. I checked the law about private schools, though, and found that the 1986 date applied only to state schools. Private schools could carry on beating the living daylights out of kids for another 12 years.'

'Blast.'

'Not the word I used when I read this, but similar.'

'There was more blood as well as the weals from the cane, you know.'

'I know, but this didn't show clearly enough in the photo. That would have been disputed by the defence. As it was, the main evidence against Stanhope is sitting in front of me. If you had done what so many victims do and remained silent, that man wouldn't be sitting in Carluccio's in Reading right now. You're the one whose determination got him to this point. If all goes well, this will be his last visit to a coffee shop for quite a while.'

'I was really struck by the state Richard was in. There are other boys who went through it, too. There's Grant Baxter and Michael O'Hare.'

'If they've been victims, let's hope they read about this. I wouldn't be surprised if one or more makes contact with you. You might consider giving an interview if the verdict goes the right way. People who want to make a complaint about their time at that place can reach you via whichever paper gets the exclusive or via me.'

'But then everyone will know.'

'They will know that you've been the utterly blameless victim of a crime and that you've been brave enough to stand up against *the criminal. You have to get in your head that you have done nothing wrong.'*

'*I kept silent for almost thirty-five years.'*

'*The other victims will have kept silent for longer. It was the gross nature of the crime that stopped you saying anything until you felt able. That's why there's no time limit on these cases. You will be a shining example to others. You'll see.'*

'*I think others have contacted Paul. I'll tell him I'll help.'*

'*Great. You know what it's like first hand. Other victims are likely to relate to you more than anyone. OK. Just hang on. They're leaving. Good. So they should. This my longest text exchange ever.'*

'*Me, too. Sorry for being a wimp.'*

Hugh pocketed his phone.

'*And don't fish for compliments. You know what I think. I won't say it again. Hang on a mo. I'm vibrating.'*

He pulled out his phone again.

'*Now I know why they left. I was engaged with you, so I didn't get the message as quickly as they did. The jury's coming back.'*

Chapter 27

'The thing is,' Michael leaned back, pushed his sunglasses over his head and let the sun shine full on his face. I've never been happier.'

'Or more indulged,' Jed suggested. The cricket match carried on in the background unobserved.

'Well. Isn't this heaven? The soft thwack of leather on willow; the sunshine dappled through the trees; the immaculately mown greensward. What more could one want? '

'God's in his heaven. All's right with the world. Is that it?'

'Pretty much so. Who am I to rock the boat?'

'Is it likely to stay afloat?'

'I really don't know, but I have all his attention now and, you know, I go places, and I do things. ' The last words came out as a ditty.

'You disappear to Alex's. I disappear to Alan's. We're spoiled. It's fun. '

'Sure.' Michael O'Hare had no idea what his slavery was like. Jed didn't think to enlighten him. He wondered what line the boy might take. He would probably tell him to approach it differently. 'Just be nicer to him, and he'll treat you well.' That or some such platitude.

'We never see you. Well, only in class.'

'I suppose my interests are a bit – what's the word? – exotic.'

'I think you may mean esoteric.'

'Yes. That, too. No, silly, I know the word; I just couldn't bring it to mind. I'll run it past Alan and see if he knows it.'

'Alan understands the similarity between Kylie Minogue and Johann Pachelbel, you know.'

'I know. I told him. I read about it in 'The Telegraph'. He's more of a 'Guardian' man himself.'

'It came up in class the other day.'

'I told him it would do his street-cred no end of good. Did it?'

'Very probably. Look, Michael, I thought I should have a word with you about something he's asked me to do.'

'I'm sure you don't need my permission, but I understand. I'm the teacher's pet, and you thought I might be jealous.'

'Not quite. It's that I thought I should tell you what he suggested to me, so you don't see yourself as quite so special.'

'Gosh, you're making me curious. What on earth did he say?'

'He asked if he could draw me.'

'Did you agree?'

'I went to his room to see what his drawings were like.'

'Did he show you?'

'Oh, yes. He was really proud of them. And I have to say they were good.'

'So you agreed to sit for him?'

'No. I said I'd think about it. What I didn't say was that I'd have a word with you. I think you know why.'

'He showed you those drawings, did he?'

'Yes.'

'So now you know.'

Jed paused and looked quizzically at the face in front of him. 'I don't think they're a good idea.'

Michael leaned back, luxuriating in the sunshine. 'But I do.'

'Why?'

'Because they don't matter. They don't bother me, and they don't bother him. I think they're rather good.'

'I'm sure they are, but aren't they rather personal?'

'Totally.'

'If you didn't sit for them, do you think he would treat you to dinners and trips and things the way he does?'

'Probably, but I won't test the theory. I assume he didn't show you the ones I do of him. '

'God, Michael, isn't all this just too much?'

'Nah, I like it. Look, I'm older than you. I can deal with these things.'

'A few months, but that's not the point.'

'So what is? That I'll hit 14 and be over the hill? Nope. He says I'm charming and appreciative. I am. That's very easy for me. Both are true. As I said, I've never been happier. Hang on. I think he's out. I'm next. See you.'

Michael had already padded up in anticipation. He strode out, passing the last man out. There was a ripple of applause. Jed joined in. Good luck, mate, he thought. You'll need it.

'You were miles away.'

'Oh, was I? Yes. Just dozing.'

'Jed, you were back there, I sense.'

'Uh-huh. I was back with Michael. You remember, Michael O'Hare?'

'Ah yes, smooth-talking one. Alan Watson's favourite.'

'Yes. Richard called me yesterday and told me Watson was dead. Seems he was under investigation, and he took an overdose. You knew, didn't you? Has Michael been in touch with you?'

Paul put a finger on the tip of Jed's nose. 'Nosey. Anyway, it was a few weeks ago. I need to talk to him again. Shall I ask if he'd agree to your coming along?'

'Sure,' Jed paused. 'Six and a half years. It isn't much. Divide that by two, and he'll be out in three.'

'He's hoping to be out in less than that. You know he's lodged an appeal.'

'I suppose he hasn't much else to do inside. That was such a time – the verdict, the sentencing, the eleven to one and the juror who came to the sentencing and shook my hand. He was great, so supportive. I seemed to spend all my time in tears that week.'

'You did. Your emotions were all over the place.'

'It was all so new. Suddenly, he wasn't in my head. Just knowing he was in prison was enough. He was gone. I knew he was locked away securely. There was this amazing feeling of liberation. Hugh was right in thinking it would be good for me to talk to the papers. I had nothing to hide. And the first thing I wanted to do…'

'Was to find out if you had the scars.'

'Which I do.'

'Well, faintly. Brett Poynton must've dug deep.' Paul's finger traced the line from start to end.

'Which led to us. I had no idea.'

'Nor me. None whatsoever.'

'No inhibitions now.'

'You, Jed Massie, can be called any number of things. 'Inhibited' is, I have to say, at least from what I've seen, not one of them.'

'No longer. Yup. I think I'm 'apt to forget to remember' now. 'I don't know so much about only the snow explaining it. I think I'm working it out myself. Here we are, 'all by all' and nothing to hide. Jed pulled the cover back and stood up in one movement. "Never been happier.' That's what Michael told me way back. I knew it would end in tears.' He paused and looked for assurance. 'This won't, will it? Never been happier.'

'Consenting adults, Jed. Middle-aged consenting adults. There's all the difference in the world.'

Chapter 28

'I get up in the morning. I get in my car. I say goodbye to my wife and drive off. Ten minutes later, I reach the common. I read the paper, listen to the radio, go for a walk and kill time. Kill time, that's good. Told the doctor I wanted to kill myself. She got me onto pills pdq. They're what keep me going. Wife doesn't have a clue. I've been living a lie for years. Lost my job four years ago. Bag of nerves. Nothing can hold my attention.'

'Was it Watson?'

'Oh, yes. And I remember how I used to be. So sure of myself; that it would all last forever; that Alan was so liberal, and I was liberated. Yes, Jed Massie, I remember our conversation - me all smug and sophisticated, and you were spot-on. It couldn't last. It was all so intense, so all-consuming. Every day at school right from age 12. Several times a day. I was taken to galleries, shows, dinners. My rewards. My treats. He got to know my grandparents, who were ersatz parents to me while mine were away, and they loved him so much that they paid for most of the trips he took me on in his car. That bronze Cortina GXL. Remember that one? How well I got to know that car. Ended up doing most of the driving myself at the end of these nights when he was so bladdered he couldn't stand. God knows how we got away with it.'

'So did he find a younger model?'

Michael O'Hare laughed mirthlessly. 'You must be kidding. Shall we put it this way? His tastes changed. He fancied an older model. Nick Boyce. Handed down from Cassell. He never had him, though. Poor Nick Boyce. Threw a knife at Cassell once in the dining room, I heard. Missed him and hit the mirror. Blond-haired chap, Boyce. Went in front of a train. Best out of it. And Watson, too. That's what sticks in the craw. You had the immeasurable joy and relief of seeing your tormentor get what he deserved. How I wanted justice for what Watson did to me. I haven't told you. He passed me around. I was a sort of trophy. When the teachers had finished with me, I did the rounds of the churches. I was very into religion at that time. Still am, more or less. Well, anyway, I showed an interest in religiosity, and you can imagine that the clergy showed an interest in me. You know what I was like. Being anointed by Peter Ball, being released from my sins, having all worldliness taken away: I was used and chucked.

'Paul knew this. I made contact with him a couple of years before you did for very much the same reasons. You look at your life, know it's rubbish, need to pin down a reason for this and come up with the same answer every time; that place. I talked. Then, for once, I listened. 'You were never guilty'. But I was. I felt guilty. No one pushed me into Watson's room or dragged me up the stairs. That was my choice. I wanted to go. What Paul did was tell me I shouldn't have been presented with the sort of choice that was likely to result in only one action. And the person who presented me with that choice was someone in charge, someone whose job it was to tell me things. When I grasped that, the way forward was clearer.

'What did I want? For it never to have happened. How to achieve that? To get help to put me back into the state I was in when I came down that drive for the first time. Therapy. Expensive therapy. I couldn't afford that. How to pay for it? Insurance money. How to get the insurance money? Sue the school. They should have looked after us. I learned all about 'duty of care.' Now there has to be proof that they didn't exercise that. They wouldn't just take my word for it so, now that I knew, really knew in my heart of hearts, that I was innocent, had been innocent and wanted to be that person again more than anything in the world, I had to go the police and get my case investigated. To do that, I would have to open up parts of my memory that had been closed off to me for decades. Prise open compartments with shut-off safety-valves that had protected me. That was the hardest job. I had to do it on my own. No one could be suspected of giving me the language to use. Paul knew that he would have to leave me to do this on my own.

'I imagined it would be some uniformed clod asking, 'What you been up to then?' It wasn't. I was listened to carefully and for as long as it took, and it took a long time; such a long time. There were so many people. For you, Jed, it was Stanhope. He was new to it. You were lucky. Watson was pretty new to it, too, but not the people he passed me on to. I don't know, but I suspect it was Cassell pulling the strings. I got to know the word 'vicarious.' That's how he operated. Not always, but mostly. He surrounded himself with people who would act for him. Half the teachers. Brookfield was always in the background, too. Some you wouldn't have suspected, Jed. Vaughan and Martin. My god, they were two-faced.

'So there's the police investigation, and there's Paul checking on the insurance. With Cassell dead, it's hard to find who the insurers were, but in the end, there was no point. His heirs knew what might be coming down the train track and dissolved the company. Poof. Gone. Everything. No chance to make a claim except the Criminal Injuries Compensation people, and that's not much. So all I'd be left with would be the result of the investigation: an arrest. And the hope that one thing would lead to another. I convinced myself that's what I really wanted.

'Next thing I hear is that he's taken an overdose. Someone tipped him off. The morning they were due to arrest him, they found his body. Watson took the coward's way out. I was left with nothing. Has getting it out helped? There needs to be an end product. That's what the trial and conviction would've been. Now it's more amorphous. I just don't know. My life has been a lie. Not a problem while I was in the circle of those who know what it's like to live a lie, but with Veronica, it's different. She's into truth. You'll see.

'But here I am. I'm a person. I have feelings. These are mostly bitter, of course, and my only pleasure has been taken away from me. Now the man is dead. He has even taken that small satisfaction from me. Ball, too. Dead. All dead.

'I think I became an alcoholic at school. It numbed the pain. So there you are. No arrest. No court case. Write a story. Say how easily it can happen. Show the effects, but don't mention my name.'

'And your wife, Veronica?' Paul asked.

'Hmm. My wife. She'll be home shortly. She knows you're both coming. I primed her with the press cuttings. She doesn't know I was there. You're old friends. No idea about our real connection, although she may suspect. Hasn't put that two-and-two together yet. Doesn't know about the job. Knows that I'm vulnerable – tough time at school - and supports me. That's what's important.'

In front of them stood a young fogey. Tweed jacket with patches on the elbows, check shirt, woollen tie, brown brogues. No doubt there was a cloth cap for his walks on the common. Green wellington boots stood by the door of their semi-detached farm cottage.

'All hers,' was his answer to their unasked question.

Paul and Jed stood to greet Veronica O'Hare. 'Just back from work. I hope Michael has been looking after you. Oh yes, I see I've caught you off-guard. I'm a deacon. The church is where I work, and this is my uniform. Tea anyone?'

Daylight faded. No one thought to turn on the light. They sat in the gloaming; Veronica transfixed by the story her husband was telling, empowered by the presence of his classmate who had been through a public wringer and his erstwhile teacher who had supported him. She had sat in silence through every twist, turn, variation thereon and explanation thereof. She remained composed, demure, attentive. The story ended. She remained poised and silent until it was clear that there were no more words.

'So, that's alright, then.'

She got up, walked to the front door and opened it.

'Except that it isn't. At all. Thank you for giving Michael the strength to tell me what has been the truth that he has hidden me from the day we met. I wonder if you would be kind enough to wait in your car for him. He will just be packing a few things. He won't be taking the car. He'll be leaving me the keys to that - and to the house.' Her open hand waited to be filled. 'Then he will ask you if you will please give him a lift to wherever he is going to. It is probable that, when I have had the chance to collect my thoughts and recover from the unutterable catastrophe he has presented me with, he may hear from my solicitor. I am in favour of forgiveness, of course. My job makes this somewhat essential. I can forgive a mistake, several mistakes, but when every part of my husband's life turns out to have been a lie – everything apart from his name, I think – then I have to ask myself what remains, and I give myself the answer – nothing.'

She remained by the open door, bidding farewell to her two visitors in a formal way with a slight bow of acknowledgement. 'Goodbye, Michael. I assume this is your name. Please try to see how I have been so completely deceived that there is no other way.' She was unbending at his exit from his home and her life. The door shut purposefully.

'Well, that went well.' Michael was matter-of-fact. The others sensed that he was used to an element of disappointment. 'Thought she might have been more charitable.'

'Where can we take you?'

'Well, I suppose there's my ex's place. I'll give him a call.' Michael had a number on speed dial. 'Benny, dear boy. It's happened. She's given me the boot. Yes. No. Not entirely unexpected. Did I mention you? No. Not to anyone. Thought it might take them by surprise. Funny thing is, she almost guessed. 'Goodbye, Michael. I assume this is your name' was her rather cutting parting shot. She went for the wrong name. Yes, OK, 'Bunny' was short-term, can't count that one, but I did take on yours at the ceremony. And I don't think I've ever legally relinquished it. Look, Benny, I'm not completely sure which side of the tracks I'm on now, but if you haven't... OK. Good. Just for a few days possibly, and then we'll see. I'll get a train and call you when I'm close. Yes, she's taken the car. Well, it is hers. See you.'

'Benny? Benny Jamieson? The boy who was good at history? He wasn't one of the chosen, was he?'

'On and off. Mainly off. He resisted them. He warned me about Watson, too. That's how we got to know each other. He could see what was coming. He wanted to talk to you but somehow never did. It can go that way. You didn't notice him, did you? He was deep in his books, so no one saw him. You know he's Professor Jamieson now? Anyway, I thought, now that I'm no longer in my 30s, maybe I'd better think of a family, so I sort of spread my wings. Or maybe it was the pills I was on. Veronica was a sweetie. She's a friend of Benny's. He's one of her flock. Yes, you never can tell. Well, he was until I left him for her, but I told him it might not work out, so it's not entirely unexpected. It's been quite a day. I was hoping for a legal session with Watson, but now it looks like it'll be one with Veronica. All things pass.'

Whatever bravado Michael had assumed lasted for just a few miles. It was to the sound of quiet sobbing that the car pulled up outside the station.

'Good luck.' Paul shook hands formally. He was back to his teacher role.

Jed hugged him.

'Well, at least I'm on the train and not in front of it. On balance, I would say in my case, honesty may not have been the best policy, but neither you nor I were to know. Maybe she'll calm down. Maybe I'll want her to, but I think not.'

The door closed, and the car was silent.

'Should we see the next one? Sleeping dogs and all that,' Jed had been quiet for some while.

'Some people can live with it, accommodate it, subsume it into their lives, but, you know, it's always there. Anyway, they contacted me. I didn't force the issue. They knew they wanted to get rid of it. At least they did then. If they still do, we press on. If not, we stop.'

Paul knew that once the ball had started rolling, it was bound to hit something.

"I am in blood stepped in so far that, should I wade no more, returning were as tedious as go o'er."

Jed knew just what he meant.

'Christ, Paul. Benny Jamieson. Why didn't I notice?'

Chapter 29

'It would've been a takeover bid: Cassell's school for his freedom. The younger Poynton told the older one what he was finding out. The brother told Stanhope, and Stanhope told Brookfield. Boyce took the photos. I was a bit on the side. Come to think of it, there were quite a few bits on many sides. I was cleaning up after my first paid-for session with Brookfield when we met. Actually, I was feeling pretty awful. It wasn't me at all. I wanted to be seen for who I really was.'

'I certainly saw that, Grant.'

'Yes, you did. And it didn't bother me. What did – slightly then and much more since - was that I should've told you there and then not to set foot inside the place.'

Grant Baxter was the manager of the boutique hotel in which they were meeting. Smart, besuited - and penitent. The handshake was firm, given that it was with his left hand. His right arm was in a sling.

'Went over on a patch of grease in the kitchen. Just a sprain, but that can be worse than a break.'

'Good to see you, Grant, injured or not. Thanks for calling. You were going to tell us how it all came crashing down.'

'I was. You need to know the full story.' He pulled the knees of his suit trousers up a touch and sat down, motioning them to do the same. 'Those photos. That's what ended it for Brookfield and Stanhope. Boyce had the same make of camera as Braine'. Braine picked Boyce's up. Boyce ended up with Braine's, and when we had the film developed, it was all trees, fields and fluffy lambs. Maybe not the lambs, but you know what I mean. Hardly the sort of material they could blackmail Cassell with. Ten shots of him, though, on the camera Braine thought was his. With Boyce. Never occurred to us that he was an adult. Not until the police pointed it out.

'He wasn't the first with Cassell. Just the first I photographed. Brookfield wondered why a man in his 70s would want to own a school, so he did a bit of checking. Cassell was the black sheep in a rich family. They didn't know what to do with him after he'd been sacked from ten schools. I think it was ten. Maybe more. So they suggested he buy one. Then he couldn't be sacked. Finchingham came on the market, and he snapped it up. It was never a going concern, but that wasn't the point. It kept him happy. All he had to worry about were the staff, so he took the line that they either lumped it or left. The ones he employed to replace them were teachers who couldn't get jobs elsewhere and, as he wasn't fussy about references, it was easy to find them. Brookfield suspected this as he had been recruited the same way.'

'So which of the two wanted to take the place over?'

'Brookfield's plan was to be nominated Cassell's successor with Stanhope as Brookfield's right-hand man and Headmaster. Brookfield was in it for the money. I doubt that I was the first he paid for. That's how he got what he wanted. Stanhope wanted the kudos and power. That was really what he was into. Yes, he wanted Poynton – god knows why, he was loathsome and stank – but most of all, he wanted power. If it's any consolation, Jed, I'm pretty sure that what he did to you was to have power over you more than to have Poynton by proxy.'

'There's a relief.' Jed was not entirely serious. 'You know, I had the feeling that might have been the case. I could tell the difference between how he looked at Poynton and how he looked at me. He wanted to break me. Nearly did.'

'What Brookfield wanted was money, and he thought he had a clever way to get it. He sold boys. If someone wanted someone, there was a price to pay. At first, it was all within the school. Then he branched out. That's how Kempson started with Braine. All laid on by Brookfield. Then when Brookfield found out about Kempson's colourful past, the price went up. If Kempson wanted to keep on with Braine, it would cost him for Brookfield to keep silent. Kempson was raking it in with the private tuition, and most of the cash went straight to Brookfield. It wasn't the money Kempson wanted from the tuition, though. If you talk to Richard, he may tell you. Anyway, in time, Kempson's contribution became less important as Brookfield expanded his business.

'Brookfield was why Michael O'Hare had such a bad time. Michael was a saleable commodity when Watson started looking elsewhere. You know Brookfield's religious side? He had plenty of contacts in that field, so Michael was sold on. Many times. He wasn't the only one. There was big money in this. He wanted to sell me on, too, but one session with him was enough to tell me this wasn't my thing. No thanks.

'So Brookfield was into selling kids on. He almost forgot about Kempson, but when you, Paul, got wind of what Kempson was up to and wanted the parents involved, Brookfield thought it would all come out. In the past, when he'd felt that he was going to be exposed, he would find some peccadillo he could use or even create, but you were squeaky clean. You were the only one he was afraid of. How he hated you. To dispose of the danger from you, the only way was to get you out. Difficult to sack you, but he banked on your resigning if you didn't get your way. He was right, but what might you do then? He thought you'd go down the legal route, so he put it into Cassell's head by telling him that you wanted to expose him. That's why Cassell put a note in with your final cheque that you should take legal advice before going any further with talking to Braine's parents.'

'I did. It wasn't because of his veiled threat. I thought I should check the legal position anyway. Yes, he could sue me for damaging his business. I sensed that there wasn't much of a business to damage, but I couldn't take the chance. I think Richard's parents are still unaware of what was happening, at least his mother is. I believe his dad died. He called me before the trial. It was a painful experience. He can hardly talk. He knew he was going to be called as a witness, but said he wasn't bothered. He needed to tell me something there and then, in case he wasn't able to later. I think he thinks he will die soon. God, he's younger than me and thinks he'll die. I told him that even if he didn't bother, I did, and it was possible that I'd be called as a witness, in which case our contact might be revealed and damage the case somehow. You know how much I wanted to reach out, to be cried on even, and you can imagine how hard it was to hold back. I've tried contacting Richard, but his phone won't accept calls from mine. I'll have to use Jed's.'

Grant was on a roll. 'Stanhope knew what Brookfield was doing and vice-versa. I imagine they hated each other, but they were yoked together. They know too much. The one will never tell on the other.'

'So if the police were to follow up on Brookfield and take evidence from Michael and Richard, there'd be plenty of cases to investigate?'

'Guess so. Which is probably why they won't. It's just too big a scandal. They could get actionable statements from half the staff and most of the kids. You could follow it up.'

"O that way madness lies,' I can't speak for Jed – well, maybe I can – but that's something I won't be doing. I know there are some who consider it a crusade to get these people stopped, and it's a noble aim. We know they probably won't stop until they're stopped, but the whole thing is a horror show that can swallow you up. I feel for Richard, though, so maybe just his case and then that's an end to it.

'How about you, Grant? I sense you're in your element,' Paul was solicitous.

'Great job. Yes. Can't complain. I thought I knew what I was getting myself into, but at that age, you think you know it all. I wasn't forced, but it was the most wretched experience ever, and I can only imagine what the forced version is like. I wanted to see you again, Jed, to apologise for saying nothing then, at our first encounter and all those occasions later in Stanhope's room. I saw how you were being treated and said nothing. I have often wondered why. Why did I say nothing? Why did I go there? Why did I want to be friends with Poynton?

I have no answers. Only apologies. It was all so horrendous. I am ashamed. All of this just – what shall I say? - eats you up and vomits you out.'

In the silence, Paul was finding words to thank Grant for his straightforwardness.

'You were keeping his secrets, weren't you?' Jed's intervention was sudden, and his tone had changed. A coldness had crept into his voice with a tightness around the lips. 'The wine and fags in a master's flat. The smutty conversations. From the first sip and the first puff, you were in cahoots with him. At first, it was neither here nor there. Just a drink, just a smoke. That's when the conspiracy started. You couldn't object because you were already trapped in the deceit. No matter how it developed, you were powerless to stop it. The only way out was not to go in. So, Grant, why did you go in? Why did you keep on going when you knew what was happening?'

Jed had taken Paul by surprise. 'That's pretty harsh when all Grant wanted was to apologise.'

"Thou art too full o' the milk of human kindness to catch the nearest way.' You know that I respect you, Paul. You know that there is, was and will be, no one closer, but there is one big difference between us. You have never been violated. The touching you have known has been good touching, the touch of those who want to show their emotional closeness physically; the touch of those you trust. Bear with me.'

Jed turned away briefly. He didn't want a moment of weakness to take the tension out of the moment.

'I thought it might be that you really wanted Poynton. I doubt that. I don't think Stanhope interested you either. So what was it that kept you going back? It may have been as simple as the drinks and fags and smut, but I'm not sure that was the allure. Always, Grant, with you, it's been what you didn't say. In Stanhope's room, you played along with it when he was demeaning me. You never said a word to me or about what was happening to me. Now we meet on equal terms as adults, and you have plenty to say to me. All the right things. Nothing is spared. All the dramatis personae are up for criticism, even you. At least when we first met, you were hiding nothing, but this time you slipped up.'

Jed paused to let the significance of the verb take effect.

'Shall we say your jacket sleeve slipped up? You remember? When you shook hands with me.'

Grant Baxter's hand instinctively went to the cuff of his jacket and pressed it to his wrist.

'You saw it.'

It was more a statement than a question, but Jed wanted to explain.

'Paul didn't. I did. It's very 'you'. You're the archetypal man-about-town, aren't you? I guess the suit is made-to-measure. The stitching is very precise, and the fabric falls softly into it. The shirt, too. Burberry to judge by the logo. The shoes, the cuff links, all seem to be of the finest. The tie is silk. Maybe your underpants are, too. I think we're talking more than a thousand pounds worth of clothes. Perhaps two. All very appropriate for the manager of a luxury hotel. Would they be tax-deductible as a uniform? I wonder. But, no, Grant, you guessed. It's the watch that gives the game away. £60,000 at least of Patek on your wrist. Really, Grant, how did you come by this? By this whole ensemble? And how does this tie in with your request for a meeting with my friend Paul?'

Jed paused. He knew he was creating an effect.

'No need to answer. Paul, I know you say that if anything's worth saying, Shakespeare's already said it. You're right, of course. Here's one for you: 'But 'tis strange. And oftentimes, to win us to our harm, the instruments of darkness tell us truths, win us with honest trifles, to betray's in deepest consequence.' Let me explain it to you, Grant. I think we can forget Stanhope. Cassell's dead, and when we see Richard, we'll find out about Kempson, but it's Brookfield I'm interested in. That was a – how do they put it in the films about thieves' parlance – 'nice little earner'. Not so little, though. I often wondered how these people found their prey. You told us: Brookfield and his ilk and their contacts. There was the truth. We believed it, and rightly so.

'When I first saw you, way back then, I have to say I was shocked. You tell us it was a ritual cleansing. You were washing away your sin. What a wonderfully intimate small truth that was, too. Who knows? I almost felt sorry for you. Perish the thought. Dissembling is second nature to you now, I guess. So what is the 'deepest consequence'? You wanted to know how serious we are with all this. Will we really follow up all the leads and get Brookfield investigated? You know Paul's answer. It may change, though I doubt it. When you've rolled around in the filth at the bottom of the barrel long enough, there's a time to get out. I feel this. He does. So you know we're unlikely to have Brookfield in our sights. He must be approaching 80 by now anyway. But how about you, Grant? You've got years left in you, and I know how flexible your conscience can be. And what a setup! A hotel in the heart of London. What an upper-class meeting place. Oh yes, you took Paul in. But I'll be the one to decide if you need to be followed up. You shouldn't sleep easy in your silk sheets, Grant Baxter.'

Out in the roar of the traffic and away from the hotel, Paul waved down a taxi.

'How did you know?'

'I didn't. I made it all up. Convincing, wasn't it? I spent hours while I was washing, sweeping and dusting, looking at him. In his eyes, I could see no fellow feeling. No ability to relate to anyone. But he took what was offered and more. Cigarettes went into his pocket for his use later. How I wanted him to stop the torment for me. How I loathed him for doing nothing.'

'He seemed to be so open.'

'For thirty-five years, I had an incubus on my back. Now I don't. I don't hide anything from you. My trust in you is total. You know this. I'm open. I know you are, too. I see it. I didn't see it in Grant Baxter then, and I don't see it now. Am I right? No idea. I don't think he's quite so smug now, though.'

Chapter 30

'That's a big yawn. They're contagious. I'm doing it now.'

'I'm tired, Jed. I just want to stay here. As we are. A quiet life without all this 'stuff'.'

'Let this one be the last. It may not happen anyway.'

'The thing is, he was so keen to talk. Even though what happened is far worse than anything that happened to any of the others, he was frank.'

"And open.' Is that what you were going to say? 'There's no art can find the mind's construction in the face."

'This is just one big Macbethfest, isn't it? Anyway, I didn't see him. It was all done over the phone.'

'Haven't we already explored the bottom of the barrel?'

''Fraid not. This barrel has a hidden depth.'

'Touch my scar.'

'No. I want to get there before lunch. One thing'll lead to another. Hang on a sec. I've had an e-mail. Goodness me, that takes me back! I put an old school photo on Facebook years ago. I must've included the names of the staff. Here's the message. *I've seen Keith Kempson's photo on the internet. He's come into my thoughts recently. I wonder if you know if he's still alive. Rob.*'

Yes, Rob. He certainly is. I have the feeling I may know why you're enquiring after him. Please feel you can tell me about how he has come to your mind now. Paul.

'I think that's an open enough reply. I have a feeling about this one.'

'Did you charge the car?'

'I did.'

'He won't see us. I'll bet on that. He wouldn't answer my phone - or any other. He was pretty ill last time. We don't know if he's still alive even.'

'We won't find out if you don't get up.'

It was after mid-day when they arrived at an unprepossessing semi that a combination of 118 dot com and Google had identified as Richard's home.

'You won't push too hard, will you?'

'Like with Baxter G.? No chance. Baxter's in a special category of things that live under stones. The only true thing he said is that while he was standing starkers in front of me, seeing my reaction, he could have given me a clue what that place was about. He was a pretty boy. I was, too. I was bound to be chosen. It was as if he wanted this to happen.'

'Richard lived in a mansion when he was a boy. His parents were well-to-do.'

'Hard times now, it would seem. OK. Out we get.'

The doorbell wasn't working, or at least they couldn't hear it ringing inside the door, so Paul tried the letterbox.

'Someone's coming.'

The door opened a crack. 'Richard. It's Paul Mason and Jed. We'd really love to see you.'

'Please just go. I can't cope with this.'

'We know. We're really concerned for you.'

'If you are, you'll just let it rest.'

'But you talked so frankly over the phone.'

'That was when Velia was alive. I've nothing to live for now. Just let me be.'

'Richard. This Jed. You remember. We haven't spoken. You mention Velia. Was she your wife?'

'My partner, Jed, and my best friend. She went two months ago. She knew all this wasn't good for me. She worried for me. And now she's the one who's gone.'

'That's not fair, we know, but look, Kempson's not going to stop unless we stop him. Just think what a ruthless man he was. Paul and I, we want to have children, and we'd hate our child to encounter someone like him. What happened to you and me was terrible. You just need to say what happened. Can we come in? Please.'

The crack in the door frame widened slightly, just enough to accommodate part of a wheelchair.

'If you come in, I won't be able to stop myself, so you can't. Let me tell you one thing. Just one, then, please go. Promise me.'

'You're the one calling the shots, Richard. We have no choice, but isn't this a bit public?'

'It'll do. Now listen to me. I was abused by Kempson every day for more than three years. I was abused at school and at home. My parents were often away. I was abused in every room in the house. And in every way, but the worst thing was… The worst thing…' He breathed into a mouthpiece and recovered his voice. 'That man made me abuse another boy while he was abusing me. A younger boy. So you see, I'm as bad as him.'

'You aren't.' Paul was quick to contradict him. 'You were forced.'

'Forced or not, I abused. Jed'll know. That feeling. That horror. Double it. That's what I felt. On and on it went.'

'All the more reason to get the man in prison.'

'All the more reason for me to leave it behind. There will have been other victims. Find them. They'll get him behind bars. My day is done. I'm sorry. Please respect my decision. I can live with it if you'll tell me you'll find other victims.'

'We promise,' Paul said.

'That's news,' he said later in the car.

'What is?'

'Having a child.'

'Not quite what I said, mate.'

'Yes, you did,'

'No. I was very careful. Think back. 'Paul and I, we want to have children,' That's what I said. Because it'll be one with yours and one with mine.'

'OK.'

'Is that OK we'll have children, or OK, I understand what you were getting at with the difference between the singular and the plural?'

'I'll tell you at home.'

'We are home. It's our driveway. Come on. Tell me now.'

'Jed, you'll be 49 in a few weeks, and I'm thirteen years older. I think that boat has sailed. Nothing to do with fertility, just mathematics. Add a couple of years for the procedure and another 18 for independence and what've we got. Running out of fingers. 69 and 82.'

'Just a thought.'

'A wonderful thought, but I really don't see it happening. What brought this on? Hang on; there's something wrong, isn't there? I know you, Jed. What is it?'

Jed unhitched his seatbelt and turned on the interior light. 'Take a look. Feel them.'

'Oh. Yes. I get it. That's recent. We'll make an appointment first thing. Whatever it is, we've caught it early.'

'I just thought, if it's going to happen, I should bank some. You, too.'

'Let's hold that thought. Don't be frightened. I'm with you all the way.'

'We'll talk about it inside.'

As was his habit, Paul automatically plugged the car into the PodPoint. The dashboard showed only 30 miles left in its battery. That was close. The blue light was showing as usual on the PodPoint. Not early-onset, surely. Maybe he hadn't pushed it fully home last time. He pondered about the small bombshell Jed had dropped. Not for long. A message was waiting.

'I've had a reply. My god, Jed, this is dynamite. Rob writes: *'When I was ten, I was interfered with every day at St Benedetta's School in the Lake District by Keith Kempson. I see him in dreams now. I just need to know that he can't do this to any other child. Best wishes. Rob. BTW, as you'll see from my e-mail address, I am in Australia.'* I'm typing out my reply: *I can't give you that assurance. Please skype me now at this address. Paul.*

'Good. Seems we have another victim. Can I get back to the other thing?'

'Hang on. There's a skype call. It's nearly midnight here. Rob? Can you hear me? What's the time in Australia?'

'Lunchtime'.

'I thought you'd answer 'Lunchtime, Cobber.''

'Nah. We're not all like that.'

'Look, Rob. You need to tell me about Kempson, and then you'll need to talk to the police. OK.'

'Hang on a minute, Cobber. This is stuff I haven't told anyone in the whole world, and here I am, blurting it out to someone I've never met on the other side of the world. This is creepy.'

'I'm not creepy. Look at me. Is this face creepy? If you've seen the FB page, you know what Jed's been through. He trusted me. Here he is.'

'I've just turned the camera round, Rob. Or should I say Cobber, too? I'm Jed, and I know what it's like. I sat on my disclosure for more than 30 years.'

'Look, Jed, I've sat on mine for more than 40 years. What's brought it up is that my daughter's now the age I was when all this kicked off. It's taken me right back. If there's a chance that this man can do anything like that to another child, I'll kill him.'

'Well, Rob, you won't. Anyway, your daughter would be without her dad, so let's be realistic.'

'It makes me angry. I punch walls.'

'Well, that's not good for the walls or your hands.'

'Talk us through what happened. Just to say, we'll be supportive, but we can't let whatever defence there will be say that we put any words in your mouth. OK? The object of the exercise is to get Kempson stopped and put away. Everything else has to be pushed to one side. You talk. We'll listen. We'll feel for you, but we won't say anything. Look at which police force area your school was in and e-mail them. Keep us posted. About everything.'

Chapter 31

'What does it look like?'

'As if you're ten years old. God, that's the wrong thing to say. What can I say? Different. Oh no. I meant it makes no difference. Come off it. I take you as you are.'

'Should I get a prosthesis?'

'Not on my account, but if it helps you feel balanced, yes, of course.'

'Did Rob call?'

'He's skyping us in a few minutes. I told him I'd be driving and that we'd be back from the hospital by one - our time.'

'And the other?'

'Can we put that on the back burner for a while? You don't have to use a bank, there's no panic, and we can take our time to work on the best way forward. Let's find out what stage Rob is at.'

Skype was already warbling as they opened the front door. 'Aha, here we go.'

'OK, Cobbers. I've had contact from the constabulary in the UK. They've investigated and expect to arrest Kempson shortly. He'll be charged with 23 counts in addition to mine.'

'Twenty-three? Wow!'

'Thought that would come as a surprise. Certainly did to me. I assumed I was the only one. It seems every kid in my class was touched: all 24 of us. As the offences happened multiple times, each offence is a specimen charge. Takes me back to when we started. You know I wondered if I should go ahead. Was it just to make me sleep better, or was it better to get over it and leave it in the past? I didn't want anyone to know. I felt stupid and embarrassed. 'Let me think about it,' I told you. All these considerations were slowing me down, and there were you guys saying, go ahead. They were excuses. I thought it might be easier to do nothing, but the nightmares would still be there. So, thanks to you, I did and here's the result. Twenty-three men my age, having the same nightmares. The only difference is that they didn't have you breathing down their necks.'

'Are they checking on other places Kempson's taught at?'

'They tell me this is in hand. He travelled around the country, it seems. He was sacked from two schools for shoplifting and one for cheque fraud.'

'I bet other schools wrote him a glowing reference just to get rid of him.'

Jed joined in the conversation. 'Did they tell you which year the offences apply to?'

'No, but it was the early '70s. Why do you ask?'

'It's the tariff. They have to imagine that there's a potential criminal thinking about committing a crime. Before he does so, he thinks, 'now let's say I'm caught, what sentence may I get? And he looks it up in a non-existent list and thinks to himself, 'is it worth it for this stretch' and decides on that basis whether or not to commit the crime. The tariffs keep changing from year to year, so the tariff used to determine the sentence is the tariff in force in that year.'

'I see where you're coming from, and back then, no one knew about this kind of abuse.'

'Exactly. Well, it wasn't as well-known as it has become. In fact, the idea of such a crime wouldn't enter the head of most right-minded people, so the tariff was set pretty low.'

'Well, if that's how it is, there's nothing to be done.'

'Actually, there is. He'll be asked if there are any other offences to be taken into consideration. If he says 'no' and other offences come to light, and they come to trial, and he's found guilty, the tariff for these crimes will be added to the first one. We know he's guilty of many crimes. When the current trial finishes, we hope he'll be arrested for more offences.'

'Fingers crossed for that. Look, Cobbers, I'm planning to come over to the UK for the trial, so we'll meet up.'

'Christ, Paul. That's a record.' Jed was pouring a celebratory bubbly. '23 people who can let go of their secrets. And it's been so long. 40 years. More. How on earth did they manage?'

'Some of them probably quite well. This shakes things up for them and their families. I sense that everyone in Rob's class would've been interviewed, nightmares or not. For those who'd managed to suppress the memories, their ordered lives will have been turned upside down. I'm remembering a hymn I used to sing at school. How did it go?'

Paul recollected the threads of a distant tune: "Take from our souls the strain and stress, and let our ordered lives confess, the beauty of Thy peace.' When I sang this, I felt a stillness, a relief. The music suited the words. There's something beautifully predictable about an ordered life. And the absence of surprises makes it peaceful. You know I've never had the radio on in the car. I just listen to the silence of no engine noise. And the aloneness.'

'Is this the 13-year difference coming to the forefront? It can't be retirement beckoning, surely? Where would you put all that energy?'

'It's the barrel, Jed. We've been in it too long. All the people we ever meet, it seems, are either damaged or twisted. You're in recovery after thirty-five years of trauma, but I really feel untouched. And yet, given all I've heard and had to deal with, I wonder if I am. I wonder sometimes if I have become just pragmatic. When someone tells me a ghastly thing that's happened to them, I just think of the best way forward for them. I don't feel their pain. Should I? You see, if I did, I think I'd be useless. I suppose my reaction to everything now is a kind of professional detachment, except that I'm not a professional. I'm just detached. When you told me what had happened to you at that place, my first thought was about how to get this man put away. While I felt for your pain, I didn't actually feel your pain. I knew I couldn't contact you until all the evidence had been given in court, but my only thinking about this was how correct it was that justice was served in that way.'

'And how many minutes did it take that day? There I was, sobbing with relief, and there was your hand on my back. Back to the hotel and how we wanted that closeness.'

'It was so unbelievably sudden that I didn't think. It was bizarre and spontaneous and unconsidered and wonderful and something that I didn't realise I was. You know that. Neither of us had any idea. Had I thought about all the possible ramifications and complications, I'd never have acted on it. That's a side I never thought I had. This is my other side. It's how logic constrains me. The right words and actions are what come out. It's the outcome that my mind is focussed on, not the sadness or the hurt or any of the human things. I know that I can come across as ruthless. Someone said to me, I think it was one of the staff at that place, 'You really don't care about the means. You're only interested in the end,' and I took it as a compliment. What I see are others' frailties, and I assess the best way to tackle them. It was the same when we had to confront the cancer. I thought only of the need for excision and what effect the outcome would have on your well-being. I know you must have been frightened, but it never occurred to me to indulge in that emotion with you.'

'We deal with crises differently, though, don't we?'

'Yes, that's true. The thing is that I see a crisis as just that - something to deal with; something to overcome. My approach is to remove the obvious emotion from the situation because it gets in the way of managing the practicalities.'

'You mean you think you lack the human touch?'

'Exactly.'

'You touch me. I mean in all senses.'

'But I think my own feelings are not touched enough, whatever 'enough' is in this sense.'

'Is it that you feel desensitised?'

'I think so.'

'Then it's how you cope.'

'Quite probably.'

'So it's you being you.'

'I think I would prefer a more sensitive me: a me who can let go.'

'And fall to pieces? Leaving me to pick them up? I don't see it. You're tough.'

'Resilient, I hope.'

'That a better word.'

'OK. Then I'm cured. Thanks. Let's say 'I have supped full with horrors.''

'But I think 'direness can still start you' if we have to do it Macbeth's way.'

'So let this be the last one. Yes?'

Rob was full of it when they met. 'He was frail and crinkled. Now, why does that word come to me? That's what he called it when he wanted me. He'd say, 'Time for crinkling, boy. I did what I was told by my teacher. That's what I was expected to do.'

'The papers are full of it. '93 offences' all over the headlines.'

'And just under seven years.'

'What did I tell you, Rob? He'll be out in three and a half. All it'll mean to him is that someone else cooks his meals and pays for his stay.'

'No, Jed, it means that Rob has seen justice done, and the man is removed – yes, albeit temporarily – from society.'

Rob was miles away. 'Look, I'll tell you this. Something else I said to no one. For my whole life, from the time I was at that school, I've had real problems with my temper. With drink, too. Lost my first family to those. I knew I was going to lose my second family when I reached out for help. Well, my wife told me to. I went to a psychiatrist. For hours I told her my story. It all came out, the abuse at school, the drinking, the fights, the prison time – I never told you about that – my violent outbursts, my problems with women and my connection to you two. It all came out. She sat, and she listened, and she let me talk. She wrote a report with her findings. I'm going to e-mail you a copy.

'She traced everything, every thought, feeling, every action, back to the time I was ten in that classroom with that man and what he did to me. I didn't know what was happening to me; I felt disgusting, dirty, perverted and, in a word, not manly. You can imagine how important manliness is, especially where I come from. So I asserted my masculinity. I fought to show my strength; I went with women to prove my prowess; I argued with men to show myself that I was a match for any of them; I became argumentative, pig-headed and generally vile.

'My violence extended to my first family. When I lost them, I had thoughts of self-harm. How my second family tolerated me, I have no idea. They put up with all the stuff that was inside me, all the rage. And it was the fury about what that man had done to me to me that drove me to that state of despair, that wretchedness that shaped my entire life.'

Rob wiped his eyes. 'And made me start looking for him. Oh, yes, it was to kill him. That's what I wanted to do. And then I met you two, and I started seeing another way.'

He paused, looked at his feet and sighed. 'It took this lady psychiatrist to tell me that this man, this evil man, had ruined my life. All this has vindicated what I did. I have never hated anyone as I despise him. He needs to die in prison.'

The three men sat in silence.

'You did a wonderful thing for me. Thank you. From the bottom of my heart, thank you.'

The following morning the e-mail arrived with the psychiatric report attached to it.

'Here you are, as promised. BTW, you need to read the papers. You're the news now.'

Chapter 32

'Quite a hatchet job.' Hugh took the offered coffee. 'Thanks. Words and pictures. Clear, too. Fortunately pixilated. How did they get them?'

'That's what we asked ourselves. Well, after we'd taken in the hate that motivated it all. How on earth did they come by it all? It isn't as if we broadcast these things. Then we realised that all the words used came from conversations in the car. The photos, too. Hang on, I thought. I remembered that the charge in the car seemed low one evening, which it never is as I plug it in after every journey. It's a habit. I didn't think any more of it. Assumed I hadn't pushed the plug fully home.'

'Isn't the I-Pace all-electric?'

'Yes. It's like a computer on wheels. The police think someone cloned the key signal, got into the car and either put devices in it or manipulated the car's devices in some way. They couldn't move the car without disconnecting it from the mains, so maybe they didn't reconnect it properly afterwards. The car records every journey automatically, no matter how short, so they'll be able to tell exactly when it was moved. What whoever did it may not have realised is that I also had extra cameras fitted in it, front and rear to record the outside of the car, so they may have captured people around the car.'

'A clever sting.'

'Clever and ruthless. Someone's got it in for us. It's the reference to a ten-year-old that hurts the most. It was just a throwaway remark. I knew there and then I shouldn't have said it.'

'So there you are. 'Gamekeepers turned poachers.' That's what they're saying.'

'Not only are we doing what we've accused others of doing, but we're planning to have a child of our own, too, it seems, with a good chance one or both of us will be dead before that child's an adult. Sexism, ageism, the lot. Jed's an exhibitionist, and I'm a fraud. No one will believe a word we say now.'

'And you can bet that Stanhope will use this in his appeal.'

'It just gets worse.'

'What do you want to do?'

'First reaction - this can't be happening. Disbelief. Second reaction - disappearance. Make us disappear, and it'll all go away. To lie low. Let it all die down. Today's headline news is tomorrow's fish and chip wrapper. But no. It didn't take long for us to become indignant. My car is my private space. What I say in it is my choice. What Jed shows me is his choice. We weren't on a public road. We have done absolutely nothing wrong. Our words have been edited. The pictures cropped. Yes, they must have been thrilled to get these unguarded comments and explicit images, but it's all just smut. It's taken a few days to get over it and to rationalise everything, but we've decided not to be ashamed, to hold our heads high – and sue.'

'You can,' Hugh was giving a considered legal opinion, 'the question is, will it do more harm than good?'

'That's why we wanted to see how you think it might go. We want the police to make a big thing of this. Our freedoms have been interfered with. We have been libelled. My I-Pace is a crime scene. There will be traces left; prints, fibres, equipment even and recordings. We want to go big on this one. What people can do with electric cars is part of the future. What happens if someone controls the car remotely? It's two tons and instant torque that accelerates it faster than almost anything else on the road. We need to stop it happening now. Yes, OK, I'll get off my soapbox.'

'Any suspects you can think of?'

'Oh yes. Just one.'

'The one mentioned in the paper by an initial. One you mention, Jed, as the one you saw under the shower on your first day. The one you are supposed to have always wanted to get to know. The 'pretty boy' who spurned your attentions as a child? That one?'

'Baxter G. The one with £60,000 on his wrist.'

'He's not the general manager of the hotel, you know? I did some checking after Jed had a go at him and all this happened. He owns it.'

'You think it happened the night before you visited Richard Braine. Shall I assume you inputted his address into the sat nav before you left the car that night? OK. Then that should be your first port-of-call. They'll have got to Richard Braine before you did.'

'Ah, Richard, poor chap,' said his neighbour whose door they tried after getting no response to their knocking.

'He's not...'

'No, young man, he's moved. Into a care home. Just a couple of days ago. Far the best thing for him. He was never the same after his dear Velia passed away. It's a good home, best in the area, they say. I'd love to book a place there myself for when the time comes, but it's fifty thou a year. Out of my price range. Must've been a relative who came to collect him - big car. I even remember the number. I never notice numbers, but I remember this one COV 1P. I did a double-take, thinking no one would want a plate like that, but it wasn't what I thought at first glance. Big car, though. Oh, yes, the name of the home. It's 'The Alders' on Borough Road. Just a few minutes by car, my dears.'

'Jed. This is a petrol station. In an electric car? Have you forgotten?'

'Just need to do something. Won't be a minute.'

He sprinted in the direction of the loo, returning a few minutes later. He drove. Paul dialled a number.

'Hugh, can you get them to check who owns COV 1P, please? That's the car that spirited Richard away. We're going to try to see him. Just pulling into the drive now.'

Jed turned to him.

'You know we haven't said a word in the car since we left home. Is this how it's going to be? We have to assume we're bugged? I haven't taken this car out since well before seeing Baxter G. I'm sure they haven't got to this one, too.'

Paul got out of Jed's car.

'Let's not make assumptions. Whatever's going on is far bigger than just a few teachers and pupils at a closed-down school. Someone's shelling out £50,000 a year for this place to keep Richard onside. I thought it was just Kempson he had information about, and, vile though he is, I sense he's not worth that amount of money. We need to see who else is in the frame.'

Richard Braine had shed several years since their last meeting. He was moving around the garden under his own steam and enjoying animated conversations with other residents.

'Richard!' Paul waved cheerfully. Richard waved back and beckoned them to join him.

'I know what you're thinking, and you're not wrong. I've heard what happened to you, and it's not fair. You're decent people, and you're trying to do the right thing by all the kids who were caught up in this. It started with kids and teachers, but it broadened out more than you can imagine. Sorry to appear suspicious, but I have to assume I'm not being recorded, so can you open your jackets, please, and turn round? Yes, that's fine. I'm really sorry things have taken this turn. As I said, you are good people, really altruistic, and I can see why you want to figure out what's happening.

'Let me just tell you about Kempson first. I know that he's been convicted, and all credit to you for that. He's a beast and deserves more time than he got. What I told you was the worst part of what he did to me, and I shall never recover from it. What I am now is what Kempson did to me. It's also what, through me, was done to someone else. I became a self-pitying shadow of what I was. My parents thought I was worthless enough to start with, and when I deteriorated under his tutelage, they were in despair. They sent me away to a sanatorium and, although they saw this as a punishment, I saw it as a huge relief.

Detachment from Kempson. I loved it. I ended up working there, in fact, and that's where I met Velia.'

Richard lifted a small flask to his lips. 'Helps me in times of stress. Where was I? Yes. The boy whose life I thought I had ruined. He changed because of this, but in a different way. When we reached an age that was no longer of interest to Kempson, he dropped us both. The other boy became driven by revenge. He wanted to wreck Kempson's life, but he chose to do it so that Kempson would end up paying him for what he'd done. He did some research on him. Did you know Kempson's been in prison several times, mainly for fraud? This other boy threatened to expose him to the school he was at after Finchingham School folded - unless he supplied him with boys. He became a pimp, supplying high-class people with boys with posh accents. Soon he didn't need Kempson's services any more, but he wanted to make him suffer, so he made Kempson work for him as a prostitute, giving him a fraction of what the punters paid.

'They were all in it. This boy controlled all of them by threatening them with exposure. He probably did the same with his customers. I was just left with my guilt. He never came near me again, until recently. He told me that he regretted not having been in contact with me as we had shared experiences, and he knew how I must have felt. He told me he had the choice of either giving way to self-pity – which he could see I had done – or getting even. That's what he's been doing for years and raking it in.

'All this is guilt money. It makes him feel better, and I'm not complaining. All he wanted is for no one ever to know the name of the 'other boy', and that's what I've promised him. If

I were to have made a complaint about Kempson, his existence would've become known. I had given you a clue back then, and I think you're sensitive enough to be able to work out what I meant.'

'Is that when you came out with, 'he wants me to be like him?' I think that's what you said back then. It's stuck in my head for some reason. I wondered why you said it, or whether I'd misheard it. Would I have brought it to mind if I'd been questioned about you and Kempson? Maybe so.'

'Richard,' said Paul. 'If he's convicted of another offence he didn't ask to be taken into consideration at the original trial, you know he'll be sent down for longer.'

'Even so, please don't connect me to Kempson. You see what I'd lose if it came out and the other boy were ever identified. This is my life now. Let me enjoy it. You see – no more aids for my breathing. I might even find love.'

'I do hope so, Richard. Paul and I are getting married soon. Thank you so much for seeing us.'

They bade farewell to a rejuvenated Richard Braine for what they assumed would be the last time.

'Let's get in the car quickly. You drive.'

'Jed, is it possible that you will ever do anything that doesn't take me by surprise?'

'Well, take it as a proposal. You want to, don't you?'

'Yes, of course, but...' Paul stopped. 'What on earth are you doing?'

'It's getting a bit painful. I need to get it out.'

Jed had unzipped himself and was reaching into his underpants. He pulled out a small dictaphone.

'Thank goodness he only asked us to open our jackets.'

Chapter 33

The phone rang as they drove home. Paul pushed the accept button.

'We're in Jed's car. He doesn't think anyone could've got to this one, but we aren't saying anything, so whoever it is, please give us a couple of hours and call back.'

He mouthed without a sound: 'Yes. I'll marry you. Thank you.'

'Put the key somewhere safe. No, not there. In a metal tin. We're going to be relying on the Polestar for a while. Aha. I'm vibrating.'

'It's Hugh. I've got a name for you. The car's registered to a firm called Covipale. I've checked with Companies House. Looks like a shell company, so I've done some more digging. Covipale is more like a cover-up, but there's a name that keeps appearing. It's a certain David Baxter. Is that any help?'

'Oh yes. They're in it together, the Baxter brothers. Might've known it. Hugh, we'll come and see you. We have a recording for you. And a wedding invitation.'

Paul clicked the phone down. 'David seems to be the human face of the Baxter brothers, though, wouldn't you say?'

'I'd say he's the one who feels guilt. I reckon his humanity doesn't stretch further than that. Look what they're involved in - procuring for rich men. Ugh. Turns my stomach.'

Jed paused. 'You know, we haven't mentioned what's been done to us for hours.'

'Well. That's mainly because we were afraid we were being bugged. It hasn't gone away, and we're drawing more attention to ourselves by getting married. It's like raising two fingers to them. Or is it one middle finger? I've lost touch with what's current. We're the victims. What's been done to us is a crime. It's the same conversations I've had with the victims at that place. And you. They tried to make us feel dirty. To imagine that we were means they've won. We know we aren't. They are. They are the criminals.'

'And Richard?'

'Let's hope David Baxter feels guilty enough to carry on paying the fees when he's in prison. I guess £50,000 a year is chickenfeed to him. If this ring is as big as we think, we're talking millions.'

'Is that your way of saying 'collateral damage?''

When Jed was in bed, Paul let his memory roam. It went back to his classroom to the lessons he remembered with the young Jed Massie. There was Jed, in his mind's eye, in his school jumper and grey trousers, asking him questions about words and quotations. What had he thought about him then? Did he like him? Yes. Did he want him as a friend? No. That never entered his head. Did it not enter because it was forbidden? No. The concept of having 12-year-old Jed Massie as a friend simply did not exist. The thought was not there. How about the feeling? Did he feel for him? Yes. But just that he was too clever for this school. And if his 25-year-old self could imagine that Jed Massie would eventually be the most important person in his life, his lover, his partner for the rest of his days, what would he think? He couldn't bear the thought.

Yet they were the same people. How could it be? Paul had never felt this type of attraction. Not even when they were sitting in his car and Jed was pouring his heart out did he have any idea how it would end. So what happened? He knew he was overthinking it, and if he carried on with this analysis, he would convince himself that their relationship was wrong, but in no way was it wrong. It was the most right thing that had ever happened to him. Jed's happiness mattered more than anything else to him, and he knew that their happiness was shared.

How had it all come about and so suddenly? After the sentencing, all that had been no longer was. There was only the future. Not a word had been spoken, but in that hotel room in Reading, they found a togetherness that both seemed to have waited for so long. If anything in this world could be perfect, Paul knew that he had found it. Neither hid anything from the other, and he knew he would externalise that if he had thought of Jed's 12-year-self in this state... He recoiled in horror. The 12-year-old no longer existed; he had vanished. If there was something wrong, he wanted to find it and right it before they married, yet he knew nothing was wrong, and he was inventing predicaments. He had a stock of *bon mots* at his disposal. Which to choose? '*Vivre pour le moment, c'est la seule raison d'être*', or the words of John Lennon – 'all you need is love'?

'Are you awake?'

'No.'

'Do you love me to the moon?'

'Yes – and back again.'

'I've been on a journey in my head back to when you were 12.'

'I was a child.'

'I wasn't.'

'I'm not now, and you're even more not. Now you've made me awake. Why do you think so brainsickly of things? Look, it's growing back. I'm a man in my middle years. You're a man in your slightly more middle years. We are friends. We are lovers. We have no secrets. If we were marooned on a desert island, we'd make babies one way or another. How much better can it get? When I was 12, you were an old man to me, and I was a young boy to you. Time changed us. And here we are. Simples.'

'As ever, you're right,' Paul started to sink into sleep. 'Oh, I think we should see Brookfield while he's still around. He's more a part of this than we imagine.'

Chapter 34

Footsteps shuffled behind the door.

Paul twitched his hands. 'By the pricking of my thumbs…"

"Something wicked this way comes,' You don't stop, do you? Aha, the locks are opening.'

'Yes.'

'Hello, Mr Brookfield. You said to get in touch when we were in town, and here we are.' Jed found the lies came as second nature now.

Brookfield looked momentarily perplexed. 'You'd better come in then.'

He stood back from the door to let them into a stone-tiled hall and then to a small drawing-room.

'Thanks. We thought we'd have a reminisce about Finchingham. We were wondering how you felt about your role in its closing down.'

St. John Brookfield's smile vanished in an instant.

'You roll up on my doorstep – unannounced, I might add - and expect me to give you the time of day? Who are you again?'

'Mason and Massie, sir' Jed wondered why he added 'sir'. He was going back to boyhood again. The face in front of him was aged but recognisable. The effete mannerisms were identical.

'Mason and Massie' made them sound like a latter-day 'Cagney and Lacey'. He wondered how they would have tackled this.

'Never heard of you.'

Jed was jolted out of his reverie. 'We were at Finchingham School, sir. Many decades ago.'

'So what are you after? A refund?'

'No, sir, we'd really like some of the background to what went on.'

'"What went on?" Teaching went on. That's what went on.'

'But there was rather more than that, sir. Wasn't there? There was a scandal, and the place closed down a year later.'

'A fuss about nothing.'

'Many people thought different. There was an enquiry. Crimes were uncovered.' Now he was thinking of 'Dalziel and Pasco.' Why was the spelling of Dalziel so odd?

'Crimes? Rubbish.' Back to reality.

'But there have been convictions.'

'For nothing. For peccadillos that were so trivial that they were over before they started. The 'place' as you so patronisingly term it was a school that shaped young people.'

'How would you say it shaped them?' Jed decided to drop the 'sir'. He didn't think Brookfield deserved it.

'It made them upright citizens who could withstand whatever knocks the real world would give them. And reality hits everyone from time to time. What they received at my hands was a rounded education in the classroom and on the sports field.'

'And in the dormitories and teachers' flats?'

'Those, too. That's all a part of real life. They had the chance to experience life.'

'It took me thirty-five years to recover from this real life you say was so good for me.'

'Then, if I may say so, you are weak. You succumbed to a lack of backbone.'

'I succumbed to cruelty and disdain.'

'Part of living is dealing with things without running to some higher authority. 'Get on with it' - that should be the motto of a school. Should have been the motto of that school and would have been, had not some leftie do-gooders taken a sledgehammer into their hands to crack a walnut; to kill the patient by dissecting him. I mix my metaphors. They went into nooks, crannies, crevices. They poked around and found a few things they thought weren't quite politically correct. They tore into the very fabric of a decent – yes, decent – establishment that was sending out young people equipped to face the world and made them feel guilty to have had had this privilege. They were guilty of nothing. Guilty, maybe, of not standing up to the prying and fault-finding system that sought to control them. It won't happen, Mr Massie. There's a real world that's far more powerful, and these justice warriors will never get close to that.'

'You mean corrupt people, Mr Brookfield.'

'I mean people in power, Mr Massie. Little people who slip up may go to prison. I gather some have – probably at the hands of people like you – but you won't come close to the people who matter.'

'You mean 'the establishment?''

'I mean what I say. Things will always remain as they were. You won't change human nature. It will change you or finish you. Haven't you gathered that?'

'What I've gathered is that Finchingham School and places like that are training grounds for an endemic corruption.'

''Corruption' rubbish. It's the way things are and always will be. If you can't accept that, as I said, human nature will change you. It will eat you up and vomit you out.'

Jed stopped. He knew. At that precise moment, he knew. Oh yes. 'Eats you up and vomits you out.' Grant Baxter's words. Learned from his mentor.

'It was all your doing, wasn't it? The others were just patsies. You pulled their strings. I wondered what you got off on. You taught them. That's what gets you up of a morning. It wasn't money. It was creating a legacy. Now you're coming to the end, you can look with satisfaction at your creations. I see them as grotesques, all of them. You see them as successes. Created by you, sustained by you.'

'Just a cog, Mr Massie. Small cog in a big wheel that will keep on turning long after you and I are gone. We understand each other. And, yes, I do remember you. Both of you. Mr Mason, you failed. You may have had some small achievements, but ultimately it ended in failure for you. Mr Massie, however, has reaped the rewards. You are a spoke in the wheel. Listen to him, Mr Mason. Join with him. I think you have done so already.'

He walked to an adjoining kitchen and put a kettle on the hob. He opened a larder door and took out a black metal caddy and a packet of ginger biscuits. The kettle began to whistle.

'Tea? I think we can be civilised to each other now. This is how life can be, and it's infinitely preferable to struggling against slings and arrows that really don't exist. I'm sure you're both utterly charming under all the bravado. Shall I be mother?

There you are. Restraint, delicacy, sophistication - they're what make life worth living. You see how life can be? Just let it wash over you.'

St. John Brookfield held the teapot delicately over each bone china cup. 'There's milk and sugar. Aha. I see you're not 'mif.' You've read your Nancy Mitford. Milk in first would be so non-U. Just not upper class at all. Funny thing is there's no 'U', I think. Like 'uncouth'. There's no 'couth'. But we know how things should be, do we not?'

The smile had returned to his lips. It was now beatific. He held the tips of the fingers of his hands together.

'Mr Brookfield, you have educated me. You are in error, though. You are a conjuror, not a teacher. You trade in smoke and mirrors that soften the suffering not one iota. Some might call you a trickster, though that is too lightweight a term. Truth, decency, honesty – I think you don't know the import of these concepts. For you, nothing is but what is not. Good things of day are drooping and dying wherever you set foot. Frankly, whether you squeeze my balls between two velvet cushions or two concrete blocks, the excruciating pain is very much the same.'

The smile broadened.

'Your legerdemain – for want, I assure you, of a better word - has spawned any number of creatures like you whose humanity has been sucked out of them. Your salvation is that you have not the faintest idea of what you have done. In the struggle of truth with falsehood, I believe truth will prevail. Thank you for the tea. We shall not meet again. I shall remain charming – and retain my integrity. This is possible, Mr Brookfield. Goodbye. We'll see ourselves out.'

They closed the door with the lightest of clicks.

'It's not in my underpants. Brookfield would've noticed. See how I used the plural? A bit of licence. God, you could see he fancied me. It's in my jacket, by the way.'

'I didn't say a word.'

'No need. In his eyes, you're one of them. He saw me as a kindred spirit who has made you part of me and so part of him.'

'Is he right?'

'Maybe.'

'Does it matter?'

'Not to me.'

'Can we finish this? Please. Finally, it's 'the future in the instant' moment.'

'And all the rest? The evidence? The recordings? We let it all go?'

"That way madness lies."

'Until the next time?'

'Of course.'

Chapter 35

'Mrs McAllister, may I have a word?'

Mrs McAllister was starting to put away the Bunsen burners and Petri dishes. She turned to the speaker.

'Let me help,' said Grant Baxter.

'Sure. Thanks. I think you know which cupboard they go in. What can I do for you?'

'I, or rather my dad...' The boy paused. He so wanted this to come out right that he wondered whether the following verb should be singular or plural. He had never bothered with grammatical niceties before, but he needed to strike the right note this time, and a clumsy expression could ruin everything. He continued with a correction made possible by the hiatus. 'My dad wonders if you can give me some extra lessons to help me with the exam? He tells me he's happy to pay you whatever you charge.'

Frances McAllister hung up her white coat and looked at him quizzically.

'I rather think that if you were more on board with the lessons you already have, anything extra wouldn't be necessary.'

'The thing is that when I want to understand something better, I don't like to put my hand up and ask. I'd look a fool.'

'Street cred?'

'Something like that.'

'I'll put it to the Head and get back to you.'

'Well, no. Sorry, I didn't mean it to come out that way. Dad and I were hoping it would be something we could arrange just between ourselves. We really want the school to think I'm just improving under my own steam. It might help me get a Prefectship if they see that I'm doing better academically. That's what dad thinks. He's given me the money to pay for the lessons, so it'll just come out of my pocket money. No need to involve the school.' He paused to see how this idea was being received.

'A man on a mission. I can see the way he's thinking.' Frances McAllister opened her handbag. 'Tuesday morning break and Thursday lunchtime seem to be free. I could see you then, if you and dad wish.'

'Great. That'll be perfect. Here?'

'If you don't want the whole school to know, we can use the prep room at the back.'

'Perfect. Thanks.'

She smiled, opened her compact and glanced at her reflection. 'Still OK for facing the world. My husband's taking me out this evening. Tenth anniversary.'

'Congratulations.'

'Thank you, Grant.'

'And thank you for not calling me Baxter G.'

She smiled and left the room. Grant Baxter drank in the smell of perfume she left. One way or another, he would eke out his pocket money to afford the lessons.

Six weeks later, he was still pondering how to do this when it was brought to his attention.

'Your work has really come along.' She put her red pen down. 'Much as I enjoy our sessions, Grant, and I know talking about money is vulgar, but I really think it's time to open your dad's treasure chest. After all, the labourer is worthy of his hire. Or her in this case.'

'Mrs McAllister,' he began.

'It's OK for me to be Frances outside class, Grant. I told you this.'

'Frances,' he continued. 'The thing is, I haven't been entirely straight with you. It isn't my dad who's paying. It's me. Well, it would be if I could. And I wasn't so worried about my exam, although what you've done has worked wonders for my chances. The thing is, I just can't stop thinking about you.'

Frances picked up her pen again and studied it closely.

'And I wonder if I could possibly do this.'

He leant across the desk and kissed her gently, tasting her lipstick. Her lips were warm, and he sensed no resistance. His hands moved to her blouse. His whole being was pounding, and he knew he could no longer contain himself.

'I'm sorry. I'm so, so sorry. I can't stop it.'

He tried pulling his trousers away from the stickiness.

'Are these what you're after?' She smiled. 'Next time.'

Grant walked with some difficulty to the showers. He let the cool water flow over him and saw himself slowly detumesce.

There was a gentle noise at the door.

'Hello?'

'Oh, hello. I'm sorry. I didn't expect to see anyone.' A boy was looking at his face.

'It's OK. I'm Baxter G.'

'That's a strange name.'

'No, it isn't. Oh. I see. There's a space between 'Baxter' and 'G'. That's so you know I'm not 'Baxter D'. He's my brother.'

'Is that your first name?'

'No. We don't have first names.'

'Oh?'

'We have them, of course, but we never use them.'

'Oh. I'd better go. I'm on the tour.'

'OK. May see you if you come.'

Grant knew that he felt no shame. A grown woman wanted him. He was an object of desire, and he was happy for anyone to see what was being desired. He left his stained clothes to be collected later, put his towel on a hook, grabbed his sponge bag and walked naked up the stone steps.

'And that's how it started,' Grant put down his coffee cup. 'That's when we first met. I was washing my sin off me. Or her sin. It wasn't Brookfield. Not that time anyway. It was Frances McAllister.'

'Is that why you came to see us, to tell us that?' Jed took the lead. He was the one who was most surprised to see Grant Baxter after what he had said and done to him. 'That you were getting rid of your ejaculate?'

'No. I wasn't honest with you, nor with anyone really. I know that you are helping people get over what they experienced at that place, and I want you to know that there are different kinds of violation. I don't blame you for despising me. I am despicable. I have been a pimp, a gigolo, whatever you can think of, that's who I have been. And as much as others have been violated, I have been violated, too. I know what violation is. There I was, having it off with a woman twice a week. Yes, I led her on, but I was a boy, a headstrong boy with his brains in his pants. She wanted a baby that she felt her husband couldn't provide and the sort of sex he couldn't give her. It was all the time. I just wanted a conversation; wanted to be a person, not just an object. He left her, and then she left me. Maybe she had the baby she wanted. I could be a dad and not know it. I had no idea how to be with anyone if not for sex.

'I went into these tuition sessions twice a week. There was no conversation. Sure, I was up for it, but it was just sex. I was seventeen. Seventeen. I knew nothing. Yes, I led her on and made the first move. But she was the adult in that – how do you call it? – 'relationship'. She was 34, for Christ's sake. When it wasn't Frances, it was Brookfield. At least with Stanhope, he had no expectations. He thought I was stupid, and I'm sure he was right, but not in the way he thought. Being in his place was a relief. At least I could keep my clothes on. I had no conversation. No one wanted me for that. He didn't want to know what sort of a person I was. I'm not sure there was much there at that time. There's not much there now. At school, it was just doing what Frances wanted or what Brookfield wanted. I suppose, at first, I thought it was what I wanted, at least with Frances, but it was the same with both of them.

'When you saw me that first time, I was proud of myself and wanted everyone to see how desirable I was. I think I even wanted you to desire me. But I expect I repulsed you; I just didn't care. On and on it went - with both of them. Eventually, I couldn't tell the one from the other. It became my life. It was boring; it was repetitive; it was all I was. I didn't know anything else.

'I was a commodity that Brookfield passed on. I was anyone's. Men, women, old, young, they were all the same to me. I wore smart clothes. Some of them gave me presents. The watch that gave me away to you that day, Jed, was from a satisfied customer. I can't remember who it was, whether a man or a woman. I liked to look good. Still do. I don't know what it was that made first realise how utterly shallow I had become. I know that I asked a client if we could have a conversation first. 'You talk?' he said. 'Yes, I talk – and I think, and I feel, and I have opinions and standards and… And I actually have a personality,' I almost believed what I was saying, and then I knew that they were things I wanted to have and no longer wanted not to have. I never got to talk to that one. He just wanted my clothes off, and I ended up doing what I did best. I was really good at it, but it was the last time. I repulsed myself.

'That was when I went to evening classes. Yes, Paul, I knew I had a brain. I went into business with the hotel, and I tried to put everything that I had become behind me. Brookfield kept tabs on me, and that's why he targeted you after you saw me. Or it may have been David, my brother. I haven't seen him for thirty years. I know he worked with Brookfield.'

Grant Baxter looked from Paul to Jed and back again. 'I've never had love. I have no idea what a relationship is. That's what that place did for me.'

'And that's why you sought to end it?'

Grant looked Jed straight in the eye. 'So, you saw more than the Patek that day?'

He took off his watch and held up both hands.

'Christ, Jed. You saw that and still went on the attack?'
Paul's tone was accusatory for the first time.

'The one thing you will never be able to understand about
me, Paul, no matter how close we are, no matter how we feel
at one with each other, is how the very essence of my being
has been defiled. Yes, 'defiled' is the word. I have been entered
against my will. This is what marks out those who been abused.
It's not a feeling that those who haven't been abused can really
understand. Yes, you can imagine it, but you can't experience
it. I don't blame you for not trying. It's just that you can't and
never will.'

Jed turned to Grant Baxter.

'I loathed you then, and I loathe you now. Night after
night, you saw me being humiliated in that man's room. You
did nothing to stop it. You didn't even tell me what I should do.
You just let it happen – and you laughed. I was twelve. I was a
child. I was raped. I had to manage all this on my own. And
worse, you connived with Brookfield and his lot to ensnare
more kids. Yes, you should have killed yourself. The sooner, the
better. And don't come at me with your sob story that people
were attracted to you and you couldn't help yourself. Yes, you
were a pretty boy. I was a pretty boy, too. And you may say
that you were such a pretty boy that you didn't stand a chance.
But you did. You had the chance to say 'no'. To see that one
action was right and another action was wrong. You had no
moral compass. If you're lost and alone now, you brought it
on yourself.

'You could have changed my life at that moment when
I was in front of you in that shower room. I was a little boy
who needed to be as far from the ghastly grown-ups in that

place as possible. You knew what people like Brookfield, Stanhope and McAllister were. You knew what was in store for me. And all you wanted was for me to see you as a naked hunk. I was embarrassed for you and thought you were a fool for leaving the door ajar. You can sit there crying, and I don't feel your embarrassment. I don't think you're a fool. I know it. And I know you're vicious and venal with it. This pretty boy survived. You became a monster. Paul, get him out of our house, please.'

Chapter 36

'He'll get over it.'

'Doubt it. I deserved every word. I could quite easily lie here and do it again, properly this time.'

'Well, you won't. Don't even think it. I guess it will all wash out. I have to watch the cashmere, though. I've put them on pre-wash to get rid of the smell. Vomit is really pervasive.'

'What he said was all true. I can't remember the last time I cried – or was sick – and now they happened together. I'm sorry.'

Paul was sitting on the edge of the bath.

'I think this is the best place for you at the moment. I've checked to see that there aren't any sharp instruments. I think I'll just let the water out and refill it. There's still some of what looks like lunch floating around.'

'Naked and humiliated. My God, it's come to this. Lying in your bath picking diced carrot off myself.'

'Yes, it's a low point. You know that you and Jed have shared experiences, don't you? He doesn't see you as a victim, but actually, you are. You were a child, too. This isn't to detract from anything Jed went through, but you were abused.'

'I let it happen. With Frances, I instigated it. With Brookfield, I took the money. I was no victim. I went for it.'

'And if there had been no Frances McAllister, no Brookfield, no Stanhope, would you really have sought them out? I'll put some bubble bath in there so you won't be quite so naked and humiliated.'

'I loved the sex with Frances. I wondered if I would, but it was great.'

'You mean after Brookfield?'

'No. I mean after you, Paul?'

'How come 'after me?''

'OK. Here goes. It's been a long time coming. You had no idea, but I fancied you rotten. Quite a few of the boys did.'

'What! I certainly did nothing to encourage it.'

'That was what was so appealing about you. You didn't have a clue. There you were all clever and good-looking and well-dressed and educated and with a great voice – and a snazzy car. I had such a crush.'

'That's hilarious.'

Grant swished the water to make more bubbles and piled them high.

'You mean, you're...'

'Sorry.'

'OK. Not sure what the etiquette is for this, but I am sitting on the edge of the bathtub with you in it. What I was saying is that all the criteria that applied to Jed work for you, too. As for Frances McAllister, she abused you. She should have just stopped it. It was wrong and unprofessional, and she should have called a halt before anything began. Her actions were criminal, too. Here. Have some more bubble bath.'

'I've never seen it that way.'

'Well, start now. You need to make a complaint about each of the people who should have looked after your welfare but instead used you for their own ends. You know this was what Brookfield was doing, and now you can see that McAllister was doing the same. I assume you talked while you were doing it. Did she tell you about her marriage?'

'Yes. She regretted not having a baby and told me they were doing IVF. She said I was a much better lover than Edward, her husband. I really liked that. Made me feel like a proper man.'

'Stud, more like.'

'I think she felt guilty about the age difference. She told me not to shave, that she liked to feel the roughness on my face. So I stopped shaving. Took a few weeks before it showed, then she took a picture as a keepsake and said I could shave again.'

'We noticed that. Designer stubble hadn't come into fashion then. You just looked scruffy, and then - you didn't.'

'There's something else, though. It seemed odd at the time, but now I can see the sense in it. We had some pretty frank conversations, or, rather, she was pretty frank with me in comparing me to her husband. Everything was compared. I felt I knew the man. Well, bits of him. She told me she wanted to see what my sperm looked like compared to his. She got me to ejaculate into a jar. I quite liked that as she was looking and, well, I produced quite a lot. Then I had to do it again the next session. She'd dropped it.'

'I bet it was right at the end of the session each time.'

'It was. I left a week later. I didn't think any more of it. In fact, she never did tell me whose was better.'

'Are you getting the picture now?'

'You mean, she took it off to the IVF place and used it?'

'Or a DIY in case the natural method didn't work. Did you use protection?'

'No. She said it felt better without.'

'I expect it was more satisfying in more ways than one. Do you know where she is now?'

'It all happened at the end of the term. My last term. The place imploded the following year. I didn't see her again. Heard she took up with a boy called Tom Dunstan after me. She had him on the first day he was there. He was the one who saw Nick Boyce end it all.'

'She got around. Let's do the maths. All this happened in 1987, I think, and you were 17, so you're getting on for 52. She was twice your age, so add on 17, and she's 69 or so. Young enough to still be alive, and if, as 'Who's Who' puts it, 'there was issue,' the issue will be in his or her mid-30s. Good lord, Grant, you may be a grandfather, let alone a dad. Now do you see how you were used? I don't think you need the bubbles any more. Have this towel.'

Grant Baxter rubbed himself dry.

'I don't think I've ever felt my emotions so all over the place. I've been abused, used, corrupted and may have a child. All in one afternoon and all while lying naked and talking to my teacher.'

'Well, you never can tell how your day might go.'

'I still do, you know?'

'Still do what?'

'Fancy you. Jed's lucky.'

'The luck's all mine, Grant. I think we'll be frank with him and tell him we'll pursue an abuse case similar to his. Let me have a list of who did what to you when and we'll take it to the next level. It sounds quite stark, but that's what it boils down to. At least I know you won't be shy. OK, yes, I'm being matter-of-fact, but I can't do the emotion. That's something for you to deal with. Don't kill yourself. I'm coming round to you now. No need to tell Jed about what you feel about me, as that really would complicate things. We just need a straightforward trajectory to get this thing off the ground. No hurry, but the day after tomorrow would be great. Meet me here.'

Chapter 37

'After all these years…' Should it be a handshake, a kiss on one cheek, two or another for luck? Paul resorted to the hands together and head slightly bowed greeting that had become de rigeur recently. 'It's good to see you.'

Frances McAllister extended an arm to invite her erstwhile colleague into her home. Paul took it in at a glance. A seventies house in its own grounds, spacious rooms and a minimalist design. Its owner handsome, silver-haired and smartly trouser-suited.

'Something to drink? Coffee's ready, but I can do tea or whatever.' She motioned to a sculpted leather chair by a stone table on which a black coffee pot and chunky black cups were placed. Her taste was exquisite.

'Coffee's fine. Just black and no sugar, please.'

'You've worn well, Paul. I wondered if all that publicity might have taken its toll, but no. I'd have recognised you in the street.'

'Let me repay the compliment, Frances. And thank you for seeing me.'

'Shall we cut to the chase? I assume it's about that place. I have to tell you that I've moved on. I suspect you have not, and I'm really not sure what help I can be to you.'

'As ever, Frances, you state the situation clearly. I recall that in that past life, in staff meetings, you always used to be able to go the heart of the matter with a few well-chosen words.'

'Well, Paul, I can repay that compliment, too. I remember the quotations from the Bard that livened up those dreary get-togethers. What was it you used to say? 'If something's worth saying, Shakespeare's already said it.' I think that's how it went.'

'Indeed. But, again, to quote, it's a forgone conclusion that we will be talking about that place, so maybe we should start. Let me just say 'Grant Baxter."

'An interesting young man. Have you met him since?'

'He's wondering if he fathered your child.'

'Now, what would make him think that?'

'I had hoped that my putting it that way would short-cut my getting to that point. I can go the long way round if you wish, but then you know that I know, so is there really any point? I can play guessing games with you, if you really want. Or you can simply answer my question. Or you can throw me out. As you will have guessed, I've done my homework.'

'Is there any point in going back over old ground? The past is another country. We were different people then.'

'I've always found that Popeye the Sailor Man got it right.'
'How so?'

"I am what I am, and that's all that I am. I'm Popeye the Sailor Man,' We don't change. We just build on what we have always been.'

'Let's put it this way; I am a happy and fulfilled grandparent. I had a long and mainly unhappy marriage to a man, now deceased, whose approach to the noble institution was to see it as a way to get a meal on the table several times a day, and for whom children were a noise and a nuisance, so he didn't do all he could not do to have any. I've used too many negatives, but you may catch my drift. I had other ideas.'

'So the answer to the perfectly natural question that Grant posed to me is 'yes'. Thank you for this. But it's the 'other ideas' you mention that interest me. Here's where I had to work harder to get at what had happened. I sense that your initial idea was a family for yourself. That didn't require much depletion of the goods that Grant gave you. You are a chemist, and you are resourceful. You found a way to get a plentiful supply of a valuable commodity for those who would benefit. I assume that, like carrots, fresh or frozen didn't make any difference. Yes, it was the quantity you required that got me thinking. And the photograph. He had almost forgotten. It seemed so inconsequential. It was just your telling him not to shave that made it stick in his mind. He was a child. Good-looking, but a child. Put some stubble on him, and he would look older. So there he was for you to present to your clientele – a handsome young man. You even dressed him in a smart jacket and tie. It all came back to him. He has no idea why that was a useful recollection, and I am really not sure how he will cope with the knowledge that he has - how many children would you say? Could be several hundred.'

Frances McAllister flicked a hand at the idea dismissively. 'It was material that would have gone to waste.'

"'Material' is one word to use for it. It wasn't your material, though, was it? And that young man had to put in some effort to produce it. It, having been produced, was then put to use in a way that he could have no knowledge of, let alone control over. The ethical and moral niceties will be overshadowed by the legal implications, of course.'

Frances sighed, 'Which would cause enormous unhappiness to many people whose settled lives would be thrown into chaos by such a revelation. I gave happiness. You would give misery. Do you really want that to be your legacy?'

'I wondered about that.'

'More coffee?'

'Thanks. But then there's the aspect of misrepresentation. That's given me something else to think about.'

The rictus smile that had characterised Paul's host since his arrival flickered slightly. Frances McAllister remained composed, her silver hair matching her suit and shoes. She was power dressing on legs; a self-made woman, articulate, intelligent and serene.

'I have some shortbread you might like to try. I wish I could say they are homemade, but I confess to M and S.'

'I do, too, frequently. Life gets in the way of baking, doesn't it?'

Paul took the offered biscuit.

'Gorgeous. Thank you. As I was saying, there was Grant Baxter, young, virile and good looking. He became quite upfront with me, but then he hasn't ever hidden much of himself from anyone. Your extra-curricular tuition made a real impression on him. An older woman from whom he felt he was learning and honing his technique. A woman he thought he was helping, too. In fact, you were, of course, helping yourself. But, as you knew, the place was imploding, and your time was limited. Your protégé would move on to pastures new and other passions. He would be out of your control, and you knew him enough to assume, correctly I think, that he would not wish to assume mass-fatherhood at one remove.

'Who could take on his mantle and not be troubled by moral scruples? Who wouldn't know what these words even meant? Who would do anything at all for money? Having seen him recently and realised that nothing about him had changed, the answer was rather obvious. There was another budding entrepreneur on the premises, albeit not with your panache. A mistake you made, as I'm sure you realised later, was going through an intermediary. You could have gone direct to the source. Brookfield was a procurer. He made the arrangements, maybe even suggested him for the reasons I have given and, I am in no doubt, took a cut, but Jerome Poynton would have been delighted to deal with you direct. The point is, though, would any of your clients wish to jump in a gene pool with the likes of Jerome Poynton? Appearances can be deceptive and are superficial, but that's how most of us are first attracted, and Jerome Poynton was no oil painting. Indeed, there was precious little else to commend him, apart from his being able to deliver as and when required.

'I believe you started with him when he was 13. That's what he tells me anyway. As I said, he will do anything for money. I had no idea what 'a monkey' was until I came across the expression when he used it in court. I'm not sure there's much he wouldn't do for 'a monkey', but when I offered it to him, he told me the whole story. He'd had some practice with Dotty in the kitchen, who wanted to get a flat from the council and needed a baby to achieve this. Then came the offer from Brookfield. All he had to do was pleasure himself. And he did. Over and over. All his Christmases had come at once. I asked him if he had his photo taken. If you remember, he was at the time troubled with a ripening pustule. No photo. So your clients assumed that the material contained the building blocks of hunky Grant Baxter rather than lumbering Jerome Poynton.

'I doubt if any protested that the outcome wasn't what was promised in the photo. A tiny baby for those desperate will receive their unqualified love, and that's what should happen. The misdescription is hardly the child's fault, but that sort of legerdemain is bad for business, should it come out, and might well be actionable.'

Paul took another shortbread, unasked. The moral high ground was his and the self-righteousness unaccustomed.

The smile remained. The woman in front of him was as calm as the Mona Lisa. Paul resumed:

'So, Frances, you have committed many crimes. Grant will not be able to un-know that he has progeny. He will be forever changed. Those families to whom you provided a service would be, to a greater or lesser extent, devastated, and I cannot imagine the effect this knowledge would have on their children.'

'Which, Paul, is precisely the reason you will do nothing,' Frances smiled broadly. 'That you use the conditional tense - oh yes, I know these things as well as you - makes it clear to me that you have already come to this conclusion. You would be wracked with guilt were this to come out. The only person you need to be concerned about is Grant. You might tell him that he was a wonderful lover. One of the best. You can tell him he can meet our children and grandchildren and develop whatever relationship he wishes with them. He may regret that he wasn't given the chance to know them sooner. He will have to live with that. As to the rest – no one will ever know that.

'Hundreds of children have the Poynton boy's genes, but they are blissfully unaware of this and will remain so. You won't dare to tell. And do I have regrets? No. I don't do regrets. A married woman who can take on a 17-year-old schoolboy as her lover finds it easy to gloss over minor irritants. Yes, I am amoral and all the other things you are thinking of, too. I'm sure you are absolutely right, but you're stuck with this, and there is nothing you will do about it. I see no danger coming from your direction.'

'And will you continue in this line of work?'

She swept her arm towards everything in view. 'See the Roche Bobois sofas, the Foscari lamps, the Warhols and the Picassos, the Aston in the drive? It keeps me in the style to which I have become accustomed. Are you offering your services as a donor? I can fix it for you and Jed to conceive whenever you wish. No charge. We can make it one for each of you. I'll throw in a post-natal DNA so you can be sure. I'd offer myself, but I'm afraid that ship has sailed, and I fear you might not rise to the occasion anyway.'

'You are undiminished, Frances. Meeting you is an experience.'

'But not one you wish to repeat? No need to answer. Let's see.'

Chapter 38

'Well, at least you were a wonderful lover. She was clear about that.'

'I can't take it in.'

'No. That's why I thought it best for me to come to yours. It's a shock, I know.'

'You can't know how much of a shock it is to know that you have a few hundred children.'

'Well, it may not be that many.'

'However many or few makes no difference. This morning I didn't know I had any.'

'Go and see her. Get it out of your system. You can meet her children if you want.'

'God in heaven. Grandchildren. I suddenly feel so old.' Grant looked at his reflection in the white glass of his larder door. 'I've got creases. I haven't been sleeping. Oh, how I crave sleep.'

"Great nature's second course" The quotation was lost on Grant. 'So, as I understand it, you were a father at 17. That's the plain, unvarnished truth. It's happened, and it's a fact you can't do anything about. I just knew I had to tell you.'

'I can't get my head around it. What was she thinking of? Don't answer it. Herself. That's who she was thinking of all the time. I was just a horny idiot. Such a fool.'

He took two mugs from a cabinet and poured coffee into them.

'Just black, please.'

'You know…' He continued to look into the glass and stretched the skin on his face as if to smooth it. 'Come to think of it, that spotty boy, Jerome Poynton, could've been a father at 13. Years after the school closed, Brookfield told me he'd been asked to be a donor. I told him that'd be impossible.'

'Well, undesirable, but not impossible.'

Grant Baxter was in reflective mode. His kitchen was as he imagined Frances' would have been had he progressed so far into her house; sparsely but tastefully furnished. Two steaming mugs of coffee were on the kitchen counter. The washing machine was chuntering. Two eggs sat near the hob, ready for boiling or frying. Paul had declined Grant's offer to make them both breakfast.

'No. Impossible. Brett told me about the Huntington's.'

'I've heard of that. Isn't it – or wasn't it – 'Huntington's Chorea?''

'Yes, he told me that when he was at school. He had a 50-50 chance of having it. He was pretty sure he didn't have it, but it was pretty clear to me that his brother had it. He'd run the risk of passing it on. It's an inherited disease.'

'What made you think Jerome had it?'

'Come off it; no one could be that clumsy all the time. He'd fall over his feet every time he went through a door. He had real problems with his coordination. That was why people thought he was too stupid to walk and fart at the same time. I told Brett he ought to tell him, but he said, why make his life complicated? He's happy enough in his small world of money-making activities. I left it there. It wasn't my place to tell the boy something that might devastate him. I haven't seen him for years, so who knows how things may have progressed. I guess that if he ends up falling over all the time, even he might think he should get checked out.'

'Christ!'

'Why are we talking about Jerome Poynton? I can't imagine you'd have much time for him. Anyway, did you speak to Jed about me?'

'Jed? Me? Oh yes, you. Sorry, I'm adjusting to what you told me about Jerome. Jed. Yes. Or rather, no. He hates you. Apart from Stanhope, I've never seen him hate anyone like this. I told him that to understand all is to forgive all, but he just told me that I didn't understand.'

'Sorry to hear that, but I can't do more than cry and vomit about what I let happen. I was in despair. He saw it. What more does he want?'

'I don't think he wants anything except you out of his life. Look, I know Jed. I know every beat of his heart. I know how he thinks. There's something else. He's protecting me from you. That's the only reason for this. If there's something I don't understand, it's because it's being hidden from me. I'm not exactly a shrinking violet. I do know about things. What I don't know about is what it is that keeps him hating you. It's not good to feel such never-ending hate.'

'Well, I don't know about it either. I can go through every moment of my life there if he wants, but we've been through how horrible I was, how unthinking, how...' The voice trailed away as realisation began. Grant slapped his forehead. 'Oh. No. Not that. He can't know that.'

Grant walked into the sitting room and sank into a chair.

'I had no idea he knew. Don't ask. I can't deal with this right now. I need to go inside myself and work it out first. You think back to when you're young; you do stupid things and just never imagine what the consequences might be. The thing is, there is always a reason for doing something. It's never just one of those things, is it? Bear with me. Actually, it's easier to verbalise this than keep the thoughts in my head. I did something because I could do it, and I knew it would have an effect. I knew what the effect would be. I have to work out why I wanted the effect then and why I needed it just for that moment. I must have wanted to be in control, to be in some way meaningful in that pathetic and brief instant. This must have been because I saw myself, my life, as meaningless. It was. I was. Still am. I thought when he saw me that first day, he had seen it all. I thought she had. I thought that's all I was. I was proud of that. Not now.'

He pulled at his sweater. 'I know what's really underneath all this. I have to keep it down, control it, change it into something good and positive. I know what shame is. I'm ashamed of myself. Who else can I blame? The place? The people who should have cared for me? No. It was my bad. My fault. My weakness of character. What to do? No, Paul, it won't be what you think. That doesn't make anything right. I need to make things what they would have been if I hadn't been the stupid, self-centred, mindless prick I was.'

He took his keys from a dish by the door. 'I need to see Jed and beg, yes beg with every bit of my being, his forgiveness. Not for me. For him.'

Chapter 39

'Paul, please ask him to leave.'

'Just give him a moment, please, Jed. For you. For me.'

'No, Paul. Whatever it is, it's for him. He's bad for me, for us. He watched it all happen and loved every moment. He won. I was tormented, humiliated, raped. He got it all. Now he wants more. He's not having it. I won't listen.'

Jed walked out of the room. Both other men, still in their coats, tried to follow. The door to the kitchen slammed shut.

'Go away. Leave us alone. You aren't in our lives. You don't exist,' Jed was sobbing.

'I can't bear this. Please go.' Paul was insistent and pushed Grant towards the front door.

'Salt!' Grant shouted.

The sobbing stopped. The door opened.

Grant fell to the floor, pulling off his coat and sweater. 'Beat me, draw blood, rub it in. It's what I deserve. Do it now. Here. My back. My legs. My buttocks. Here you are. Wherever. Get some. Cut me. Make me scream in pain.'

'For God's sake, stop. This is ridiculous. You can't do this. Get up. Put your clothes on.'

Jed's lip curled. 'On yes, he can do this. And something inside me wants to do exactly what he says. I want him to be in agony.'

'Jed, I'm trembling. This is our home. I don't feel safe with you. I don't know this you. I don't want it. Stop it now. What is it?'

Jed's chest was heaving, and he was ashen. He fixed his gaze on the prone figure. His voice, when it came, shook with an emotion Paul had never heard.

'It was the ultimate humiliation. I've never told you or anyone, but he knows. He didn't know I knew, but I've known all along. I'll tell you. Wait, I need to catch my breath.'

Jed filled a glass and took a sip.

'It was after I'd been beaten. You know, by those animals. I had wounds all over my back, my backside, my legs. I sponged the blood off, but they hurt so much, so very much. I cried myself to sleep that night. The pain was so great that I couldn't put my pyjamas on. I just moved onto my side and hoped some sleep would come. Eventually, it did. I thought I was in a dream, a horrible dream. My sheet was being pulled back, and something was falling onto me. Something soft, yet gritty. I opened my eye to see that thing there disappearing, and then the agony hit me. It was like something I had never known. I couldn't scream. Everyone would hear. I just needed to get it off. I bit my lip and ran to the shower room. I turned it on. It was like ice, but I just needed to get it off me, out of my wounds.

'Yes, Paul, that excrescence on the floor there had poured salt into my wounds, had given me a more exquisite agony than I have known. I still cry at the memory. There's a recollection that never varies. Never has left me. Never will, What had I done to deserve it? Nothing. I just was there. There to be bullied, humiliated, to writhe in agony. Because of him. That's what he did to me. And now he's sorry and wants me to shake hands with him or cut him and pour salt into the wound because he knows I won't do it. I'm a human being. The same little boy, the same innocent little boy whose life you made hell, who ended up raped and scarred – and for what? For nothing. Nothing. Because that's what you happened to want to do. And you lie there on my kitchen floor, all vulnerable and want to be shriven in some way. Well, I'm no pardoner.'

Jed wiped the tears and snot from his face.

'Cover yourself and get out.'

Paul hugged Jed close to him.

'Don't hate,' he whispered. 'Remember 'A Poison Tree', how we read it and agreed what a positive message it contained? 'In the morning, glad, I see my foe outstretched beneath the tree.' Hatred will eat you up. Yes, I know you hadn't brought it to mind until he came back into our lives and, yes, it would maybe have been better if he had never come, but it's out now and mustn't be put back as it was. It's been with you for nearly forty years. That's time enough. We can get rid of it for good.'

'I hate him, Paul. I just want to be the little boy I was before I went in through that front door, before I met Freeman and Cassell and the other grotesques. They messed with my head, Paul. I want it all gone.'

'Yes, we'll get it all away. We'll put it in a compartment and lock it up. We may visit it from time to time to see it getting smaller. We'll take the positives. You and me. We were there and could easily have been nowhere else. But here we are, and we don't want it any other way. We have love, and we will give love. We will learn how to love others. That's the only way. We will understand, empathise and remain true to our values. We will take this man from the floor, and we will lead him gently to our bed. We will let him sleep and help him grow stronger. We will forgive. There is no other way.'

Jed looked Paul straight in the eye and, in that moment, understood what his lover's values were and how he needed to match them. They half-carried Grant to the bedroom, laid him in bed, pulled the covers over him and stroked his hair.

'I have no words,' he murmured.

'You lack the season of all natures', Jed said.

Paul kissed Jed gently. 'You're back. Thank you.'

'I mustn't keep anything from you, 'Jed said as they returned to the kitchen. 'You're right. I nurtured that hate like an old friend. I used to think of all the pain I could inflict on him.'

'Not as much as he wanted to do to himself, Jed. He's plumbed the depths.'

'God, we're all so damaged. Every one of us. How can we make ourselves better?'

'Well, first of all, by seeing he's OK.

'I'll go in in a few minutes,' said Jed.

'He'll cry.'

'Yes. I'll probably do the same. It's odd; hate and love are so close. I suppose the opposite is indifference. We've seen human nature in the raw, you and I.'

'I think we'll keep on seeing it, but we're strong, and we'll manage. We just have to think logically and believe in ourselves and each other.'

'You make me cry.'

Paul tasted the tears. 'Speak to him gently. There hasn't been much of that in his life.'

'I'll be guided by you. I'm washing my face first, though. Can't let him see me like this, or he'll think he's won. No, don't say it. I didn't mean it.'

Chapter 40

———∿∿———

'Did you?' Paul asked.

'Did I what?'

'Cry? You were ages. What happened?'

Jed had taken the initiative and had brought a coffee into the bedroom. He put it on the bedside table. Grant opened one eye.

'Thank you. I don't deserve it. I meant what I was saying. I deserve to be punished.'

'I think you deserve to live a normal life and to see how boringly normal people can be.'

'I think I'm being punished anyway. I need to tell someone and, well, I think you're the best person. Here goes. I've had this pain for a few months now. I know from the media what you've been through, and I expect it's the same, but I've not done anything about it.'

'Let me look.'

Grant hesitated. For the first time in ages, he would make himself vulnerable. He would let someone into something that was personal, intimate, private even.

'Don't be shy. I won't laugh.'

Grant smiled and pulled back the sheet.

'May I touch?'

Grant nodded his assent, and Jed took his testicles in his hand one by one and gently felt each all over.

'One's bigger, isn't it? And it hangs lower.'

'That happens,' said Jed, 'but there's a lump, and I could tell that you felt some pain when I touched it. It needs to be checked out.'

'What's likely to happen if it is cancer?'

'It'll be removed. Don't worry. You'll still be fertile.'

'That's not what bothers me. Will I still be a man?'

'You know, Grant Baxter, most people you meet think you're a man and they've never seen your balls. Yes, of course, you'll still be a man. And are you going to ask me if you can still get an erection? Yes, I can get erect. I do. Frequently. The only thing was, I thought I'd be lop-sided.'

'Are you?'

'Hang on,' Jed slipped out of his jeans and underpants and pulled up his T-shirt. 'You see, the hair's grown back now and covers everything, but if I lift it away, you'll see that my scrotum looks pretty normal. Feel it. Yes, you can. Don't worry. I know you won't want to hurt me. Just squeeze a little, and you'll feel just the one ball there. Part my pubic hair just there,' he pointed, 'and you'll see the faintest scar. And that saved my life.'

'How can you be so,' Grant hunted for a word, 'completely bloody open?'

Jed zipped himself up. 'Well, why shouldn't I be? I haven't lost anything. In fact, I've gained your trust. I always was open. When I was a child, I was encouraged to be trusting, and it never occurred to me to be anything other than accepting of other people, but then again, everyone around me was doing their best for me. That all changed when I was 12 and didn't leave me until I met Paul again. I felt so secure with him, so safe, that it all came back. I was sorry that I had lost sight of who I really was for so long, but now, well, I'm in love, and that changes everything. I have given Paul everything I am, and he has done the same.

'What you did to me was the only thing I've kept hidden, and you see where that got me. So I try to be open with everyone now, and it isn't hard. It's a different kind of openness with different people, of course. With you, I can be open in that I can show you my body, even the most private parts, because I have good reason to show you, but I won't show you my feelings, nor would you expect me to. I don't think Paul and I would kiss in front of you because that's just something for us, so I think it's a matter of appropriateness. We haven't talked about it, but we just know how to be at different levels of openness with different people – and with each other. We respect the boundaries. Because of our background, Grant, I can be more open about sexual aspects than with most people and, as I have taken the lead, you should know that you can be, too.'

Jed took the coffee Paul was holding for him. 'That's what we talked about. Then I thought we'd change the subject and I talked about hate, and how much I had hated him, and what you said about how destructive it is and how I agreed. I think he has only ever hated one person. He blames himself for everything that has happened to him. Like me, he was a shy young boy when he started at that place, and from the first day, he was swept up into the corruption that festered there. His shyness didn't last long. He said he was felt up every day, told he was special and believed it. Also told he was thick and that the only way he'd make it in the world was using his body. The kid never had a chance.

'I remembered that he had lots of different clothes, expensive ones with foreign labels. He told me they were bought for him so that whoever bought them could take them off him. 'I wanted them so much, I didn't care. I just let them do what they wanted. After a while, it didn't hurt so much.' That's what he said. Seems that several of the staff had him. It was mainly Brookfield and Cassell, but there were five or six others – male and female. A couple of the older boys, too, except that he didn't let them have much as they couldn't give him anything. He told me he never felt anything by way of emotion. Never had. Doesn't know what it's like to have a friend or feel for someone. Can't understand why we're looking after him when we don't get anything back. I tried telling him that it was human kindness. He assumed it was because it made us feel better about ourselves. I think he understood that it isn't like that, but I don't think he knew how to feel that understanding. He just trusted me enough to take my word for it.'

'Biscuit?'

'Please. I guess that now that I've let him touch my balls – oh, God, the plural comes so easily – and I've touched his, our relationship will be easier. At least it's better than the tight knot of hatred. Thank you for your wisdom. I was wrong and hadn't thought it through. I need to let your pragmatism become part of me. I hope we've caught it in time.'

'He's sure to want to make an appointment as soon as he wakes up.'

'How did your meeting with Mrs McAllister go, by the way? I haven't had a chance to catch up.'

'I'll give you the packet of biscuits. It'll be a long story and a dilemma for us to think through. It's one that I have no idea how to tackle. Whichever way we deal with it is going to be wrong, I fear.'

'Talking about becoming part of each other, I also think we should sort out the wedding, don't you? I feel I want us to be one legally as well as spiritually.'

'Of course.'

'And you'll remember that we spoke about children?'

'Yes, and then life got in the way. We didn't do any banking, and neither of is any younger,'

'69 and 82. Oh yes, I have those figures firmly in my head, but there are two of us, and we're not there yet.'

'But we will be, and we have to think - are we really the right people for a child to rely on? Might it be just a way to normalise our position?'

'I'd never thought that way. I was just thinking that, if I could, I would be happy to carry a child myself. In fact, I'd love to. I'd feel there was part of you inside me and, when it was born, I'd see it as a physical manifestation of our love. Then I wonder if this is sufficient reason. It's certainly selfish, but does that make it bad? It isn't that it's just selfishness; it's also that it makes us a family, and I think we can bring so much wisdom to any family we might create.'

'Quite a bit of which is how not to bring up a family, of course. You've said it yourself, 'we are all so damaged.' Those are your very words.'

'But, then, who isn't? We all get bumps and scrapes in life. We repair ourselves. I think we've done a good job of being back to brand new. That's what I feel. Raped and scarred, but back to as was and part of a fantastic duo. So happy and secure that I want to give that to our child.'

'Let me tell you about my meeting with the remarkable Frances McAllister and what she said about this very point.'

Chapter 41

‘We meet again. And so soon. I had wondered if you might have had enough first time. You didn't exactly get what you wanted, did you? Here you are with your beau. You take me back a while. I remember you both as you were. Paul, a correct, fresh-faced, young teacher at a place quite unworthy of his talent, who sensed that this was an establishment he would be better off leaving, but who stayed out of a misplaced sense of loyalty to his pupils. It was all going on around you, and you knew there was something wrong, but you never spotted what it was. I wondered why you didn't see what I realised on day one. I think it was because you were so pure that you never imagined others in the same profession could have standards that fell so short of your own. Either that or you were particularly deluded.

‘And Jed Massie. Sweet boy. I could have eaten you up; you were so nice. I almost felt like telling your charming aunt to get back in her little car with you in it and drive like hell all the way home and never come back. But I didn't, and you were almost broken there. I look at you, and I look at the Poynton boy, and I wonder how you two can be on the same planet. I would no more have thought of asking you to pop into that pot than

I would have suggested you fly in the air. The progeny would have been remarkable, though.

'The perfect teacher and the motivated pupil. Now together. Impossible then, and I just can't imagine it now, but you're big boys and able to follow your hearts. Congratulations.'

Frances had selected something sparkling for this meeting. The glasses were crystal, and the bottle a 2008 Amour de Deutz Blanc de Blancs.

'You have exquisite taste, Mrs McAllister.'

'We've both left school, Jed. I won't be calling you 'Massie'. So you are allowed to 'Frances' me, if you wish.'

'You have exquisite taste.'

'So, you are sizing up the opposition, young man. Probably a sensible move considering my history with young men. But I do you a disservice. You must both be well into middle age now.'

'The proverbial water has flowed under the bridge, and we are both older and wiser.'

'Yes, Paul, and am I being too sensitive – never a trait I was accused of – in sensing an undercurrent there? Have you come to discuss my suggestion? I assume you are an item.'

Jed responded. 'We are lovers, and we will soon be married. Paul has accepted me as his husband and I, him.'

'Thank you. That makes everything clear. Shall we proceed to my suggestion?'

'Shall we talk about Jerome Poynton instead?'

'Oh, Paul, why spoil the ambience? What can possibly bring the name of that boy into our conversation?'

'Huntington's.'

'What's that?'

Paul passed his phone to Frances. He had keyed the word into Google and selected the Wikipedia article.

'By all means, read it aloud.'

Frances cleared her throat as if for a speaking engagement. 'Huntington's disease (HD), also known as Huntington's chorea, is a neurodegenerative disease that is mostly inherited.'

'Please now read the first line of the third paragraph.'

'There is no cure for HD, and full-time care is required in the later stages.'

'Please read the entire article to yourself.'

The sound of three people breathing filled the room for several minutes. Frances passed the phone back to Paul. He clicked it off.

'Jerome Poynton has HD.'

'Well, he didn't have it when I knew him.'

'Actually, he did, but you didn't notice it. I imagine you were more concerned with the quantity of the supply than its quality.'

'So?'

'It's an inherited disease. He inherited it from his parents. He stands a chance of passing it on. One of the other significant sentences in this article is 'Cognitive abilities are progressively impaired and tend to generally decline into dementia.' Does this give you pause for thought?'

'No one's complained that anyone's gone mad.'

'Well, that's hunky-dory, isn't it?'

'OK. You've made your point. If I'd known that half the potential progeny might inherit this, I would have chosen someone else.'

'What you did was everything I said it was when we first spoke, and now I can add the word 'dangerous.' This could be a big news story.'

'Another glass?' Frances lifted the Blanc de Blancs.

'For Christ's sake, do you really have no idea of what you've done?'

'Mr Massie, if you won't call me by my first name, I shall refrain from using yours. I am now completely aware of what I have done. I have helped make many people very happy and fulfilled.'

'And given some of them problems that will last for the rest of their lives.'

'I have already told you that, had I known, I would have looked elsewhere. I wasn't to know. The boy didn't tell me.'

'The boy was a child. He didn't know.'

'So I couldn't have known, then, could I? I could hardly contact his parents and tell them I was thinking of getting their son to jerk off into a jar so that he might father an untold number of children, and could they please, kindly vouch for the absence of degenerative diseases. I don't think that would have gone down too well.'

'You could go to prison.'

She poured herself another glass and inclined the bottle in the direction of her guests. They declined. 'Sure. And it would be a huge news story. It would knock your little to-do with the media into a cocked hat. Sad, in a way, that it'll never see the light of day.'

'There's my quandary. Do I tell or do I not? Tell, and you're stopped. Don't tell, and you go on and on. Tell, and lives are ruined. Don't tell, and they're still ruined.'

'As I said before, that's why you won't tell. That way, only unhappiness lies.'

'Yes,' said Paul, 'a real Robert Frost dilemma. 'Two roads diverged in a wood, and I — I took the one less travelled by, and that has made all the difference.' You see, in 'The Road Not Taken,' it's not certain who has the joke on whom. Was it that he did or didn't take the road less travelled? We will never know. So I'll think about which road to take.'

'Then I'll know when they come to take me away to lock me up - or don't come.'

'You will. Tell me one thing, though. Do you still use Brookfield?'

'He has his uses.'

'He knew about Poynton.'

'Then he's lost his usefulness,' She looked out into the garden and said as if to herself, 'Just as well his secrets are buried.'

'And there's the other matter.'

'Oh yes. My generous offer. How do you want to do it? Go into the same pot and take your chance, or two pots and make a baby each. Your choice. I use a top clinic in London. I'll tell you which one. The choice of donor and surrogate will be yours. There will be a DNA test afterwards as you might possibly have doubts about my bona fides. All told, at least £100,000 of IVF and all with my compliments.'

'And if you're in prison?'

'Maybe trickier to arrange and less complimentary.'

'So,' said Jed, 'you have us by the balls.'

'Thank Christ,' said Frances. 'You have a personality. I was starting to have my doubts. Most people think I have a pair of my own.'

'Others might think you're an amoral procurer.'

'They might, indeed, Mr Massie, but I sense that you're more into balls yourself.'

Frances opened the door where she had hung their coats on arrival.

'Maybe, Mr Massie, you should, as they used to say, 'adjust your dress before leaving'.'

Jed made a grab for his zip. It was closed.

'Gets them every time. Bye boys.'

Chapter 42

'Kiss me, Paul.'

They had stopped on the road just outside Frances' house.

'I just need to feel normal. God, I want to make love to you now.'

'I can tell.'

'Stop it, Paul. Oh no, don't stop it. Just a bit.'

'She is something else.'

'Isn't she just?'

'Heart of steel.'

'Do you remember her when she taught you?'

'Apart from the animals, I only remember you, Paul, and I never dreamed that we'd be making love in broad daylight in your car at the side of a road.'

'Enough. 'Adjust your dress.''

'I just want to go on snuggling into you for ever and ever until I become you and you become me.'

'Christ!'

There was a sharp tap at the passenger's window. Frances was smiling at them.

'Thought you'd stopped. Just wanted to give you this. Must've fallen out of your pocket.'

Jed rolled his window down and took the small electronic device from her.

'Thanks.'

'I'll let you get back to it. Bye.'

'Is it?'

'Yes.'

'Was it on?'

'All the time.'

'Is there anything on it?'

Jed had it to his ear. 'Wiped clean as a whistle.'

'Not sure about her balls, but she certainly has nous.'

'Did she see anything?'

'No. Dress suitably adjusted in the nick of time.'

'So what shall we do?'

'Go home, get into bed and make love until we fall asleep in each other's arms.'

'You know exactly what I mean.'

'I think a pot each and two babies.'

'And the illegality, immorality and all the crimes?'

'As she said, you won't take it any further.'

'I think it's going to be whatever we decide. Not just me. Let's look at some fundamental truths. Brookfield is a criminal. We know this. It's not just that he is a pimp. We know who his early victims were, and we have recorded evidence that he is still engaged in everything that the UN's Trafficking in Persons Protocol lists as human trafficking. Yes, I looked it up. He tells us it's so ingrained into society that it can't be stopped. That's what those who dealt in slavery may have said a few centuries ago. It seems that more needs to be changed.

'And what about Frances McAllister? We don't know as much about her dealings, but the way she operates goes way beyond what Trading Standards might describe as bad practice. I suppose the issue is that given all the information we have, should we do something, or can we in all conscience leave it there and get on with our lives?'

'No recorded evidence on her, though.'

'Credit me with some sense.' Paul dug into his pocket.

'You sly dog!'

'I got the first meeting on tape, too.'

'We know what the media can do to people like us, though. If we took up McAllister's offer and exposed her at the same time, the media would have us for breakfast, wouldn't they? Ditto Brookfield. Here you are, a teacher, screwing one of his pupils. That several decades have elapsed since those two roles were delineated can easily be glossed over. Maybe you were hankering after me right from the get-go. Fantasising over me in the classroom. Watching me change for games. No smoke without fire. I'm sorry, Paul. That was crass.'

'You see what it does to me, don't you? You see the tears, but you don't see what goes on inside. It's an issue for me. You know this. You and I met in a privileged position. I was not allowed to develop a relationship with you. I have developed a relationship with you. That's the blunt and, OK, yes, too blunt, distorted truth. I am a teacher having sex with one of my pupils. That's something I have to live with, and sometimes it's really tough. Oh yes, anyone who has a mind to can really drag me over the coals.'

'I know you have these meltdowns from time to time, and there's nothing I can do about what's in your head. There's thirteen years between us. Fact. You used to be my teacher. Another fact. We are grown men, able to make our own decisions, and we are in love. I would die for you. I love you more than my life. There is nothing about me you don't know. Nothing is hidden. Our relationship is perfect and will never end. What else can I say?'

'Maybe I torment myself because it is so perfect. Sometimes I wake up and see you and think, how can I be so happy? How can I so love someone with every fibre of my being? When I try to verbalise it, all I have are clichés, so maybe that's why I externalise all the negatives because they're unusual, special and, ultimately and perversely, wrong. At least, in my logical brain, they are. But there's nothing logical about love, is there?'

'Nothing. And what's also special is that for each of is there has never been anyone else. It's as though we were waiting for the moment. My first time with you was the first time for you, and it was just wonderful and electric and an experience to be treasured. My life changed in that instant.'

'I know it did. I was there. But the perverse side of me thinks, what if you had been 17 and I had been 30?'

'But I wasn't. How far back do you want to go to make it wrong, and how far forward to make it right?'

'Is our having a baby something that will help make it right? Something we have achieved in the here and now, and nothing connected with our past? If that's the reason, we shouldn't do it. If we think that we can give all the love we have for each other to a child we create, then, and only then should we go ahead.'

'Then we should go ahead. £100,000 is more than we can afford. The offer is the only way to achieve it. Unless we go for adoption and then we have a few potential problems – your age, our orientation, and goodness knows what else.'

Paul sighed. 'The issue I would have about adoption has some similarities with the one I was just externalising so self-pityingly to you. It's someone else's child. As a teacher, I dealt with other people's children and kept my professional distance. I never had to think about it. It became instinctual. I have a hang-up about loving someone else's child. I would love my child, and I would love your child because you're – well, you're me. So it would stop some angst in me if we could go down that route.'

'We get back to one pot or two?'

'In that we are one person, one pot.'

'Or, as we are both only children and know how lonely that can be, one pot each. Why not?'

'It's all a bit contrived, isn't it?'

'We could substitute the word 'logical'.'

'The media would use 'businesslike'.'

'If they were being kind. 'Selfish,' 'creating orphans,' I could go on. We are not going to modify our behaviour to please them, though, are we? Should we give the idea of being disloyal to McAllister any credence? She's hardly virtuous herself. I wouldn't feel guilty if we take up her offer and shop her to the authorities at the same time.'

'Realistically, it would have to be a year after. To make sure the babies are born and DNA tested to see we don't have a couple of Poyntons in the nest.'

'So we deal with clinic rather than her? Yes? Let's turn the car round.'

Chapter 43

'It's a while since I last did this,' Paul remarked casually as he manoeuvred the heavy Jaguar 360° back to its original spot. 'My driving test, I think.'

'When I said 'let's turn the car round,' I imagined 180°.'

'So did I. Then when I was pulling out, your words stuck in my head. 'I just want to go on snuggling into you for ever and ever until I become you and you become me.' And then other words you used just now, hit me. It was when I asked what you wanted to do, you said, 'Go home, get into bed and make love until we fall asleep in each other's arms.' And then I thought, you know, that's exactly what I want to do. I want to snuggle into you until I become you, and yes, I want to go home, get into bed and make love with you until we fall asleep in each other's arms. I don't want anything else. I know every bit of you, every cadence of your voice, every undercurrent of meaning in your words, and I know that's what you'd be happiest with. So I turned the car round.'

'I'm sure she's watching us. She must think we're mad.'

'I'm sure she is, and I'm sure I don't give a toss what she thinks.'

'I'll have to get to know you better. Yes, all I want is you. You knew this, but – I'm really stuck how I can say this and I don't want it to come out as more selfish than it is – but I want you so much that, if anything should take you away from me, I couldn't bear your not being with me.'

'To have a child as an ersatz me?'

'That's why it would have to be your sperm.'

'You're assuming that I would predecease you.'

'I have a few years' advantage.'

'And you would never be able to tell the child that this featured in your thinking.'

'I'm just being honest.'

'Which you could never be with our child.'

'I would love the child unconditionally.'

'On condition that it was my sperm that made that child.'

'If you put it like that, it's incredibly selfish. But the concept is born out of love. Love for you and love for the child.'

'But, Jed, we're talking about a child, not a concept.'

'Just as you have a hang-up about your having been my teacher, I have one, too. I'm just scared that at some point, I won't have you. For years, I was my own boss. Then I became part of a couple. It's changed me. I'm sounding like The Beatles' song now, but I'm half the man I used to be. You're so much a part of me now that you're the other half. I can't imagine life without you.'

'Nor me, but you know that I'll never leave you. Yes, physically, of course. We've come to each other late in life, but long enough to grow as one and then, when it happens, we will have grown into each so much that, while you and I will still be individuals, we'll know each other so well that we'll exist as a whole. We can wait another thirteen years to make the decision, of course. Maybe I should use Frances's good offices to bank some now in case I become too decrepit. Or, if you're really set on the idea, we'll go ahead, but I know that right now we are so into each other that we're all we need.'

'Your hang-up is all angst and navel-gazing. Mine is a fact. Oh God, did Lady Macbeth really have a baby? These are saucy doubts and fears that we are rapt withal. I suppose it's all to do with how contrived having a child would have to be. If only we could have sex and get pregnant. Then it would be a result of our love. As it is, it has to be supernatural soliciting.'

'I see Frances more as Lady Macbeth than a supernatural solicitor, but what we could do is go along with everything to see how she does it up to a certain point and then wade no more. Jed, I'll have to stop thinking about that play, or I'll end up like that dead butcher or his fiend-like queen. But all these quotes are so apropos.'

'So, another 180°?'

'No. We'll do it over the phone. We can go home and have an early night.'

'I doubt we'll get pregnant.'

'It won't be for want of trying.'

Paul pushed the voice control button. 'Call Frances McAllister. Home.'

The voice was crisp. 'McAllister. Aha. Have you come to a decision?'

'We'd like to proceed to the next step. Maybe you can tell us what this is.'

'On the assumption that there will be a baby each, we will need both of you to make a donation. This will be at a London clinic. I'll text you the address and the date of the appointment, which I shall make on your behalf. The timing is important as there will need to be abstinence for three days prior to the donation. This is so that the quality will be optimal. If I can make the appointment for this Thursday, the abstinence can start now, so I suggest you assume that Thursday will be the day. Is this OK with you?'

'Understood, Frances. Thank you.'

'I wish you well on this journey, Paul. It's a big step and a life-changing experience. All being well, you should be parents in two years. How does that sound?'

'Daunting.'

'Let's say 'magical', shall we? This is modern science working for you. You'll be in the hands of the clinic from here on in, so goodbye and good luck.'

Paul pressed the phone down symbol.

Jed exhaled. 'Well, that's put paid to our night of passion.'

'We'll do it properly and see how this goes. Even allowing for the quid pro quo, I have the feeling that there is something else going on here. She knows we're the enemy. She needs to neutralise us.'

'I have to say it, Paul. It's all there in 'Macbeth.' I said it to Grant. 'Oftentimes, to win us to our harm, the instruments of darkness tell us truths, win us with honest trifles, to betray's in deepest consequence,' This what we're doing to her, and you can bet she has something up her sleeve for us.'

'So, Jed, we proceed in the knowledge that nothing is but what is not.'

Chapter 44

———∼∼∼———

Indistinguishable from its expensive West End neighbours, the address they gave the taxi driver was in the most fashionable part of London. Limousines lined the road. The clinic announced itself with a small brass plate beneath which sat an intercom.

'Massie and Mason. I believe we are expected.'

The mechanism whirred, and the door clicked open.

Reception was signposted upstairs. The room was softly carpeted. On the silk-covered walls were framed photographs of smiling families – one parent, two parents, different genders, same gender, all races. It was the picture of inclusiveness. The lady behind the counter smiled at them and greeted them by name.

'Lovely to meet you. How are you today?'

'Fine. Thank you. Perhaps a touch nervous as this is rather a different experience for us.'

'It's all very straightforward, and it's important that you feel relaxed. Mrs McAllister has completed the formalities on your behalf, so all that remains is for you to make the donations and sign them over to our care. The donations will be then be analysed and frozen so that we can proceed to the next stage when you feel ready. I understand that the importance of the three-day abstinence period was made clear, and I assume that you have followed this instruction. These are the pots for the donations. The room is over there.' She indicated a door to her right. 'Would you prefer to donate separately or together? OK. Would you like magazines, videos, other materials to assist you?'

'Thank you. We'll manage on our own.'

'Perfect. There is a hand basin in the room and towels. Please clean the outside of the pot and put it in the sealable bag provided. As you see, each pot is individually identified.'

She handed the pots over, opened the door for them to enter and switched on the light. The room resembled a clinically clean kitchen. A vinyl-covered seat and table on which magazines were scattered were the only free-standing furnishings. The floor was tiled and evidently heated from underneath. A TV screen filled one wall, and a large cabinet occupied another.

Jed and Paul stood there, pots in hand.

Jed laughed. 'OK, it's not funny; it's just that it's so bizarre. I actually feel embarrassed to do the job in front of you. Shy, even.'

'Christ, Jed. You're making me feel like teacher Paul again. Here you are in the school changing room, and I'm looking at you. OK. Easiest if I'm not fully clothed. Right, here I am, Jed. This is me with nothing to be embarrassed about. Hug me. Good. That's more like it. I'm snuggling into you and, ah good, hard now, and here it goes. Wow. That was good. Thanks. Now you.'

'Is that I really just want your baby? Is this what's holding me back?'

'Just as long as I'm not your teacher and you're not back at that place.'

'Oh, sure, there you are in the classroom, and I'm getting a hard-on. I never did. Never saw any of the teachers that way until Stanhope, and then, after the court case, after that man had been put away, there was you. And I just ran to you in the hotel room and buried myself in you, and we cried, and it was all so natural and beautiful and pure and good. As this is so contrived. OK, here I am. Hold me. Love me. I can feel it… OK. Done.'

They stood under the fluorescent light like Rodin's 'Kiss'.

'Oh my God. There's more. Wow, we've cracked it. Together we can do everything. I love you, Paul Mason. Here's your pot again.'

'I love you, Jed Massie. Here's yours.'

They sponged down the pots and each other, dressed and went back to the reception room. The young woman smiled at them. 'I won't ask how it went. I can see that the donations are substantial. Would you care to meet one of the counsellors here to talk you through the next steps?'

Jed hesitated. 'I think that may be enough for one day.'

'On the other hand,' said Paul, 'As we're here…'

The counsellor was informed and articulate. 'It all depends what kind of pregnancy you'd like. It can be a partial surrogacy or a gestational surrogacy. Shall I go through the difference? So, a partial surrogacy is one in which the egg donor herself is the surrogate and is impregnated using her own eggs. The gestational surrogacy uses the eggs of another woman implanted into the surrogate. In this case, there is no biological connection between the birth mother and the baby or babies. Your choice, but most of our clients choose gestational surrogacy. In either case, we will present you with descriptions of potential surrogates, and you can make your choice. Look, here's one. She writes, 'I have never done anything special in my life, but this gives me the opportunity to do something that will elevate me above normal women.' We make our surrogates think very carefully about why they want to do this. It's a year out of their life, and they have to know that they will never get to know and love the babies they are carrying. You stay in telephone contact with them and then collect the baby from here.'

'And if we go for gestational surrogacy. How do we choose whose eggs we use?'

'Again, we choose egg donors carefully. You will see photos and CVs so you can see whose genes your child will inherit. It's not an exact science, of course, but we have many graduates among our donors who are happy to donate eggs that would otherwise go to waste. This is why the majority of our clients choose the gestational route.'

'Sorry to appear over-cautious, but it is a decision that will remain with us for the rest of our lives, so how do we know that the eggs are, in fact, from the donor we have chosen?'

'I've never been asked this, but it's an interesting question. There is no contact between the intended parents and the donor. It's all a matter of trust. The DNA will show that you are the parent.'

Jed asked. 'Do you also recruit sperm donors?'

'We do and, to anticipate your question, again, it's photos and CVs.'

'And trust.'

'Indeed. We have many testimonials in this folder here, so you can check us out. I am aware that Mrs McAllister is providing our services, so you are free to choose whichever route you wish. We will also let you have sperm analyses.'

'You have no web site.'

'No, sir. What we do remains discreet. Please take a look at this file. You see, late 20s, graduate - PhD, in fact. British and Dutch ancestry. Clean bill of health. Blue eyes, blonde. Read her rationale. She has just come onto our books, and I think you will find her rather suitable. All our donors are known by their numbers. This one is ED 344.'

In the bright sunshine and roar of the traffic, they looked for a passing taxi with an illuminated sign.

'Hang on,' said Jed. 'Look at that parked car right opposite us.'

'The black BMW?'

'Look at the number plate.'

'Well, that's a coincidence.'

'Except that it can't be. I told you she'd be up to something. I have the feeling that we may not have to wait long to find out what it is.'

Chapter 45

'You may not remember me. It's been a while.'

Their doorbell had rung that same evening. They had only just returned, and Jed was still wearing his leather jacket. The black BMW was in their drive. A well-built man in a black overcoat was at their door.

Jed, for it was he had who answered the ring, looked into the face and saw traces of the boy whose face it had been decades earlier.

'You aren't Grant's brother, David, are you?'

'Well done.'

'Please come in. Paul,' Jed called to Paul, who was in the kitchen. 'It's David Baxter.

'Thank you. No, I'll keep my coat on. I won't be long. I think we need to have a conversation. No, I won't have a drink, thank you. Good though it is to see you again, this isn't a social call. I think we need to clear the air and best to do this in person, I would say. Now to the point of my visit. Jed, I'm sorry about that business with Stanhope. He's an arrogant fool and a nasty piece of work, best off in jail. What he did was rough on you. But, and it's a big but, it seems you've been looking into various areas that are – shall we say – not your concern.

'I'm sure you have your gripes with Brookfield, but he never touched you, and, as for Frances McAllister, she has only shown you kindness and remarkable generosity. The services you have been availing yourselves of today are perfectly legal in much of the US and elsewhere, but not yet in this country; more's the pity. They should be. We see ourselves as trailblazers who must, for the moment, operate in a quiet way. This is why we would appreciate your silence about this. We are giving us what you want, and you will give us the silence we request.'

'Silence about the clinic?'

'About everything, Jed.'

'Including Brookfield?'

'Let me put it this way; we provide services to people. The service we are providing you is giving you parenthood. We provide what people want and can pay for. It is to everyone's benefit.'

'And the boys from Finchingham?'

'Were well-rewarded for their efforts.'

'They were children.'

'That's what some of our clients like. They prefer the unspoiled.'

'Then you spoil them, and they live with the consequences.'

'As I said, they are amply rewarded, and they can go on to provide other services.'

'The kids who fell into Brookfield's clutches had no choice.'

'They didn't complain when they saw how much money they were making. Many of these boys would have had problems getting a job flipping burgers. They made money doing what wealthy people wanted them to do. Cash in hand. Some of these boys made vast sums of money.'

'Your brother being one of them. We've seen what it did for him.'

'Grant didn't know which side his bread was buttered. He was weak. He had it all and then threw it away - for what? I have no idea. I can't deal with him. Haven't seen him for decades.'

'We've seen the scars on his wrists.'

'Tried that, did he? The idiot. Look, there are many rich people in this country. They have particular interests which may not appeal to you – or me, for that matter – but they are powerful, influential people, and they get what they want. This is big and not something that you are able to stop. I know Brookfield gave you that message loud and clear. Now I'm giving it to you louder.'

'Thank you, David. I rather think that's it. Message delivered.'

'Not quite. We will be happy for you to carry on with your adventure into parenthood. I've seen the material you left behind. Quite a quantity. More than enough for embryonic fertilisation purposes. Sperm donation is, as you know, one of the areas we cover and high prices are paid for the right seed. I don't imagine that either of you imagined fathering more than a baby each. With what you have provided, it's possible that, were it to be marketed, hundreds of babies could be created. I fear that might pose a moral dilemma for you. But there it is. Just a little to provide you with the offspring you need and plenty left over, which would otherwise go to waste. What a shame that would be – for you. Quite a profit for us, of course.

'And just in case you're thinking of turning us in, please bear in mind that what you have been doing is an illegal activity. If anyone is in any doubt as to your involvement in this criminality, they can always listen to your words. Here are Jed's: 'Maybe you were hankering after me right from the get-go. Fantasising over me in the classroom. Watching me change for games. No smoke without fire.'

'And from Mr Mason – I can't first name you, I'm afraid, for me you are still my teacher: 'You and I met in a privileged position. I was not allowed to develop a relationship with you. I have developed a relationship with you. That's the blunt truth. I am a teacher having sex with one of my pupils.' There's plenty more, of course. Photos and videos, too. I feel I know you quite intimately now. I think your credibility and whatever holier-than-thou attitude you might strike wouldn't last long were this to be given to the media.

'So, just let us get on with what we do best and stop your nonsense. We will provide you with parenthood and whatever else you might fancy. No charge. We have you, as one says, by the balls. Good evening.'

David Baxter gathered his coat around him and swept out of the room towards the front door. 'I'll see myself out.' Jed was reminded momentarily of Brian Freeman and his gown all those years ago. The world was full of dangerous people, all of whom had, in one way or another, tried to wreck him. Time to put a stop to it all.

The front door slammed shut, and the car's engine started. Jed ran out just as the car was reversing and launched himself at it. He fell under it with a thud.

'Film it!' Jed screamed. Paul punched at his phone. The car drove over the prone body and accelerated away from the house.

'Which service do you…'

Paul shouted over the speaker, gave his name and address and screamed, 'A BMW, COV 1P, has just deliberately run over my partner, Jed Massie. Please send an ambulance and get the police to stop the driver. He is David Baxter. There will be evidence under that car that I'm sure he'll try to wash off. Please get him and that car. He tried to kill Jed. He may be dead. I'm with him now.'

Paul felt the prone body and looked in desperation for signs of life. Blood was running from a head wound, and he could see seepage under his clothes. Never had he felt so useless. If he moved him into a recovery position, he might do more harm than good.

'Should I move him? His airways? Is he breathing? I'll look. Not sure. Shall I breathe for him? OK. I'll do this.'

Paul cradled Jed's head off the gravel and blew air into his mouth. The seconds ticked by. Then the minutes. He sensed that life was slipping from Jed. Distantly he heard a siren. It was getting nearer. Thank God. Hands lifted him from Jed. Green-suited paramedics went to work.

'Is he alive?'

'Just. Leave it to us, sir. Did you see which part of him went under the car?'

'I think all of him. I can show you. I have it here on my phone. Sorry. I'm trying to hold it still, but I'm shaking.'

'It's shock, sir. We'll be treating you, too.'

Paul could see that Jed had become caught by something under the car and was briefly dragged along until the fabric tore and he was released. The gravel was disturbed for more than twenty yards. Shreds of clothing lay on the drive. The paramedics were using language that he had only heard on TV medical soaps, but that they were still working on him had to be a good sign. He couldn't lose Jed. Jed had to live.

'Please don't die, Jed. Please!'

'Come with us in the ambulance, sir. We'll have you both in hospital soon.'

Chapter 46

'Two broken arms, a broken leg, a few ribs and some tissue damage on the back. That's what they told me. I think they should be looking for brain damage. You wanted him to hit you.'

'He had us over a barrel, Paul. The recordings, the photos, the semen, all of it. He'd worked it out like some sort of military operation. We didn't stand a chance, and he knew it. The first thing I thought of was let's get him for attempted murder, so I tried to get his reversing car to give me a bit of a knock and instead, he went backwards right over me, and I got dragged under it. You know, I think he really did want to finish me off when he shot ahead with me under the car.'

'Says he didn't know you were there.'

'Somehow, I don't think the police are going to believe that. One of the back lights was smashed, and part of the bumper was pulled off in the impact. That was no gentle tap. He had his foot right down. My jeans caught on the exhaust, and they're what dragged me until they ripped, and I fell free. Then the rear wheel caught my arm. My leather jacket rode up and protected most of my head. It was my shirt being ripped off by the gravel that did for the skin on my back.

I had nearly taken that jacket off. If he had rung that bell just half a minute later, I would have, and I'm sure I'd have been cut about far more.'

'Talk about quick thinking, Jed. There you were doing your kamikaze act, and as soon as you yelled 'film it,' I knew what you were about. I caught almost everything. The police have impounded the car and, would you believe it, the car has drive record on it. Because it's top-of-the-range, it has all the bells and whistles. Drive record is one. It films what's going on outside the car, front and rear.'

'Hang on a mo. I need a wee. Can you press that buzzer? Thanks. It's going to be interesting for a while with two arms out of action. Thanks. It's OK. Paul can hold me while I wee.'

'That's OK,' said Paul. 'He's my husband.'

'We must get round to it, so at least one of us can die a widower.'

'It just saves explanations, but, yes, I'll arrange it as soon as you're out.'

'Or before. David Baxter may want a second pop at me. I sense that he's not someone to be underestimated.'

'If you mean he's a serial criminal and psychotic killer, I'll agree. If some of the torque hadn't been transferred to the gravel, that burst of speed could've pulled you apart.'

'Have you given a statement yet?'

'They wanted one about the attempted murder while the events were still fresh in my memory - not that I'll ever forget it. They've got everything on paper. I told them there was a reason Baxter was at our house that night and started to tell them the whole story right back to Finchingham days, but they said they'd rather record it at the station, so that's what I'll do tonight. I told them they should get him for human trafficking. I gave them the address of the clinic, so I hope they'll raid it before they take it all away.'

'It'll be a long night.'

'They're going to pick me up from here. I'm still shaking and don't feel right enough to drive.'

'You should get them to look in the I-Pace. Those recordings Baxter played were from our conversation in the car. I know it was checked for devices last time, so maybe McAllister slipped something in when she was giving me back my recorder.'

'Oh, what tangled webs we weave… Yes. Good thinking.'

The nurse returned to collect the used bottle and smiled at them both. 'It's so sweet,' she said. 'I mean, it's so sweet to see you both so devoted to each other.'

'But he lied to you.' Jed's voice was hushed as if communicating a secret. 'He's not my husband. Yet. We've been meaning to get round to it, but somehow things kept getting in the way. We like to do it. Um, sort of now, please. Can you pass on the request?'

The nurse's smile broadened. 'You really wouldn't want this,' she said.

'Oh, but I would. I really, really would. Do I sound like the Spice Girls? I really, really don't mean to.'

'It's clear you're feeling more yourself now, although you have to allow for some of this to be the medication.' The nurse's tone was reassuring rather than patronising. 'No. I said you wouldn't want this because, although we can arrange for marriage services to take place here, it's because we believe that the patient will soon die.'

'So, denying my request is an indication that you anticipate my survival. Well, that's good news and gives Paul something to do. Please, love of my life, make the arrangements for something so quiet that no one will notice me walking down the aisle – which there won't be as it won't be in a church – with a plaster cast and a stick. Where you'll put the ring, I have no idea, but that's a bagatelle. Please just arrange for us to be married without delay. I want to be made an honest man of.'

'You're making me cry.' The young nurse slipped away, full bottle in hand.

'She's a toughie, that one. How she can be affected by romance while carrying a bottle full of wee, I can't imagine, but they're all brilliant. What have I done to myself? I just acted on instinct. I knew he had to be stopped, and I used my body to stop him.'

'Except that he didn't stop.'

'But in going on, he absolutely incriminated himself.'

'There is a fly in the ointment, though, isn't there? Have you spotted it? That car has a recording device which will show you launching yourself and telling me to film it.'

'Sure, after he had threatened us and stormed out. Of course, I had to carry on our conversation, and I wanted you to film whatever he might say or do after I had told him to stop his intimidation. Perfectly natural, and you knew this as well as I did, didn't you?'

'Now you mention it, yes.'

'I'm getting light-headed. I don't know what I'll come up with next, but all this has taken us in a completely different direction.'

"'This murderous shaft that's shot hath not yet lighted…'
I can't stop. Sorry. At least we are the ones who are aiming it.
I imagine we'll be meeting David Baxter again. In court.'

Jed had slipped into the relief of sleep. Paul kissed him on
the forehead and aligned his angle prior to the interview.

Chapter 47

David Baxter placed both thumbs on the lapels of his dark suit jacket and pulled the fabric slightly forward to exaggerate the proportions of his upper body, striking, as he thought, a more commanding presence in the dock. He elevated his head and looked Prosecuting Counsel firmly in the eye. He had spent his several months in custody convincing himself that he had nothing to hide. He was now firmly of that belief.

'Do you accept, Mr Baxter, that you knew Mr Massie was under your car while you were in control of it?'

'No, sir.'

'The camera at the rear of your car shows Mr Mason waving at you to stop.'

'As I recall, the camera shows Mr Mason on his mobile phone filming the incident, sir.'

'The recording shows Mr Massie at the rear of your car as you reverse it towards him. Do you accept this?'

'Yes.'

'Is there a reason you were reversing towards him at high speed?'

'I was reversing the car to leave his property. He may have been trying to prevent me from doing so, but that is just my speculation. I believed my car did not strike him,' he paused, 'Sir.'

'Mr Baxter, do you accept that the front camera of your car shows Mr Massie prone on the ground as you reverse away from his body?'

'Yes. This is a view I did not see at the time as I was looking behind me while I was reversing.'

'Mr Baxter, various pieces of fabric from Mr Massie's clothing along with blood and tissue which have been identified as his were found under your car when it was eventually stopped. Do you accept that Mr Massie was dragged under your car?'

'That may or may not have been the case. I was certainly unaware of it at that time.'

'Mr Baxter, fragments of glass which have been identified as coming from the rear light of your car were found on Mr Massie's driveway. When your car was stopped by the police, your car's rear bumper was partly detached from the bodywork, both of which items of damage indicate that your car had suffered an impact at the rear. Mr Massie's blood was found on the partly detached bumper. Mr Baxter, the damage suggests that this is an impact you would have heard and felt. Is this correct?'

'It may be that I should have heard it, but I did not, sir. The car is well-insulated from road noises, and I had the car sound system on at the time. I believe the bumper was damaged while the car was parked in central London earlier that day.'

'What are your feelings towards Mr Massie and Mr Mason?'

'I hardly knew either of them. One is a former classmate. The other is a former teacher.'

'Can you tell the Court, Mr Baxter, why you visited them that evening?'

'It was a brief stop. I was in the area.'

'Would you describe your interaction as friendly?'

'It was purposeful.'

'When you use the word 'purposeful', this assumes that there was a purpose rather than just a sudden inclination because you were in the area, as you have just stated. Was there a purpose?'

'While I there, I may have happened to remark that I did not approve of their relationship.'

'What did you think was relevant in your approving or not approving of any relationship they might have?'

'It's not right for a boy and his teacher to have a relationship. That's what I thought then, and that's what I think now.'

'That they are now both in middle age does not, in your opinion, remove any impropriety?'

'No. The teacher and the pupil met in a privileged position. The teacher was not allowed to develop a relationship with him. He developed a relationship with him. He is a teacher having sex with one of his pupils. Disgusting.'

'Where do these words come from, Mr Baxter? You show a considerable knowledge of the legal situation.'

'Just what I think, sir.'

'Let me play you a recording, Mr Baxter. It was found on a device located in Mr Mason's car. It is a conversation that he and Mr Massie had last year while sitting in their car near the property of a Ms Frances McAllister.'

There was a brief pause while the clerk switched on the recording apparatus.

'You and I met in a privileged position. I was not allowed to develop a relationship with you. I have developed a relationship with you. That's the blunt and, OK, yes, too blunt, distorted truth. I am a teacher having sex with one of my pupils. That's something I have to live with, and sometimes it's really tough. Oh yes, anyone who has a mind to can really drag me over the coals.'

'Almost word for word, Mr Baxter. Have you heard the recording?'

'No, sir.'

'Did you commission the recording?'

'No, sir.'

'So this is just a coincidence, Mr Baxter?'

'It states the situation, sir.'

'And, Ms Frances McAllister. Are you acquainted with the lady?'

'No, sir.'

'Permit me to play the Court another recording, again found on the device discovered in Mr Mason's car – words spoken just a few minutes after the words just played:'

"McAllister. Aha. Have you come to a decision?'

'We'd like to proceed to the next step. Maybe you can tell us what this is.'

'On the assumption that there will be a baby each, we will need both of you to make a donation. This will be at a London clinic. I'll text you the address and the date of the appointment, which I shall make on your behalf. The timing is important as there will need to be abstinence for three days prior to the donation. This is so that the quality will be optimal. If I can make the appointment for this Thursday, the abstinence can start now, so I suggest you assume that Thursday will be the day. Is this OK with you?"

'Are you aware of the connection between Frances McAllister and a clinic operating in London specialising in the illegal procurement of surrogate babies?'

'That is the first I have heard of it, sir.'

'Are you the listed by Companies House as the owner of a firm called 'Covipale', Mr Baxter?'

'I am.'

'This the same 'Covipale' that lists as one of its directors a Ms Frances McAllister. May I ask again, Mr Baxter, are you acquainted with Mrs Frances McAllister.'

'No, sir. You must understand that I have many interests, and I do not know who is connected with every company I own.'

'Every company, Mr Baxter? Companies Houses lists you as owning just the one – 'Covipale'.'

'I have many commercial interests. Not all are documented, sir. I am a busy man.'

'Do you know that a director of the company you own is Mrs Frances McAllister?'

'First I've heard of it.'

'The company minutes read that you appointed her. Are the minutes false?'

'No recollection of it at all.'

Chapter 48

'No recollection at all.'

Paul woke with a jolt. The small green digits in the corner of his eye read 04.04. On his other side, the soft breathing of his lover. The memory of his dream evaporated, as evanescent as a cloud. He knew it had been about the trial and shuddered at the thought of the event that had so devastated their lives. He turned on to his side, leaned over and, as he kissed the closed eyelids, a tear fell onto Jed's cheek. Jed stirred slightly and sighed contentedly, reaching for Paul's hand and squeezing it gently before succumbing to sleep once more. The tears came more readily to Paul now, streaming down his cheeks, wanting to express themselves in sobs, but checked by his determination not to let Jed know what was happening inside him.

In the bed was the centre of his world, his only love; the person who mattered more than his own life; the one who had captured him, body and soul, and from whom he could never be parted; the one whose touch sent electricity through his body; the one who knew him inside out.

Except that now he didn't.

He couldn't let Jed know how he felt, to realise that he couldn't respond as he had, that however much he longed for Jed's touch, it repelled him.

He tried to expunge the image from his brain. He knew it was destructive. The awfulness dominated his waking thoughts and now his dreams. There was Jed, trusting and open, lying by his side. All he had to do was unbutton him, and Jed would be his, willingly, lovingly. The picture remained in Paul's mind's eye. Jed open, receptive. And twelve years old.

There was the blond boy he used to teach, the school shirt, the short grey trousers. Paul pushed the image out of his conscious mind. It was disgusting, perverted. Jed was a grown man. It was not what the media broadcast in simplistic headlines. Teacher plus schoolboy plus relationship, and the rest of the prosody wrote itself. The decades between were easily glossed over.

Why did he feel guilt? He was guilty of nothing. That's what his rational mind told him over and over, but he had now worked himself up into a state of doubt that maybe, just maybe, he had wanted Jed from when he was twelve. Then again, how did he remember Jed? It was only the long photograph of the whole school from way back with its tiny faces that had brought him back into mind when he had contacted him. He had liked Jed. He was bright, chatty and teachable, but that's where it ended. He had never harboured any such thoughts of his pupils, not that he had to push any back. They simply had not existed. No, he was guilty of nothing. So why did he feel it? This was brainsickly nonsense. Jed must never know. He turned back to his sleeping partner. The eyes were open.

Jed took in the tear-stained face and smiled. 'Did you really think I didn't know?' He paused and sighed. 'Of course, I know. I know you, Paul Mason, maybe better than you know yourself. I know every pore, nerve-ending and muscle. I know how you are and how you respond. I touch you, and things happen. When they don't happen, I know it's not me. So it doesn't take a genius to know that it's you, and it's in your head. Nowhere else. Just up there. It's all the innuendoes and nods and winks from people you have never met and never will; people who don't have any idea about you and don't care; newspapers that the next day will be cat litter tray liners – all of this is nonsense. I can't imagine you want it in you, so let's try to get it out.'

He took Paul's hand. 'Is this a twelve-year-old? Or this? Or this? Of course not. This is a grown man. And this is a grown man who loves you and who wouldn't wish his life to be in the arms of anyone else. And the unspoken things. They're unspoken because we know each other. You said it to me when I was a boy. Do you remember? You said, 'You know that I know, and I know that you know I know. We're knowledgeable people,' and we should have trusted each other then. This – us - wouldn't have happened, though, and if it's the price I had to pay to get to this point in our lives, I'd go through it again. It happened, and we happened. We know everything without saying anything. You haven't entered me. We haven't spoken about it, but both of us understand that this isn't what we want. You know you can, and I know you know you can, and we both know that neither of us will. This is why it's all so perfect. We can speak through touch. When you're ready, I'll know it.'

'All very logical,' Paul sat up. 'But right now, I'm not. All this just feels wrong. What are we doing? I shouldn't be doing this. I shouldn't be here with you. I shouldn't be encouraging you.'

'Listen to yourself. You're going back to the 1960s and conventional morality. Back also to Clause 28 and the Thatcher days and children, as she put it, 'being taught that they have an inalienable right to be gay.' Well, they did; they do. People have proved this. Society hasn't collapsed. It's like being right-handed or left-handed – or ambidextrous. You are, or you aren't. We are. For Christ's sake, this may not be a joy to those who think the fifties was a golden age when people didn't lock their doors and all was sweetness. Rubbish. It was a time when people had precious little to steal and were kept in check by the authorities using guilt and shame. It was a vicious period. You know it. You've told me what you think about it, and now you can see how huge its power was, as even now, you're being consumed by it.

Let's say I wouldn't have been like this if I hadn't been raped all those years ago. So what? I'm happy now. And let's reverse it and imagine I'd turned out 'normal'. Would I have been happier? Who's to say? This is reality, not pie-in-the-sky happiness or unhappiness. You haven't turned me or whatever ideas the media have tried to put into some people's heads. I jumped on you, didn't I? I don't remember you pushing me off. We knew what we liked, and we still do. Do you really want to try not being together and see how it goes; see if we both become normal? That's where your thinking goes, and it's a desolate place that lies at the end of that path.'

'But–'

'No 'buts'. Anyway, the media has far more than us to amuse itself with now.'

'Careless driving. What a let-down. But – don't stop me, you'll like this 'but' – without this, there'd have been no investigation into McAllister which led to Brookfield, which is leading to God knows what. Ministerial resignations, questions in Parliament, shake-ups in the church. We knew it was big. It's enormous.'

'Good. Now you're starting to get real. We shot this shaft into the air, and it's taken out far more than we hoped. What hits us is collateral. We have to be pragmatic and see it like this. It isn't all going to go in the way we hoped, but the end product certainly will be the end of Brookfield, and a raking light shone into the slimy depths he inhabited.'

'No more 'saucy doubts and fears,' then. I need you to bring me back. We also need to make contact with Frances. I don't fancy her outfit spreading our seed around. Now that we're up, we may as well start.'

Chapter 49

'No COV 1P this time,' Paul's eyes had scoured the ranks of luxury cars. 'No brass plate either. Oh, thanks,' He smiled at the woman exiting the building who held the door open for them.

The scene upstairs was that of a moving-in day. The signwriter was applying a logo to the door. A man inside was moving files from cardboard boxes into a filing cabinet.

'You don't happen to have a forwarding address for the previous tenants, do you?'

'Sorry, no. Seems they left in quite a hurry. Quite a bit of mess to throw out. Small price to pay for a set of furnished offices in this part of town, though. Stroke of luck to find them.'

'It's just that we did some business with these people, and we left a couple of things with them for safekeeping, and now they've done a runner.'

'If they didn't take them when they left, I imagine we'll already have thrown them out. Sorry.'

Jed seized the initiative. 'They were a medical practice, and we left specimens with them. I imagine they would have been kept in a fridge or freezer. I think it may have been in the room through that door. Is there a fridge in there?'

'We've made it into our kitchen now. Yes, there's a huge cabinet that looks like some industrial fridge-freezer. Take a look.'

The man indicated that they could open the door.

It was almost untouched. The big TV screen remained in situ. The rest of the kitchen looked as they remembered it. They tried the cabinet. It was locked.

Paul squinted into the area between it and the wall and could see nothing. He turned on the flash on his phone and put it into the aperture.

'There's a lead and what looks like a socket.'

Jed addressed the man in the other office. 'Have you opened the big cabinet in here? Is it a freezer? Was the electricity on when you took possession?'

Momentarily thrown by the triple barrage, he paused. 'No, maybe, and yes.'

Jed then tried to remember the questions he had asked. 'So why haven't you opened it?'

'Can't find a key.'

'What do you want to do, Paul? Do we just ask them to throw away whatever they find inside when they force it open? Do we encourage them to find a professional who can open it without damaging the seal? Do we ask them if we can take away what may be inside and may have our names on it? How do we take it away? What do we do with it?'

'If I may interrupt, gentlemen? The man in the other office held up his hand to stop further discussion. 'The police forensic team will be here tomorrow to open it. They seem to have taken an interest in this suite. We were asked to leave it alone. They also asked us not to throw anything else out. That small filing cabinet over there is still stuffed with papers.'

'They asked you not to touch the big cabinet and not to throw anything else out. Is this precisely what they asked you to do and not to do?'

'Yes.'

'In those words? Paul was insistent.

'Yes. More or less.'

'Was it more or was it less? Hang on, did they ask you to leave the filing cabinet alone or just not to throw anything out?'

'It's just the big, locked cabinet they asked us not to touch.'

'Good,' Paul opened the small cabinet and looked at the labels on top of each file. They were alphabetised. 'We're not throwing anything out. We're just looking.'

The man didn't appear convinced. 'Not sure they'd approve.'

'Well, then. What the eye doesn't see, the heart doesn't grieve about.'

His eyes focussed on the 'M's. 'Massie', 'Mason', 'McAllister'. We're all here. Have you a copier we can use?'

'Waiting for the maintenance people to fix it.'

'God, it's just like thirty-five years ago. We'll use our phones. You take 'Massie' and 'Mason'. I'll take 'McAllister'. Check the backs, too.'

Their phones clicked on each sheet.

'Do you mind if we have a look at what we've just photographed, in case we need to snap other files?'

'In for a penny.' The man seemed reconciled to his uninvited guests being around for a while. 'I'm Henry, by the way.'

'Thanks, Henry. You don't know how personal this is to us.'

'I may have an idea, though.' Henry seemed suddenly just a touch smug. 'Three or four girls have come here in the last couple of days since we moved in and seemed quite annoyed that the people they'd come to see weren't here. They were young girls. Kids. All foreign and with what seemed like eastern European accents. Was this some sort of knocking shop?'

Paul looked up from the file. 'From what I see here, it may very well have been. At one remove, though. Jed, there are papers relating to a 'Besjana' in my file.'

'And a 'Lule' in mine.'

'There's a date of birth. Oh, no. That girl is a child of 15.'

'The one in mine's 15, too.'

Jed stood up and spoke to Henry. 'I'm just going to vomit in the room next door. I shall clear everything up.'

'Do you recognise these?' Paul held up photographs.

'Could be. Didn't have my glasses on, but I think these are the kids who came here. What's been going on then?'

'It looks as if these girls were going to be inseminated.'

'With…'

'Yes, Henry. What whatever may still be in that cabinet. Or it may not be if others have already been inseminated. Or others may have been, and the leftovers may still be there. Sorry, if you were going to use it as your kitchen fridge.'

'Is your jizz in there?'

'I hope so. And Jed's. But we cleaned it off the floor before we left.'

'When your friend's finished, I think I'll go in there to throw up.'

'Sorry, Henry. I couldn't resist it. You never know what has happened in premises before you move in, but I'm afraid that this one has a sordid history. You might ask for a rent reduction. I rather think it may hit the headlines.'

Henry groaned quietly.

'What business are you in?'

'Religious publications.'

Chapter 50

'Shame. I was rather getting used to the idea of ED 344.'

'Jed, you know as well as I do that any babies would have one of those girls Henry saw as the mother. I don't imagine ED 344 even knows that her photo is being used to recruit people like us. Aha, it looks as if she's in.'

They were in front of Frances McAllister's house. A shadowy form could be seen through the obscured glass.

A woman answered the door. She sounded mildly irritated. 'Yes?'

'We've come to see Frances,' Paul said.

'You're the umpteenth person who's shown up here asking for her. Frances, Mrs McAllister, no longer lives here. We bought the house and moved in last week. The agent said the previous owner moved suddenly.'

'The agent didn't say where, I suppose.'

'Didn't know, but I've done some asking around. Seems she's in witness protection and won't be contactable again. This is just the local gossip, but from what I've heard, I can well believe it.'

'May we ask what you've heard?'

'Nothing specific, but she was somehow connected with that big human trafficking case in the news now. Seems she's turned Queen's evidence and is ratting on the man they arrested. What was his name, Bookend?'

'Brookfield.'

'That's the one. Nasty business. But haven't I seen you before? Aren't you two of them?'

'No, we're on the other side. We started the investigation.'

'Well, I can't be doing with this sort of thing. I'll bid you good day.'

'Just one thing before we go. Do you garden?'

Paul shared the woman's surprise at the question. She repeated as if for clarity. 'Do I garden? Do I do gardening? Yes. I love it.'

'I'm pretty sure that your predecessor here buried something in the garden, or maybe in the house. Probably in the garden as it was deep. I have no idea what, but it was just something she said. Perhaps part of the garden looks disturbed as if something's been taken out of it, or put into it. If you could have a look, that'd be great. I suppose we could mention it to the police, but you know what they're like. They'd excavate it all. Shame to lose all this landscaping. You'd be left with a barren wasteland. Just a thought - if I dial my number from your phone, you'll have me and I'll have you. Jed Massie's the name. And yours?'

'Candice. Candice Rutherford.'

Jed's phone rang briefly, and he tapped in the name.

'Thanks. Look, don't worry, we're not stalkers. If we'd had the choice, we wouldn't be having to do with this sort of thing either, but these people have gone around wrecking lives and need to be stopped. I hope you'll see it like this.'

Candice looked him straight in the eye. 'You mean business, don't you?'

'When your life's been turned around, your childhood taken away from you, and you've been raped, yes, I would say that makes you mean business.'

'I'll start looking tomorrow when it's light and call you if I find anything. OK?'

'That's all we're asking.'

'You can come in if you like. I'm sorry I was abrupt.'

'Thank you, but I just want to get into the car. I'm going to cry and need to let it all out with Paul here, so I'll bid you goodbye.'

Jed turned and ran to the car in the roadway.

Paul reached for the app on his phone and unlocked it. Candice took his hand and squeezed it.

'I hope you'll be strong.'

'I shall. Sorry to have brought this into your life. I need to go.'

Paul ran down the drive.

'I thought you'd be in floods. What was that?'

Jed looked into the middle distance past the house and beyond it. 'When something significant happens, like someone vanishing as Frances McAllister has, you go back over every last detail. That's what I was doing when we were standing there. I was re-living the conversations we had. She was always to the point, you know. Didn't waste words. There was hardly any small talk apart from the usual politenesses. That had always been a characteristic of hers. Thinking about it now, I have to say it made her a good teacher. You were aware that she was in control. She was the one who steered the conversation in whichever direction she wanted; structured without being terse. The impression she gave out was that of a strong-willed woman, with no self-doubt, who knew what she was doing.

'I didn't notice at the time, but there was just one moment when she was reflective, uncharacteristically so, and said something, not to us, but to herself. I can't remember the exact words, but she looked way out into the garden and mentioned 'secrets' being 'buried'. I mean, she had so many secrets that her head must have been full of buried ones, but now that I bring it to mind, this felt different, and I wonder if she may have physically buried something. It was in the context of Brookfield and his usefulness. Maybe she has something on him that she could use to protect herself against him. If so, she may have taken it with her, or it could still be there for use later on. Or it may be my imagination running wild. I think I'll have that cry now.'

Jed pulled a tissue from his pocket and then thought better of it.

'On the other hand, I won't. I've got nothing to cry about. Maybe Frances' confidence is rubbing off onto me. Yes. My childhood was taken, and yes, I was raped, and we've had our semen stolen and are having to deal with the most horrible aspects of human nature, but I'm actually incredibly happy. Or is all this driving me mad? No, here we are, and we're the lucky ones. John Lennon was right.'

Paul shivered. 'Someone walking over my grave. You know, that's exactly what I thought when I overcame one of my moments of self-doubt about you and being twelve and all that. His words came to me. They are so simple. Love is all you need. I must drill it into my head. He was so right.'

'And Duane Michals. That photo. Remember? The boy with the skull. 'All things mellow in the mind."

"And even our great love will fade."

''Soon we'll be strangers in the grave."

'So let's hold tight and touch and feel. For this quick instant we are real,' Oh yes, I remember when we looked at that.'

'OK,' said Jed, 'I think I'll have that cry now, after all.'

Chapter 51

Hugh was quite straightforward. 'You won't be given a running commentary on how the investigation's going. In fact,' he leaned back in his chair, 'your part in all this is more or less over. I know what you're thinking: had it not been for us, none of this would be happening, and it's true. One thing led to another, and here we are. And here's our waiter. No, the chateaubriand's over there.'

He turned to Paul and, in an undertone, added, 'A sign of a really good restaurant is that the waiter knows who has ordered what. That this one doesn't will be reflected in the tip.'

'Look, Hugh, if Jed hadn't gone under the wheels of David Baxter's car, he's never have ended up in the witness box, and the business with Frances McAllister and Brookfield wouldn't have come to light. I think that's what you mean.'

'If your frustration is that they aren't involving you in investigating the crimes, just get over it. This is a big case with plenty of powerful people involved. That little spat you had with the media about your being a predatory teacher who had his eyes on little Jed right from the start was just their way of telling you to keep your distance. You've got targets on your backs, both of you. You've disrupted the lives of people who could buy and sell all three of us in a morning and who aren't used to people telling them they can't have something.'

'Well, they – whoever they are – have millions of our sperm, so I rather think we are involved – and more than most.'

'Not sure that those sperm of yours have any rights, I'm afraid.' Hugh was trying not to be patronising. 'You won't be expected to pay child support if any of them succeeding in fertilising an egg. Anyway, you can make more.'

'And if we don't like the idea of hundreds of mini versions of us across the globe?'

'Unless the police can recover the samples, it's an idea you can either get out of your heads or just accept. That freezer in the office building was empty, you know. Chances are that unless the samples were kept in controlled conditions, they'd be useless. Don't get all mawkish over murdered sperm, please. You kill them all the time.'

Hugh was, of course, right. Paul realised that he had been romanticising over them and of his possible chance of parenthood. That it might have been unwittingly with a child having a child made the situation repulsive, and he doubted that he would ever become a dad. His eye deliberately ranged around the restaurant, taking in several tables with families. He concentrated his mind and pictured himself being at such a table with his own. The picture would not form. Did he yearn for this, want this, need this? Would it be right for him, for them? He felt nothing. Had the mechanics of the failed effort dissuaded him, or was there really no drive to make this happen? Should he externalise his doubts? Would he change his mind if he knew that the other person in this process had other views? Should he change his mind if the passion was not there?

'Don't you think so, Paul?' Hugh was asking.

'What?'

'I was saying that Voltaire had the right idea.'

'And what was that idea?'

'*Il faut cultivar notre jardin*. You've done your bit for other people. If you get to a point at which you can't do more, you can take time out to do what you want.'

'Unless doing what I want is exactly that.'

'You can't live your life through other people, Paul. That's getting towards your needing them more than you think they need you. You've helped open people's eyes to the excesses that have become ingrained in our society. You risk being consumed by these very excesses yourself. Time to back out, I would say.'

'You know, Hugh,' Jed reflected, 'you've put your finger right on it. We need to see how jardin cultivation has been going. I know it's bad form to use the mobile at the table, but bear with me while I send a quick text to a new friend.'

Candice's reply was instant. 'Nothing yet.'

'Who's your new friend?' Hugh asked.

'The lady who bought Frances' house, Candice Rutherford. We visited her. She's nice.'

'Just drop it,' Hugh insisted. 'Frances McAllister has vanished into the protection system. It's obvious she's seen as a valuable source of information, and you can't prejudice this by trying to find her. She could be in Australia for all you know. These people just disappear and take on new identities.'

Back in the car, Jed had his doubts. 'From all I know of Frances, I have the feeling that she would have agreed to a new life only if the threat to her existing one were to have been a long stretch in prison. I'm not sure her heart's in it. That remark she made wasn't a throwaway. I'm sure of it. That's not her style. She wanted to put an idea into our heads. She'll bide her time, and then she'll make a move. I don't think it's anything for our benefit. There's something she wants from us. You'll see if I'm right.'

'I'm not sure she likes you. You were quite unbending with her.'

'No, but she feels comfortable with you. She has the upper hand. There you are, full of morality and self-questioning, and there she is – sure-footed and ruthless.'

'I don't think we should do it.'

'We won't have a choice. She'll make her move, and then we'll know.'

'No. I mean babies.'

'Aha. You looked at all the families in the restaurant and thought this wasn't for you. I knew that was your moment of inattention. I can read you. You're right. They're not for you.'

'So?'

'Then they're not for me. It was a silly pipe dream. Selfish and unrealistic. We may have families all over the world for all we know. Let's leave it at that.'

Chapter 52

'Mr Massie said you'd make contact.'

'He's bright, your friend. Good-looking, too. Maybe I should have cultivated him while I had the chance. Might have turned him.'

Paul was at the supermarket. He steered his trolley into an aisle that looked less populated and assumed an interest in chutney. The screen on his phone read 'Unknown'.

'Glad you didn't, Frances. Yes, he's the sensitive one, and he picked up on something you said *en passant*, only he didn't think you did '*en passant*'.'

'He's right. I like him more and more. If you get tired of him, let me know. Oh, actually, you can't. Frances McAllister doesn't exist anymore. She's now someone else entirely, and no one can know who or where she is. Frances has given up everything – yes, family, the lot. I imagine Mr Massie has discussed this with you and come to the conclusion that she would only do this if the alternative were unthinkable.'

'Spot on.'

'It would have been. Frances has been ever such a naughty girl in her previous existence. Never malicious, mind you. I really – and this is the God's honest truth, Paul – really had no idea that the clinic was using children. As soon as I found out, I got them to destroy the deposits you'd left, along with everyone else's. And, for what it's worth, I'm mortified about the Poynton business. If I could turn back time – I'd be like Tina Turner - but I mean it. You blindsided me with that one.'

'I think you'll find it was Cher, but I hope I can believe you. We've been feeling so powerless about what we left. You can't imagine.'

'I stand corrected. Thank you. I don't think I've lied to you. Not knowingly anyway. I've always had respect for you. Never even thought of making a move. You were too virginal. 'Purity Paul', they used to call you in the staff common room. Or 'Mason the Monk'. You were just too good. This isn't in contrast to the others, most of whom were simply evil, but you had the children's interests at heart; you were principled and, well, just too good for that place. I know you and the chaplain raised welfare issues at every staff meeting and were knocked back every time. Even your successor, Patrick Warburton, tried.

'Kempson was an excrescence, and the life Braine had with him was wretched. You tried. I'm sure Nick Boyce would be alive today if they'd listened to you. Poor kid. Patrick Warburton had a breakdown because of what he saw. That other boy, too. The one who ran away and must have died. Can't remember his name. That place should have been exposed years before, and I should have done it myself. It's spawned more awfulness than anyone can imagine, and I want to help put it right.'

'Come off it, Frances, if I was 'too good for that place,' how about the children? Weren't they too good to be in it? You knew what was going on. You were part of what was going on. Yes, of course, you should have acted. Knowing and not acting was criminal. Then there are your criminal acts. Sexual assault being one.'

'If this is your way of saying you can't forgive me, I understand. You can't and shouldn't. I have to live with myself, though, and I will change. I'll have to anyway. This is the reason for contacting you. What I'm doing must remain a secret. OK, you say, why should I keep a secret for that woman? Let me tell you the reason. I can give you information that will nail Brookfield and his masters. Yes, Brookfield isn't the big cheese. He thinks he is, but he isn't. He'll be stopped, but there are others he corrupted who are now more corrupt than he is. What you saw with the children being lined up to be surrogate mothers at 15 is just part of it. There is trafficking on an industrial scale. There's slavery and worse. What I can give you will identify others in this business. I had the feeling that I should have some ammunition in my weaponry, and I stored it up for years just in case. I thought it might come in handy, and here we are.'

'I gather there's material to be found.'

'Except that you won't find it in the garden. Candice is looking in vain. Oh yes, I know about your visit. It's the doorbell, you see. It's one of those where you're always in – even when you're out. I heard it ring, she opened the door and there you all were having a conversation. Sweet. Mr Massie is dying to get his hands on whatever it is. Maybe, it's just a USB with incriminating material. Maybe it's something in the cloud or another backup service. It's so easy to hide things these days.'

'I have the feeling you're about to tell me it's more than something virtual.'

'Oh yes. For years, I've been connected to Brookfield's liaisons. A go-between, you see. A trusted older female figure. I'd tell all his conquests to bring me souvenirs to protect themselves. It was more to protect me, but they never quite got that. Each of them had a miniature recorder for video and sound. I also gave them new white briefs. They were told to keep them on until the last moment and not to wear them afterwards. A small sealable plastic bag preserved the evidence. A larger sealed bag preserved each encounter. Video and DNA identifying each punter and documentary evidence linking each punter to Brookfield or one of his masters.'

'Useful material. So where is it?'

'Now that really would be telling, wouldn't it? Can I sense an element of salivation at the thought?'

'Well, Frances, clearly you're going to lay out your conditions for telling me, aren't you? I have to say you're always, how shall I say? - upbeat.'

'That's the only way I can live with being me, Paul. I know I'm self-serving and amoral. I know that I have precious few scruples, but I propose to change all that and remarry. Yes, remarry.'

'Lucky man.'

'Do I detect a note of gentle irony in your voice, Paul?'

'How ever did you guess?'

'I must be blessed that way. Actually, it's someone you know.'

'Oh. Who?'

Grant. Grant Baxter.'

'He never mentioned it to me.'

No. He wouldn't. He doesn't know.'

Paul had no idea how to take this conversation further.

'What can I say?'

'Absolutely nothing. Just listen. I have ceased to exist. My life is over - except that it isn't. My new me is all I have, and I'm a clean sheet. I'd like a relationship. Sure, Grant was young when I had him and, of course, you never forget your first time. It was his. It was also my first at being unfaithful, and it was great. He was a wonderful lover. I want that back. And I want you to engineer it.'

'How on earth would I do that?'

'That's progress, Paul. You say 'how', not 'why'. I will come to your home, and I will meet him there. You will have told him nothing. I will sweep him off his feet, and he will disappear with me to be reborn as Mr X. And I will tell you where to find the material. Like Hannibal.'

'Hannibal?'

'Sure. When he crossed the Alps, Hannibal told his men: 'I have two pieces of news. Do you want the good news first, or the bad news? The man all shouted, 'Give us the bad news.' Hannibal said, 'We're out of food. There's only camel dung to eat.' The men all shouted, 'Give us the good news.' Hannibal replied, 'There's plenty of it.'

'So there's plenty of material. Good. And you'll tell us when you meet Grant.'

'Yes.'

'And if Grant doesn't want to disappear with you?'

'You'll get the coordinates. I'll take the chance. Deal?'

Chapter 53

'I didn't know if I ought to speak to you, or if you'd want to have anything to do with me ever again.'

'Nor did we,' Jed said, sounding reassuring. 'He's your brother, after all.'

'He tried to kill you.'

'Not what the Court said. Careless driving. Your brother was very careless.'

'He was also very guilty. I can't imagine how he got away with it.'

'Not sure that he did,' Paul interjected. 'He's going to go down for far worse than even attempted murder. How do you feel about the investigations, Grant?'

'You know I haven't seen or spoken to him for more than thirty years. I haven't got a brother. I have no feelings for him. Whatever he gets, he deserves.'

'So blood isn't thicker than water?'

'So far as he's concerned, there's ice in my veins, not water.'

'And,' Paul ventured cautiously down another route, 'is there anyone in your life now?'

Grant laughed mirthlessly. 'I live the life of a monk.'

Jed ventured further. 'No sex then?'

'Not with anyone else, no.'

'You see,' said Paul, 'it's just that there is someone who wants to meet you, and we've arranged it. You don't have to, of course; you're a grown man and can do what you want.'

'What's this? A blind date?'

'Not at all. She's someone you know. Intimately.'

'That narrows the field. I haven't known anyone intimately for years.'

'That's her.'

'Who?'

'Your number one.'

'You've lost me.'

'You lost your virginity to her.'

'Christ. Not Frances?'

'Yup. In about sixty seconds, she'll ring the doorbell. We'll let her in. She will give us a piece of paper, and we'll leave for one hour. When we return, it may be to an empty house.'

'What's this paper she'll give you?'

'The coordinates to information about the case that she's giving us in return for a re-introduction to you. She'll explain her idea. Everything is up to you.'

'You've set me up.'

'We have. The information she's giving us should protect youngsters from predators like Brookfield. The quid-pro-quo is a meeting with you. What you do is your choice. We get the information anyway. That's her.'

Frances was radiant.

'Yes, Paul. The devil wears Prada. Not original, but the line suits me. Good evening, Grant. One moment. I have to hand this over.'

Paul opened the folded paper. 'You know that we're going there immediately, don't you?'

'I'd expect nothing less. Fold down your back seat, ready. It's Hannibal time.'

'What?' said Grant.

Frances replied, 'I'll explain later. Thank you, boys. Sadly, we can never meet again.'

The door closed.

'What I'd give to be a fly on the wall.' Jed said.

'I'd rather not. Let's put this code into the sat-nav. Aha. It's a storage unit outside Reading. 22 minutes. We should do there and back in an hour. It's as if she planned it.'

Six large suitcases and nearly an hour later, they were back. Paul clicked open two of the cases.

'As she said, underwear, tapes and notes. Must be fifty different people in there. We'll keep the cases inside and not in the car, I think. I'm sure this stuff is dynamite.'

'At least the dynamite from those two hasn't flattened the house,' said Jed. 'It's still standing. The lights are on. I wonder if there's anyone home.'

The house was silent. Paul and Jed left the cases in the kitchen and checked the sitting room. No one.

'Paul, our bed's been slept in.'

'Maybe they had an hour of passion to see if they're compatible and off they've gone to wherever to be whoever.'

'Not really,' Grant approached from the bathroom. He was wearing Paul's dressing gown, and his hair was damp. 'Oh, the bed. Yes. Sorry about that. She wanted to have one last time with me. It was a disaster.'

'So, it didn't work?'

'No, Jed, I didn't work, if you catch my drift. I told her it couldn't happen, but she thought she could turn me.'

'Turn you? You don't need turning.'

'Oh, but I do, Paul. I do. I told you.'

'Told me what?'

'That I had the most enormous crush on you at school. I told you. I told you I still do.'

'I thought you were joking.'

'Wish I were. I know you're spoken for. The bed, yes. It's clean. I just had to shower her off me. Here's your dressing gown. I'll get dressed. Yes, she told me all about her vanishing and that she wanted me to vanish with her and that I was the best lover she's had, but I was a kid, a horny kid. I didn't know what I wanted. I thought I wanted you, but I didn't want to want you. I didn't want to be what I thought I was, so I tried to be someone else. It worked for a while, but only by thinking she was you when I was with her. I almost had myself convinced. Everything else was blotted out. I was normal. Hooray. Eventually, she became you, and I was great with that. She never suspected anything, and I convinced myself that I was a stud.

'Then came the stuff I did for Brookfield. That's OK, I thought, I'm doing this because it's a job, not because I like it. It all became just a job. Just something that made money. Plenty of money. I didn't look beyond that. It was a job I was good at. The first thing I was ever actually good at. People said I was good. I believed them. It didn't last, of course. Work started drying up. Demand for a 40-year-old gigolo isn't huge. I started to hate. No because of that, but because I knew what I'd become. First, I hated the people who did things to me.

Then Brookfield. Then myself. I couldn't even do myself in properly. But you know who I hated most of all? My brother. I can't say his name. He was no brother to me. He sold me. He was… I can't say it. He saw it all happening and just made it worse.'

Paul handed him a tissue.

'Thanks. So here I am. This is me. Not much, am I?'

Grant turned round. 'Just like the first time you met me, Jed. Except for the scars. Don't either of you fancy me even a tiny bit?'

'Get dressed, Grant.' Jed spoke gently and held out his hand. 'We're your friends.'

Chapter 54

Paul put down his book and glanced at the clock. He had been reading for three hours. There had been no interruptions. He luxuriated in the silence of his study, a room he had created with this in mind. One of the few carpeted rooms in the house. The alcantara boudoir chair held him in such comfort that he hardly noticed the passage of time. Reading, learning, he hardly missed the teaching. He had never taught again after leaving Finchingham. He just felt sorry that all children would lose their innocence one day. He smiled to himself. He was a latter-day Catcher in the Rye. How silly; how idealistic. Maybe that's why he kept his innocence until he realised that he wanted, not to lose it, but to develop it into experience. That it all happened in a matter of minutes in a hotel room was not in his plans, but sometimes things just happen. Things like happiness. He thought he had known it, but he hadn't. He had never known love until he fell into it. So now, he thought, I am happy and in love. For all I know, that's what many people are, so there's perhaps no need for a Catcher in or out of the rye.

Someone in love, he thought, feels an inner beauty. No need for it to be observable. It has relevance only for those in love with each other. His love was pure. He knew this and treasured the knowledge. It was enough. He needed no one's approval. His days of doubting were, he decided, a reaction against his happiness, so unaccustomed was he to it. Now he accepted it, embraced it, let it become him - so much so that he knew it could never be shaken. No matter what, he had known perfect joy.

'Brookfield's gone down.' Jed shouted from afar. 'It's on TV. Fourteen years. Doubt if he'll be coming out.'

A few months ago, he'd have been celebrating. Not now. He had done his bit to right wrong, or at least put a number of wrong-doers where they wouldn't be able to harm children for a long while. He had 'supped full with horrors.' He knew this. He understood that what he had known could be corrosive and that it had to be shut away in a locked section of his brain. He was fully aware what happened to the Macbeths. He decided that he would see it all as a story with a beginning and an end. He would gloss over the middle.

'Great!' he shouted back to Jed. '*Es ist zu Ende.*' It sounded more final in German.

That, then, was that. He and Jed, now married, happy, in love - and childless – with no mission dominating their lives. The question of children had never arisen since Jed had answered 'then they're not for me', so perfect was their accord. At their wedding, Paul reminded him of E.E. Cummings' line in 'How Town' - 'someones married their everyones' - and told the guests that 'only the snow can begin to explain' which didn't explain anything and had itself to be explained. Jed had smiled broadly and nodded in agreement.

Paul emerged from his study and ruffled Jed's hair gently. 'So here we are.'

'And there they are. So far from our way of being that they could be out of the heliosphere which is why we shall never mention them again. *'In Momenten reiner Klarheit segnen wir die Dunkelheit dafür, uns die Mittel anzubieten um zu Verstehen, wer wir wirklich sind.'* It just comes to my mind and is so true.'

'Yes, Jed. At least that's not a cliché. People keep telling me that what has been good for us has come out of evil, that every cloud, et cetera, et cetera, but that sentence really has it nailed.'

'Maybe we should write the story.'

'That would mean going through it all again, so I feel we shall leave that to others.'

'And the media news programmes?'

'I suppose we'll have to. At least it'll give the '*Klarheit*' to others.'

'Our guests will be here shortly. I'll just check that everything is right with their room.'

'Life is full of surprises, *nicht wahr*? OK, Jed. I read your mind. No German and no 'Macbeth'. OK? But you can do a bit of E.E. Cummings.'

'And nothing about that place, or the investigation, or the trial, or the dramatis personae.'

'*Genau.*'

'Stop!'

'Aha. The bell invites me. It is a knell that summons thee…'

'No, it summons you to answer the door to our guests.'

Paul opened the door. 'Great to see you both. Come on in. Coats in here. We can take the bags out of the car later, unless you want to freshen up now. We've put you in the stateroom, of course. Tea? Coffee?'

'The problem I have,' Hugh said slowly, coffee cup in hand, 'is that I can have no idea how close to the soul forced violation comes. Those of us who have dealt with this professionally have seen them as violent assaults, but every single one of you – and, yes, you are the one I have come to understand best, Jed – has exhibited life-defining trauma and, in most cases, life-limiting trauma. I'm sure you and Paul have decided never to revisit these times, and my question is an intrusion for which I apologise, but as there are to be several trials in which I shall be prosecuting counsel, I feel I can ask for elucidation. I sense – no, I know, that the repercussions of the assault have defined your life ultimately positively, but initially disruptively.'

'We have, indeed, Paul and I, moved on, but part of this process is distilling raw experience into a narrative that can stand on its own. Paul had the issue to deal with of our relationship changing from that of professional distance to complete intimacy. We verbalised and rationalised it and then put it away. We haven't had to revisit that theme for years. Then there was my trauma. Did the event touch the essence of my being? Yes. What is the essence of my being? I don't know, but I've been there and felt it. I understood in a moment what shame and guilt were, and they remained with me for thirty-five years, removing from me the ability to fully engage with anyone. I simply didn't want anyone to see those feelings within me, let alone chance that similar feelings be aroused. If Paul hadn't existed for me before those feelings were engendered, I would never have trusted him enough to make contact. My head was at the point of exploding, so how I would be, I can't imagine, but not – in no way - as you see me now.'

'But you would go through it all again to be where you are now? Hugh asked.

'I would. Do I say this because, it having happened, there is no alternative? Maybe. Do I say it because it really wasn't so bad? No. I say it because I have been able to experience the two extremes – utter desolation and bliss. If I hadn't experienced the one, would I have experienced its opposite? I have no idea, but having experienced what came out of it, I would not wish not to have it within me.'

'You articulate these events with dexterity.'

'Yes, Hugh, we both do. I thank my mother. Paul thanks his university course. To have the vocabulary to do so concretises feelings. Vague feelings of loneliness, emptiness, desolation, hatred need to be externalised with precision before they be analysed and dealt with – at least that's my experience – and Paul's. We've been there, done that and don't need to do it again. At least we don't need to do the raw emotion bit. It's been verbalised, organised and compartmentalised. It's in its box, and we move on. Easy to say. Not easy to do, but we're there.'

'And,' Paul interjected, 'we're still discovering each other. We found that both of us did German as a subsidiary at university. We dabble in it from time to time. Jed got his from when he was a forces' child. It's much better than mine, so I'm working on it.'

'Makes a change from 'Macbeth', of course.'

'Such a drama. All life is there, I'd say.'

'Well, Hugh, how about your life? There's been quite a change.'

'Yes, I've had to declare a conflict of interest and hand over the case to another.'

'Is that really all we're going to get? Come off it; you can take your lawyer's wig off with us. How is that case going?'

'I am quite aware, Jed, that right from when we met, you have found my probity reassuring – and guaranteed. I shall not disappoint you now.'

'Surely, now that you're no longer connected to the case, you can bend a little?'

'I can only say that my connection to Frances McAllister was as much a surprise to me as it is to you.'

Chapter 55

‘Ah, Frances. We have such memories of her. She had it all organised – a new life, no prosecution and no one chasing her. Then she gave it all away.’

‘She did.’ Hugh shifted in his chair. ‘If there's another cup going, I can talk about her. That's not a problem. She is the poacher turned gamekeeper. Her conversion is truly Damascene. The information that she gave you implicated many more and verified much information the enquiry already had. She couldn't give up her family, it seems. Even if it's a matter of their visiting her in prison, she would see them. She sees what she did essentially as a service for people who needed it and whose lives were enriched by it; a sort of Mother Teresa of the IVF world. When she discovered that what she had set up had been hijacked by traffickers, she turned Queen's Evidence and spilled all the beans she could think of. Her evidence has been invaluable. What difference this will mean to the outcome for her, I have no idea, but it may be considerable.’

‘One of her plans came to nothing, though, and that may have tipped the balance, surely?’

‘Grant. Right on cue. We're just talking about your old flame. Had you agreed to go off with her, she may not have changed her mind, but you turned her down, and that was that. She became a reformed woman. And that's how you and I met. There you were discussing your connection with her, and we just clicked. Well, it was more than a click for me. Yes, I know I'm playing second fiddle here, but I do my best. Grant has been quite open about his affection for you, Paul. He realises that there's no chance, and here I am. It was a surprise for me. We don't have an interest in German in common, and I'm really not sure if we have anything in common, but we get on, don't we?'

'Seem to.'

'Your situation, Grant,' Hugh continued, 'is similar to Jed's and at the same time quite different.'

'How so?'

'Correct me if I'm wrong, but no one did anything to you that you didn't invite to happen. Yes, it was more than you thought and what happened was criminal, but it wasn't exactly forced on you, was it?'

'You mean I wasn't used?' Grant coloured, and his back stiffened. 'I just did what I wanted? No way. People were up me all the time. I did things that I look back on with revulsion. I was 17, and it was every day. It went on and on, and I saw no way out. No way to stop it happening. It became a way of life. I hated every moment, but knew no other moments. I was told I was useless at everything else. Told it so often I believed it.

'I was 17, and all I was good at was getting naked and erect at the command of grown men and a grown woman. Did it touch my soul? Did I know what my soul was? I doubt I had one. I was on autopilot. It was the same day after day. Did I know anything about what was right and what wasn't? Not a chance. The only influences I had around me were evil and self-serving. I was just used. Used for twenty years. And this is what I've become.

'The only people who have shown me any understanding and kindness are these two. Hugh, you are clever and have a way with words. You make it seem that you'll make everything right, but you haven't a clue about what has made me. You are gentle and undemanding, but I really don't feel I'm anything special, just someone who gives you what you want at the moment.'

'I didn't mean to underestimate what you went through. Please don't get me wrong.'

'But it's you who's gets me wrong, Hugh. You worked this out all on your own. You never asked me. You assumed you knew me. I know me. I may not dress it up in the language of psychology or philosophy, but I've lived me all my life, so I know how I feel. You could have had a conversation with me.'

'We're having a conversation now.'

'We're not. We're having an argument. At least I am. Maybe for you, it's just some speculation about who has really suffered more, Jed or Grant? And what's the nature of their suffering? How often were they abused? What's the difference between the abuse perpetrated on each of them? You are a lawyer, Hugh. You're clinical in your dissection. But you know, when you dissect something, you kill it.'

'I'm sorry, Paul – and Jed. I really had no idea this would happen.'

'Please, Hugh, don't apologise me away. I'm a living, feeling human being. I thought- I hoped that you'd appreciate me for what I am. I've hidden nothing from any of you. You all know what I'm not. There are so many things that I'm not, Hugh, that I'm bound to be a disappointment. Naked and erect are OK. The rest, not so good. Well, imagine me not naked and not erect, and that's the me I want to be appreciated for.'

'So, Grant, I'm not even second fiddle. Here you are with the people you want to be with, and you've pushed me aside.'

'You tell me what my situation is. Well, you don't. I tell you, and I just have. Sorry. Do you leave, or do I?'

'I think our hosts should decide.'

'Let's put it this way, Hugh. Grant has told us today and in the past about the damage done to him. We understand it and know how we can support him. I think you're the together person in this relationship. We'll be in touch, and maybe we can sort everything out.'

'You didn't even take my bags out of the car, Grant. I think you knew what you were doing.'

Hugh collected his coat and swept out. Again, Jed was reminded of Freeman's gown.

'Clothes can be such instruments of drama,' he observed.

'I didn't plan this,' Grant was insistent.

'Is it that with Paul and Hugh together, your preference might dictate your actions?'

'No, Paul, I know I'm barking up the wrong tree with you in that sense. I enjoy your company. Both of you. Hugh pontificates. He works me out but really doesn't understand what makes me tick. Which of us has been abused more, isn't the point. This isn't a competition.'

'I thought he was married.'

'He was. Children, too. She left him some years ago. He never told me why. I just took him at face value as a gent. He looked and touched. No more than that. He made no demands. I thought he wanted company. I assumed I was more than a walk on the wild side. Seems I'm just a bit of rough. What came across to me was his assumption that I'm not very bright, that he can explain to me who I am and why I am better than I can. Sorry. I hope I haven't spoiled the relationship you had with him.'

'He'll get over it. I imagine it's behind him already,' Paul said.

'I'd like to stay, if I may.'

'Of course.'

'I'm seeing Frances tomorrow, by the way.'

Chapter 56

'Of all the people I never expected to see again, you are first on the list, Frances. When Grant told us he was meeting you, I suggested here rather than some café as, quite frankly, Jed and I are fascinated by your volte-face. There you were, your new life arranged, no prosecution, I guess, and you threw it all away. If Grant had decided to take a chance and go with you, would you have gone?'

'Yes – and come back.'

Frances McAllister put down the mug of coffee and strolled around the kitchen, a lioness in a cage looking for keepers to stalk and eat. She wore a similar Prada outfit to their last meeting. She had clearly dressed for the occasion and meant business.

'That thing with the clinic. I had no idea. I used them on Brookfield's recommendation. They were your brother's business, Grant. It's babies. That's been my goal. First for me and then for other people. I know the emptiness of childlessness and the thought that I could make it possible for others to be spared - that is what motivated me. Yes, it became out of control and obsessive, but that's me, way over the top. When I knew what was happening with those surrogates, everything changed. It all had to stop. The blind eye I'd been turning to your brother's activities, Grant, and to Brookfield's had been forced open, and I took a trip to the police station.

'Everything came out, yes, including recording your conversations. Such a relief. Honesty for the first time since I was a child. Only the Poynton boy is still hidden. I couldn't expect anyone to cope with that dilemma. I agreed to go into witness protection. I saw only the positives and even toyed with the idea of running off with my children's father. You turned me down, but I think I'd already decided that I couldn't cut myself off from my family, so I told them that I'd given you a shedload of evidence they could use and hoped for the best. How this will turn out, I have no idea, but even if it's just that one special person will come and visit me in prison, it's worth it.'

'So what is it you want from us?'

'Nothing. That is that you do nothing with the information you have. I have told them about my arrangement with Grant's brother, and they have all they need on Brookfield and his ilk. So far as they are concerned, I'm changed.'

'A gamekeeper who was a poacher.'

'Aha, Hugh Kennedy has already got to you. I hear his voice. That's his phrase for me. He was very keen to get more out of me. Too keen, I gather, as his attempt to cultivate Grant for information led to his being removed from the case entirely. Sorry, Grant, he just used the methods that he thought would be most likely to succeed, helped perhaps by a hint or two from me in the course of conversation. I imagine the romance was whirlwind and unconsummated. I think he carried on after he was removed in the hope that what he found would rehabilitate him. He was cross with me anyway when his wife found out I was the source of the IVF arrangement with a surrogate who was not surgically implanted. So I finished him off, as it were.'

'Are there really any depths you won't stoop to?'

'It's all a matter of ends and means, isn't it? The ones justify the other. But now, I'm Mother Teresa, as Hugh called me, and I aim to stay that way.'

'So why on earth, Frances, should we help you?' Paul was in his self-righteous mode, Jed decided. He sensed that there would be a reason.

'You mean apart from helping an old friend?'

'I think that's stretching things, Frances, don't you?'

'Well, let me put it to Grant to see if I'm worth it. Now, as the father of your daughter, I think you should know that she is having a baby. That's the special person I mentioned. Hold off with the congratulations, though. It wasn't planned, and the father departed the scene before he knew, never, I hope, to return. My daughter had a fit last year, and she has now been diagnosed with GBM. To save you having to look it up, I can tell you that it's Glioblastoma Multiforme, an aggressive cancerous brain tumour. The prognosis is death within a year to eighteen months. Because of her pregnancy, she has declined any form of palliative treatment. She is relieved that she is predicted to survive until the birth, but only for a couple of months thereafter. Which leaves me quite possibly in prison and a baby with no relative as my other daughter is deceased and her children moved overseas years ago. Maybe you can already see where this is going? You two wanted a child. Here is Grant, who seems to be quite dependent on you who will soon have a dependent relative, if he wants one. It's a boy, by the way. He's due to be born in four months' time.'

She turned away from them, and her shoulders heaved.

The three men sat in a silence broken only by quiet sobbing.

'For God's sake, say something, someone. Please.'

'Christ!'

'Well, that's a start.'

'There's no one else?' Paul ventured a way out.

'No. My two grandchildren have become estranged from me. I have no idea where they are even. Not that I could palm the child off to people I don't know. There's no other relative. The alternative will be adoption. These are the bare facts. I won't sugar-coat them. That's not my style. Does my heart break at not being able to bring up my grandson? Well, use your imagination.'

'And your daughter. What does she think about this?'

'She has no idea what has been happening with me. I promised her I would look after the child. That's all she needs to know. Ever.'

'Does she want to meet me?' Grant uttered the words dispassionately.

'We've never discussed you. So far as she is aware, her father and I divorced when she was tiny, and he died shortly afterwards. It was simpler that way. This has been her life, and I see no reason to change her world.'

'And will she definitely die? Is there no hope?'

'The paralysis has already started. It will develop until she loses movement and then all control over her bodily functions. It's as bleak a diagnosis as is possible. Had she not been pregnant, she would have taken the route of assisted dying abroad. I would have flown there with her.'

Frances turned to face them.

'Look, I'm just about holding it together here. Tell me something, anything…'

Chapter 57

Jed sensed that this doorbell ring meant business. It held its note just a touch long and resonated insistence. At the door was a man in his thirties whom he didn't recognise.

'Yes?' Jed tried to adopt a neutral tone. The man's face suggested concern.

'You, Grant?' he said.

Although brief, the question was undemanding and almost a statement. 'Me, Tarzan. You Jane,' Jed thought and smiled internally.

'No,' Jed answered, again neutrally.

'I was given this as his address. Grant Baxter. Do you know him?'

'I do. What can I do for you?'

'Well, I need to speak to him.'

'If you let me have your name and number, I'll pass the message on.'

'But isn't he here?'

'Can you tell me what this is about?'

'It's personal.'

'OK. I'll tell him you dropped by.'

'I'm not just 'dropping by.' I really need to talk to him.'

'I'll tell him this as well. What's your name?'

'Harry. Harry Bowman. Tell him I know Denise.'

'Denise?'

'Denise. I think you know her mother, Mrs McAllister. I think he's my son's grandfather.'

Jed did a quick calculation of the relationships.

'Ah. Maybe you should come in. I'll just have a word and see if Grant can see you now. Please take a seat.'

He felt as if he were ushering a client into a waiting room. He hadn't seen himself as a bouncer before. Harry Bowman walked with the aid of a stick. He hoped Grant would agree to seeing him. He thought that a 'no' wouldn't be taken for an answer and wondered if the stick might have two purposes. Grant appeared.

'I was just changing a nappy. Maybe best not to shake hands.'

'I think you have my son here.'

'I have Denise's baby, my grandson. Yes. He lives here. I have custody.' The last point was emphasised assertively.

'I need to sit.' Harry Bowman lowered himself into the nearest chair. 'Frances did her best to distance me from him and succeeded in poisoning his mother against me, too. I can tell you that I've had quite a journey to get to this point. Quite a journey.'

'Frances can be quite determined when she had a mind to be. Yes, I can understand that. Let me make one thing quite clear, Mr Bowman. I have custody. This is all above board. I hope you haven't come to claim possession.'

'It's a little more complicated than that, Mr Baxter. If there's a cup of tea going, I'd be grateful.'

'No problem.' Jed assumed that anyone who asked for tea was at least half-way decent and that whatever was going to come out of this encounter was unlikely to result in fisticuffs. He disappeared into the kitchen.

'Look, let me make one thing clear, I've known Denise for many years. Her mother talks as if this was some one-night-stand. Not so. We go back at least a decade. She spoke little of her family. I was aware that her dad was dead and assumed she was estranged from her mother. Denise never mentioned her except to say that she ran a business. She talked generally in terms of import-export without going into details. Yes, I know now what she was dealing in, and it has shaken both of us.

'Denise had a seizure about a year ago. We thought nothing of it, but she was checked over, sent for tests, and then the full horror of her condition emerged. She knew that she was expecting and that any chemotherapy would only slow the progress of the tumour and that there was no cure. For the sake of the baby, she chose to do nothing. You can imagine that all of this knocked me for six psychologically, but also physically. My legs seemed to be letting me down. Denise made me take some tests, too. The diagnosis was frightening. Huntington's Chorea. Maybe you've heard of it.'

Jed and Grant looked at each other. Jed swallowed hard and answered in the affirmative.

'It's hereditary. Here's where the mystery is. Neither of my parents has any history of this in their family. Denise, of course, made contact with her mum and told her about both of us. From being a grey eminence in our lives, she was suddenly centre-stage. I'd imagined there would be sorrow, sympathy – maybe love. There was some of this for Denise, but for me, it was rage. She was furious. I was pushed out of Denise's life. Denise was in no state to protest. She just had to watch while this woman did her best to destroy me. She tried a protection order, accused me of abusing her daughter and, well, did all she could to erase me from her daughter's life. That's when she told her about you being her biological father. I'm really not sure how much she took in. Denise was doing all she could to keep the baby in. He was premature but healthy.'

'So, you've come to tell us about the Huntington's?'

'Yes. You need to be aware of the repercussions, but I've also come with a question.'

'I think it's about the fury.' Paul had come into the room.

'Yes. Frances was furious, but I think not so much because of me, although I was the person she directed it at. I told her I would take responsibility for my actions and the child and not walk away from everything. She just raged.'

'Could she have been angry at herself?'

'That's what puzzles me. She resented me. Not really because I was her daughter's child's father, but because I was me.'

It was one of those moments, Paul knew, that could change a life. Not just the one, but several. He knew the truth. Of course, Frances was raging at herself, because in all likelihood, the co-creator of her latest grandchild was the result of her self-servingly casual foray into life creation several decades back. Ibsen couldn't have contrived a more fitting comeuppance. Her grandson had a fifty-fifty chance of developing the condition himself. No wonder she wanted to get rid of the walking, talking, breathing, suffering manifestation of her criminal idiocy and have only the person who might and equally might not have it to deal with. At least she would be long gone before such a conclusion would be realised, so she would not have to face it at all. For the rest of her life, it was there to scourge her.

So he could, in one sentence, solve the puzzle the man sitting in front of him was dealing with. What good would that be? His knowing would not make the issue disappear. He would then realise that the father he had, Paul assumed, called 'father' all his life was no relation to him; that a cruel deception had been played out on his parents who had, in turn, deceived him, and with this deception, he had maybe blighted another life. He would know that the grandmother of his child was amoral and beneath contempt and that the mother of his child had been raised by such a woman. How would this knowledge benefit anyone?

'A strange woman, Frances,' Paul said. 'I am afraid all of us came to this conclusion years ago, and none of us knows why.' He paused. 'Do we?' he added, more as an instruction than an interrogative.

They shook their heads in agreement.

'So, if it's not on my side, is it on hers? What about you, Mr Baxter?'

'Nothing at all. You can be sure that Frances did meticulous checks. Maybe, seeing you in her daughter's life brought back shades of her own past with me. I was hardly a success story as a parent. Maybe you could ask her.'

'Life's too short. Literally. Both of us are on borrowed time. The little one may be, too.'

'And,' Paul added, 'may not be.'

'Before you ask, I won't see him. I can't. That would be too hard for me. All I feel is guilt, not love. Best he stays with you and knows only you. We won't meet again. I thank you for your time – and your frankness. I fear this is a question I shall never resolve. Mr Baxter, gentlemen.' He acknowledged them with a nod and walked out.

Paul's heart broke as Harry Bowman exited their lives.

You were right,' Jed said gently. 'That way madness lies. We've all been had one way or another. At least we've spared him, and he has no idea what he's been spared from. We've become good at it, haven't we? 'To beguile the time, look like the time."

'I wonder,' Paul said. ''Look like the innocent flower. But be the serpent under't.' That's how it continues. We are the serpents. We are the sum of all that we have been, and that's who we will be. But there we are. Popeye or Voltaire? I don't know.'

'Back to gardening, then. Or nappy-changing.'

'Hang on a mo.' Paul was checking his Facebook page. 'I've just gone into 'Messenger' and looked at 'Requests', you know, people whom you don't know but have left messages for you. This one's from someone I've never heard of, but he tells me he knows you. His name's Graham Tonge.'

'Oh, yes, I remember him. He was the one Brookfield was interviewing when I was outside his study with Poynton after he'd knocked me about in the lavatories. Brookfield was at his most smarmy, making the parents feel they were so important and that their son was something special. If they signed him up and he came, he would've been in the year below me. I don't even know if he came. I didn't speak to him. What does he say?'

'I'll read it:

'*You don't know me. You never taught me. You'd left Finchingham School before I arrived, and I had Mr Warburton for English, but I read about you and how you helped Jed Massie. He was in the year above me, so we never spoke and anyway he left suddenly, so I never got the chance. The thing is, I'm dead. Look me up on Google, and you'll see I ran away and was never found. After a long time, you get pronounced dead. Clearly, I'm not. The only one I could talk to when I was at that place was Nick Boyce. You'll know his name. He's dead, too. Except that he's not either. We've been protecting each other for years. No one other than you can have any idea what happened or why we did what we did. We want to talk to you and to Jed. We want to start to be normal people again. In case you think I'm mad or not who I say I am, ask Mr Kennedy to look at the photos of Nick – the photos that helped bring the school down, the photos shown in court that were never in the news. In one of them Nick is wearing red Calvin Kleins.*

'And then he gives a mobile number for me to call.'

'So dial the number.'

'And keep this thing on the boil? It just goes on and on. Can't we just forget it all? I'll tell him we've retired. Anyway, we'd need to speak to Hugh about the photo, wouldn't we?'

'That's who I'm phoning. Please don't wait for this. Call the boy now. Retired? Speak for yourself. I'd say 'we are yet but young in deed'.'

Paul touched the numbers.

'Are you Graham? OK. I'm Paul Mason. You messaged me.'

About the Author

Iain Welsh-Shaw graduated in English from the University of London and became a teacher. He now runs a language school in the south of England where he lives with his three children.

www.ingramcontent.com/pod-product-compliance
Lightning Source LLC
Chambersburg PA
CBHW060621100726
47907CB00006B/1708